Vengeance Lies In Wait

JANICE B. SCOTT

Beasant Books

Copyright © 2011 Janice B. Scott

All rights reserved.

ISBN-13:
978-1466234130

ISBN-10:
146623413X

LCCN:

More books in the Polly Hewitt Series:

Heaven Spent
Babes And Sucklings

DEDICATION

This murder mystery is dedicated to some very special people: Peter, Sue, Diane, Alan, Nigel, Donna, Stuart, and Mitch. Thank you all for your love, so freely given.

"Mockery and abuse issue from the proud, but vengeance lies in wait for them like a lion."

The Apocrypha: Ecclesiasticus chapter 27, verse 28. Revised Standard Version.

ACKNOWLEDGMENTS

I wish to express very grateful thanks to Sergeant Sarah Cubitt and all the officers at Norwich Police Station, who answered my naïve and foolish questions so willingly, helped me sort out the niceties of the plot, showed me around the station, and offered any more help I might need. I availed myself of extra assistance from PC Sîan Johnson, who very kindly allowed me to use details of her parents' property in France. Thank you, Sîan. Any errors in police procedures are entirely my own. My gratitude too, to former detective John Kelly, for his role as a 'critical friend' in casting an experienced eye over this work.

Thanks are very much due to Catherine Howe, who volunteered to proof read the original copy for me, and did so brilliantly. The story has changed somewhat since then, Catherine, so I hope you enjoy this final version.

My family have been unfailingly supportive throughout my efforts, so I must record my thanks to them. To my husband, Ian, for producing a splendid map of Anglesham and its environs, for his helpful suggestions over place names and plot, and for his forbearance when I'm incommunicado for long periods. Thanks too, to my daughters, Dr. Fiona Scott and Dr. Rebecca Scott, for their careful reading of this manuscript in the early stages, and their thoughtful suggestions for its improvement.

Without such help this book could never have been completed.

Vengeance Lies In Wait

JANICE B. SCOTT

VENGEANCE LIES IN WAIT

JANICE B. SCOTT

PROLOGUE

The man drove slowly down Anglesham Road, to the point where the footpath abutting the road snakes away to the east. For the final few hundred metres he switched off the engine and cut the lights. Drawing away from the road he parked carefully behind the old oak tree, thick now with summer foliage and generous with its shelter for all-comers, prey and predator alike.

Good. The place was deserted; no lovers entwined in each other's arms oblivious of the rest of the world until startled by some unexpected event, no late night dog walkers taking advantage of the sultry weather. At two in the morning the population of Anglesham (one thousand, one hundred and ten at the last census) was safely asleep.

Cautiously, the man slid from the driver's seat and approached the rear of the car. Carefully he raised the lid of the boot, pausing after every click—sounding to him as loud as gunshots on the still night air—until he was certain he was alone. Struggling more than he had anticipated to lift his burden from the boot, he wondered fleetingly whether he had been entirely wise to opt for the footpath for the last quarter of a mile.

Hefting her body over his shoulder in a fireman's lift, again he reached into the boot, this time for a shovel, but it was difficult to manage with the weight across his back. For a moment he froze in terror as the shovel clanged against the metal side of the vehicle, but nothing stirred. Still, not wanting to risk more sound than was necessary, he left the boot open as he started on his trek.

The burden which had seemed light when he formulated his plan, grew heavier with every step he took, until, when his destination finally hove in sight, he was ready to drop from fatigue. As he placed the rolled carpet gently on the ground to assess the situation, both legs were trembling from the effort of the walk, but there was no time for rest. In another hour or so the first golden streaks of dawn would begin to lighten the night sky and by then he had to be home in bed, asleep.

He stared down into the hole, shining his torch into its blackness but unable to penetrate to the bottom. The hole was twice as deep as he had imagined. Worry creased the man's forehead. He had not thought to bring a ladder. If he clambered down into those depths, how would he climb out again? Time to put plan B into action, although to be honest, he hadn't thought of a plan B. Plan A had seemed foolproof back in the comfort of his own home.

The sheer impossibility of walking all the way back to his car carrying such a weight left the man with no options. With a murmured prayer he opened the carpet, rolling his burden into the hole, trying not to retch at the thud as it hit the bottom. Then, firmly pushing all regrets from his mind, he set to work with the shovel, throwing soil from the heap into the bottom of the hole. He worked solidly for half an hour, by which time he was sweating profusely but estimated that the bottom of the hole would be covered, concealing its recent contents. The torch was virtually useless, but when he was relatively satisfied that the hole had a new, false bottom effectively hiding its addition, he turned his attention to the remaining heap of soil, digging, pushing, and patting with the shovel until there was no trace of his inroads. It was, he thought irrelevantly, like making sand castles on Great Yarmouth beach when he was a small boy.

His task completed, he murmured a second prayer, said a quiet and reverent farewell, lifted the shovel across his shoulder and returned to the car without incident.

Within the hour he was home in bed, but experiencing less relief than he had expected. Since sleep eluded him, he fetched a bottle of whiskey and began to plan for next day. The first job would be to take the used carpet to the tip *early in the morning, before too many people were about. After that he must thoroughly clean the car inside and out, washing the obscuring mud from the number plates and concentrating particularly on the inside of the boot. Then he would need to defrost and purify the freezer, before it could be used again to store food.*

His plans made, the bottle emptied, and his eyelids beginning to droop, the man fell asleep, just as the first fat raindrops began to fall.

JANICE B. SCOTT

CHAPTER ONE

"Glad to see our new rector is green!"
The Reverend Polly Hewitt laughed, freewheeling towards the speaker. She had liked Jean Bannister the moment they had met. Funny, she had thought, how you hit it off immediately with some people.
She climbed off her bike and patted Moses, the big black labrador. "I trust you're referring to my ecological credentials rather than my priestly abilities?"
Jean opened the gate. "I couldn't possibly comment! Come in for a coffee—or a cold drink if you prefer—and I'll tell you a bit about the parishes. Come on, Moses. Into the garden."
Polly pushed her bike through the gate and leaned it against the wall of the old Crossing-Keeper's Cottage. The railway had been closed years ago courtesy of Doctor Beeching in the

sixties, but the line had remained more or less intact and the Crossing-Keeper's Cottage had been sold into private hands. Jean Bannister, the third occupant, had lived there for seven years.

Jean ushered her visitor into the pretty cottage garden at the back of the property, where two garden loungers and a small, wrought iron table adorned the York stone patio.

Polly stretched out on one of the loungers as her hostess fetched lemonade and the dog galloped off, chasing pheasants. "Heavenly. What a gorgeous aroma from those early roses, Jean. You know, this garden is so delightful it's almost a cliché. Reminds me of an old boy I used to know in one of my previous parishes. He built a scented garden for his wife, who was blind. Sadly, she died before it was finished, but I used to go there often, just to chill out. It restored my soul."

Jean grimaced and ran a hand through her greying hair. "Bit like me, then. Andrew died six years ago. Only got to see one summer here. He never knew it like this; it was a tip to start with. I've done loads with the garden since then. I love to be out here."

"Your favourite hobby?"

"Apart from church, you mean? Oh, sorry. I suppose I shouldn't include church under the heading of hobbies. But it is a leisure activity for us lay people, when all's said and done."

"Shouldn't have thought there'd be much leisure about it for you as churchwarden."

Jean grinned. "You're right there! Keeps me busy, that's for sure. Especially as Chloe works.

She comes when she can, but it needs one churchwarden who can be there all the time."

"What does she do? Shift work of some kind?"

"You could say that. She's a DI—detective inspector—so she's high enough up the chain to have reasonably social hours, but when they're busy she has to muck in like everyone else."

"Good heavens! Is Anglesham a major crime centre, then? Wouldn't have thought there'd be much call for any detective round here, let alone a detective inspector."

"She doesn't work here. Well, not in the village, anyway. She's based at the Norwich station, but she can get called anywhere in East Anglia. The forces all work together when necessary. Chloe lives here in Anglesham—it's only eight miles into Norwich, so it's very handy for her."

"Was she the one with dark hair who stood opposite you at my installation service? Aged about fifty-ish?"

Jean nodded. "That's the one. You'll soon get to know everyone, although at this stage it must seem something of a nightmare."

"Well," Polly said cheerfully, "it is a lot, with eight churchwardens and a couple of volunteer staff, to say nothing of the congregations and the non-churchgoing villagers. But for me, it's new and exciting, and I'm so pleased to be here. At one point I thought I'd never get my own parish. Felt like the eternal curate. But this is perfect. Just four parishes will be like a rest cure after managing six in the interregnum at Thorpemunden. I still feel responsible for the folk there, you know."

"Hm. You might find there's more to occupy you here than you imagine. I doubt you'll be able to continue with any pastoral work from your previous benefice as well."

Polly said apologetically, "Oh no, I'm sorry. I have no intention of taking on any pastoral work from the Thorpemunden benefice. Actually, I can't even go back there. The hierarchy frowns on personnel returning to their old place. They say it doesn't give the new incumbent a fair chance if previous rectors and curates keep turning up. It's quite hard, because I left a lot of friends behind, but I suppose they're right. I wouldn't want a former incumbent breathing down my neck now I'm *in situ*. I didn't mean to imply there was nothing to do here, but I was thinking that at least the rota will be easier with four parishes than it was with six. Especially as there's a local priest—an OLM—and a licensed reader here. I've never had the luxury of staff before."

"That's true. Oswald, our very own ordained local minister, has been the proverbial tower of strength during the interregnum. Practically running the place single-handed."

"Oh dear. Is he going to find it difficult to share power if he's had it all to himself for eighteen months?"

Jean laughed. "Shouldn't think so. I suspect it got a bit much for him in the end, working full time, then taking services and preaching every week as well as coping with all the weddings, baptisms, and most of the funerals when he could wangle the time off. Of course, Cheryl helped out with matins, and she took on the pastoral work, but as a licensed reader she couldn't undertake any communion services and folks prefer those, so they were down to Oswald."

"Not surprised the people prefer communion. They're usually much better services than the non-eucharistic ones. Doesn't Cheryl work, then?"

"Part time; two mornings a week in the dispensary at the local surgery. She used to be a nurse, so she's quite well clued up in that direction. And since she lives in the Hartsheads and Oswald at Parsondale, it's really nice to have you living in our village. You'll find they'll be a great help, though. With her in the surgery and him at the high school in Riversmead, they know just about everyone in all four villages."

Polly was aware of a slight misgiving at this revelation. How well would she be able to work with an ordained local minister and a reader who knew everybody for miles around? Would they resent her moving into their patch, especially as they'd had such a long interregnum? Or would they, as Jean seemed to think, welcome someone else to take the strain? She needed to know more about these two.

"Oswald's married, I believe?"

Jean nodded. "To Nina. She's lovely. One of those background people who are the mainstay of every church. Personally I think she's a saint."

"Oh?"

Aware she had let slip more than she intended, Jean dodged. "Their son, Oliver, is one of the churchwardens at Lower Hartshead. They're lucky to have him, since he must be the youngest churchwarden in the benefice by about thirty years. The whole family goes to church there, so there's actually a children's group operating at Lower Hartshead, the only church in the benefice to have one. Oliver and Catriona have two children, Emily—she's about seven, I think—and Brent, he's five. They've attracted a few other young couples as well, so it's quite a going concern. Oswald is immensely proud. Looks upon it as all his own work, even though he's had nothing much to do with it. Catriona started the children's group because her own two were so fidgety during Oswald's services. There's a proper children's room under the tower now, so the kids spend most of their time in there leaving their parents free to enjoy the service in peace. Seems to work well, and it's the envy of all the rest of us.

"That's one thing we'd all like you to do, Polly. Build up the children's work and encourage families. Maybe start a Sunday school again—we haven't had one anywhere in the benefice for years. Richard was awfully good, but to be honest, he was clueless about children."

"As it happens, that's rather my forte. I love working with children, and the children's work in Lower Hartshead sounds like a really good start. I look forward to seeing it, and to meeting the extended Waters clan. Evidently good people."

"Pillars of the parishes. I don't know where we'd be without them. The other churchwarden at Lower Hartshead is Maureen Bagshott. She's a widow like me; about seventy, I should say. But Oliver is the driving force in that parish. The whole church revolves round him."

Polly thoughtfully digested this information. "I thought you said Cheryl was in the Hartsheads?"

"She lives in Upper Hartshead. There's only a mile between the two villages if you go by the footpath, although rather more than that by road. Our MP, Sir Giles Brewster, has the manor house which nestles in the bend of the road, but the footpath bypasses his property. Not sure which Hartshead he's in as he seems to be directly in the middle. He's an occasional church attender when he's not in London, but he flits between the two. Anyway, the two Hartsheads consider themselves to be utterly separate—until there's any sort of threat from Parsondale. Then they gang up together so you couldn't slip a sheet of paper between them."

"Why on earth would there be a threat from Parsondale?"

Jean chuckled, her faded blue eyes dancing and the crinkles at their corners proliferating. "It was the war. They were on opposite sides, and they've never forgotten it."

"They *what?* You can't mean Parsondale was in league with the Germans, surely?"

At this, Jean laughed out loud. "The civil war dear, not world war two! Norfolk people have long memories when it suits them."

"I should think they do! Whereabouts does Cheryl live in Upper Hartshead?"

"Opposite the church. You can't miss it; it's a pretty grand affair, although not quite up to the standard of the manor. Three cottages knocked into one and with enough land for their own swimming pool at the back."

"Their? I thought she was single?"

"Ostensively. But there's a significant other in the form of one Byron Henderson. None of us know whether they live together and nobody dares ask, but he's always round there."

Polly raised her eyebrows but forbore to comment. Many a time she had been tempted to move in with Tom, but as a priest had thought it prudent to observe the Church of England's official policy supporting the institution of marriage along with the rejection of any other sexual relationship. Although therefore, she had some sympathy with Cheryl, she was aware immediately of the tensions this could cause, and detected some disapprobation in Jean's tone. It seemed Cheryl Patterson, the licensed reader, was less popular than Oswald Waters, the ordained local minister.

Mentally reproving herself for leaping to over-hasty and unproven conclusions, Polly said, "What about the churchwardens at Upper Hartshead? How do they feel about Cheryl and the significant other?"

Jean shrugged. "They don't say much. Elizabeth Braconridge is the senior warden, she's been there forever. Jim Miles has only been warden for a couple of years, so he more or less follows Elizabeth's lead. Nice people, though. Always support benefice events and can be relied upon for odd jobs, cakes, things like that."

"And Parsondale? Who are the wardens there?"

"They're brothers, Alan and Ralph Talbot. Lived in Parsondale all their lives, and their dad was warden before them. I think you'll like them. Always smiling, full of fun."

"Quite a family affair then, but they sound like my sort of people," Polly said, getting to her feet. "Thanks for this, Jean. It's been really helpful. I'll do my best to remember who belongs where and with whom. Hope I don't make too many fateful mistakes."

"You're welcome, and we're a forgiving lot, so no need to worry. Come round here any time, Polly. The door's always open. Just pop in when you're passing."

"Thanks, Jean. It's good to know I have at least one friend in the parishes."

The two women hugged, and Polly made a fuss of the dog. She was aware again of how from the very centre of her being she felt drawn to Jean Bannister. Whatever the future in Anglesham benefice had in store for her, Polly felt sure she would always have support at Crossing-Keeper's Cottage.

CHAPTER TWO

"You're preaching and presiding, Polly, Cheryl's reading the lessons and I'm down for starting the service and leading intercessions. Is that right?"

Polly slipped her cassock-alb over her head and struggled into the sleeves. "If that's okay with you two. Then I'll distribute the wafers at communion if both of you do the wine. We do have two chalices?"

Oswald was already robed and waiting. "Of course. As it's a benefice service and your first sermon, we expect well over a hundred. Don't get excited, though. It won't last. Benefice services usually attract only about a third of the total congregations from all four churches. The rest take it as a Sunday off."

Polly laughed, warming towards her ordained local minister. She hadn't worked with an OLM before, but here was someone thoroughly down to earth, and having another priest she could call on when necessary would be invaluable. Since he was some twenty years or so older than Polly, she had wondered how Oswald Waters would take to having a female boss, but he seemed all right so far. Not that Polly intended to act as big chief. She was more into collaboration than lording it over her two volunteers, but she was aware that there would be times when she would have to make final decisions and those decisions might not be always popular. Still, that was all in the future, and so far at least, the future was definitely rosy. Polly shrugged off any hint of anxiety as she covertly studied her staff of two, neither of whom was paid for their work in the church.

At fifty-five, Oswald was a good looking man. Tall and lean, with a schoolmaster's slight stoop, he had wiry, iron-grey hair, but unexpectedly sported the rap industry standard type of facial hair in the form of a very thin line of brown hair extending from his sideburns, along the jawline and into a pencil moustache. Polly thought it might have looked good on someone thirty years younger but was slightly ridiculous on Oswald, an effect which was exaggerated by the spectacles on a cord round his neck. Nonetheless, aware that he taught history at Riversmead High school eight miles to the north of the benefice, Polly suspected that he was quite a disciplinarian. It was something about his bearing; despite the facial hair, he had an unconscious air of authority. There would be no trouble with unruly teenagers in any of Mr. Waters' classes. She wondered idly how long it took to maintain the precision of the beard line each morning, and whether it was worth the effort. Perhaps he wore it like that in an endeavour to keep in touch with his students.

She wondered too how he got on with the licensed reader, Cheryl Patterson. The contrast between them couldn't be greater. Although she was probably in the same age range as Oswald, Cheryl was large, and a touch brash. A good two inches taller than Polly's five foot five, she wore solid, chunky shoes with a square heel giving her another three inches so that she towered over Polly and was nearly as tall as Oswald. Her hair, dyed an improbable red which hovered uncomfortably between ginger and auburn, was worn loose to her shoulders, but billowed out around her head in an untidy cloud. With scarlet lipstick, heavy make-up, a short, tight black skirt and a white, low cut top with a frill around the neckline, she was the most unlikely Church of England licensed reader Polly had ever seen, and seemed an improbable nurse, too. Still, when her white robe, set off by the readers' long blue scarf, covered her clothes, the effect was quite impressive.

Polly smiled at her. "Okay with you, Cheryl?"

Cheryl's voice was unexpected too, low and cultured. "We usually have a lay person for the bible readings—that's why I'm doing them—and since there's the three of us on the staff now, it seemed sensible for all three of us to be robed and working together on this first occasion. Usually though, someone from the congregation would read the lessons. By the way, Polly, do you like to read the gospel yourself, or are you happy for me to read it? I know some priests insist on whoever presides at communion reading the gospel. It's all the same to me. Whichever you prefer."

"What's the normal practice in the Anglesham benefice?"

Cheryl shrugged. "Depends who's taking the service. Oswald here doesn't mind, but some of the retired priests we've had during the interregnum could be a bit stuffy."

"I expect they'd be the Anglo-catholics; traditional liturgy is important to them. Me? I think God welcomes whatever we have to offer as long as we offer our best, so I'm easy about it, Cheryl. You go ahead and do all three readings. I'm happy with that. Are we all set? Shall we have a prayer before we start?"

After the short prayer in the ministers' vestry, the three of them processed down the aisle to the east end of the nave where they had raised seats behind the nave altar, facing the congregation. Polly sat in the centre flanked on either side by her staff, and was surprised at how well supported she felt by this arrangement.

Looking at the sea of expectant faces all gazing up at her, Polly was aware of the trembling in her hands and the fluttering in her stomach. Would these people take to her? Would they support her in trying to move the benefice forward, or would she come up against immutable opposition? Unconsciously, she patted at her unruly blond curls, but today they were drawn back tightly into a bun at the back of her head rather than loose or in her preferred pony tail. A pony tail, she felt, would make her appear too young to be in charge of a benefice of four churches.

VENGEANCE LIES IN WAIT

As the enormity of her new position threatened to overwhelm her momentarily, she was glad Oswald was opening the worship, giving her time to take a few deep breaths before she was faced with the sermon.

The service had no sooner started than it was disrupted by the clanging open of the heavy oak door at the west end. Since Polly knew it was impossible to open any Church of England west door quietly—at least, not in any of the medieval churches which peppered Norwich diocese—she was unperturbed, but when the latecomer loudly and deliberately clattered his way to the very front of the church, she was aware of some irritation. Why couldn't late arrivals slip quietly into a back pew so as not to disturb fellow worshippers? Why did this guy have to announce his presence so forcibly? His arrival caused a ripple of whispering and nudging to spread throughout the congregation, by which Polly deduced either that it was unusual for him to attend church at all, or that he usually sat elsewhere. She made a mental note to quiz Cheryl later on the subject of the newcomer, but meanwhile regarded him with interest.

He was middle-aged; a heavy man, tall, thickset and solidly built, with thick black hair which was parted on the side and slicked down with some sort of hair oil. His working clothes of jeans, an open-necked red and white check shirt, and an old houndstooth check sports jacket with leather elbow patches, gave the impression that he couldn't be bothered with his appearance. His face was as heavy as the rest of his body, with weather-beaten skin, jowls which were already beginning to droop into pouches, and thick, black eyebrows, but it was his eyes which transfixed Polly. They too were black, and fastened onto Polly with a rare intensity, seeming to bore into her very soul like a gimlet.

She shifted uncomfortably, tearing her glance away from him, but was inadvertently drawn back a moment or two later, only to find that he was still staring—glaring—at her. Determined not to be intimidated by this uncouth parishioner, Polly forced herself to look away and smile at the rest of the congregation, but she could sense that something had changed. There was now an almost indefinable air of expectation, which hadn't been there before the disruption. Or rather, it had been there, but was now different. Polly mulled over the difference as she joined in with singing the first hymn. It was as though prior to the big man's appearance there had been a mild anticipation of how she would conduct herself and how well she would preach, but since his arrival that had subtly changed to a kind of unholy glee, as though perhaps something unpleasant might happen which the congregation could enjoy as onlookers but which wouldn't directly affect them. Almost, Polly thought, as if people were saying, *How will she handle this?*

Out of the corner of her eye she glanced first at Oswald, and then at Cheryl, but both were singing heartily, Oswald in a deep, bass voice and Cheryl in a strained soprano which was having difficulty reaching the top notes. Neither of them appeared to have noticed anything untoward.

Polly mentally shook herself, fired off a quick, silent prayer, and at the appropriate time after the gospel reading climbed the steps to the pulpit, clutching her sermon notes. She had had nightmares about this moment which had woken her from a deep sleep the previous night; first about tripping over her long robe and stumbling up the steps, and then finding she had left her notes behind and had no idea what she was going to say. But today, nothing unfortunate occurred.

Polly closed her eyes. "May I speak in the name of God; Father, Son and Holy Spirit. Amen."

"Amen," chorused the congregation.

It was a recognised signal for them to sit. As the shuffling died away, Polly cleared her throat. This sermon was her first test. It had to be good. She allowed a moment or two of expectant hush before raising her eyes. They were all gazing at her and, she felt, willing her to do well, but the man in the front row was still glaring, now with those black brows drawn. He looked scarily angry, but Polly reminded herself that it might be merely concentration. Some folk tended to wrinkle their brows when concentrating; she must be careful not to read too much into it. It would never do to start this new post with erroneous assumptions.

She began with a mildly amusing story which engaged the congregation and raised a few muted titters, then launched into her main theme of the pain and difficulties of change, using as an illustration of her point, Saint Paul's experiences when he tried to open the early church to gentiles. It was a way of informing the congregation that she intended to change some aspects of church, but that she understood the discomfort this might cause.

She felt it was well received, and fancied that even the man in the front looked marginally less belligerent when she had finished. She climbed down from the pulpit mightily relieved. That was the worst part over. She could cope with the communion part easily enough.

It was, therefore, with some dismay that the moment she reached her seat again, Polly watched the man in the front deliberately stand up, glare at her with an expression of extreme distaste, then slowly and ostentatiously with his head held high and that fixed expression of disgust on his face, stalk back down the aisle and out of the church.

It was a supremely effective snub. As the whole church retreated into a shocked silence, Polly felt herself collapsing inside, crumbling into a heap. Tears welled up which she fought to contain. She was a professional. No way could she let her feelings be known, but she was unable to control the trembling which threatened to engulf her whole body.

Fortunately, Oswald was up to the occasion. Used to dealing with all manner of disruptions at school, he smoothly introduced the creed, which was always said facing the high altar. With relief and overwhelming gratitude, Polly turned her back on the congregation in order to recite the familiar and comforting words. It afforded her just sufficient time to compose herself. As the creed finished, she held her head as high as the man who had walked out on her, turned back towards the congregation and smiled as though nothing was the matter.

CHAPTER THREE

"Well? What d'you reckon?" Cheryl Patterson slipped brief white shorts over her tankini, plastered her corpulent thighs with suntan lotion and stretched out on the lounger by the side of the swimming pool. She was not a pretty sight, but she loved Sunday afternoons in the summer.

"What about? The service, your legs, your new boss, or Jonathan Tunbridge?"

"All of it, really. Especially her and him. I know what you think about my legs; you tell me often enough that you like something to get hold of. Byron, do you have to sit in my bit of sun? There's little enough as it is in our English summers. Look, shove your lounger round there; I don't want to be in your shade. That's better."

Byron Henderson obediently moved to Cheryl's other side. Her demands occasionally irritated him, but he prided himself on being a practical man. As long as she paid the credit cards and serviced his needs on a regular basis, he was willing to be her slave. Besides, he liked her. In complete contrast to her upper-crust accent and her carefully modulated tones, there was a vulgar edge to Cheryl which excited him, and the fact that she held an official position in the church added an extra tang of spice. Byron was aware that Cheryl tolerated him as long as he was useful to her, but since that usefulness had lasted for four years now and he couldn't foresee it ending any time soon, he was content. The arrangement between them, he thought, was of mutual benefit.

Byron hitched up his skimpy, union jack shorts to just below his bulging abdomen, which was as far as they would stretch. He had contemplated a thong, but unable to find a large enough size, had settled for the next best thing. Lowering the back of the lounger, he stretched out next to Cheryl.

"The service was okay. I thought she preached all right, not too long, that's what matters. Jonathan Tunbridge made quite an exit though, didn't he? Good job he went before the creed. Did you see her face? I thought for a moment she was going to burst into tears."

Cheryl laughed. "That would have been fun, wouldn't it? But she is only a bit of a kid, after all. I thought she coped quite well, really. She asked me about him after the service, but what could I say? We all know his opinion of women and anyway, he made it pretty obvious, I thought. I told her to take no notice, that he was just an odd-ball."

"And did she? Take no notice, I mean?"

"Not sure. She asked me where he lived, so she may be planning to visit. Not a good idea, so I made it as vague as possible. Could hardly tell her not to go near the place though, could I?"

"Did you fill her in? You know, with all that stuff?"

"Certainly not. Not my place to bring her up to speed on scandal. She'll find out soon enough, I dare say."

Byron ran a hand self-consciously through his hair. Now it was thinning so much, he couldn't decide whether or not to go in for a toupee, but he was chary of asking Cheryl's opinion. She already had a propensity to laugh at him; he didn't want to afford her any further opportunities for unseemly mirth at his expense.

"So you're sending her into the lion's den without warning and unarmed?"

Cheryl smouldered. "I'm doing nothing of the sort. What do you think I am? I'm not sending her anywhere. I merely kept out of it. She can do what she wants. I hinted that she might not be welcome at Abbot's Farm, but after the way he behaved in church, she can hardly have failed to work that out for herself. If she wants to walk headlong into trouble, I'm not going to stop her. She's a big girl now, and I'm not a nursemaid. Anyway, why are you so concerned about her?"

Byron had felt attracted to Polly immediately and had spent the sermon pleasantly engrossed in fantasising over removing her gorgeous blond hair from its restraining bands and watching it cascade towards her shoulders prior to removing her clothing and crushing her naked body against his, but he wasn't about to admit this to Cheryl.

"I'm not! It'll be amusing, though, don't you think? Standing on the sidelines and watching how it plays out. As you say, she's only a bit of a kid, barely out of the playpen. I expect she thinks she knows the lot and can tell us all what to do, so it'll be interesting to see how she reacts to the Tunbridge clan. Good luck to her, I say."

"Mm." Cheryl was already bored with the conversation. "Rub my back with suntan lotion, will you, Byron? I'm going for a swim before the sun goes in. You coming with me or spending the whole afternoon lying on your arse?"

***

Polly decided to walk to Abbots Farm. The footpath looked solid enough as it passed behind the rectory and to the front of the church, so the chances were that it would remain navigable for the whole of its length. She hoped so, anyway.

She had discovered from Cheryl that Jonathan Tunbridge was a farmer, so he was unlikely to be home before late evening during the summer months. That suited Polly just fine. A small voice inside her head hoped he wouldn't be home at all when she called, but she tried to quell the voice. Even so she took a business card with her to push through the door, should he be out.

Polly loved the early evening in Norfolk, when the light was soft and muted and so many small creatures and birds came out to play. She heard an owl hooting from the depths of the old oak tree although she was unable to see the bird itself, and wondered whether she might be lucky enough to spot a kingfisher, as the footpath skirted Carley Wood and veered towards the river. At the river the footpath split, going east towards Upper Hartshead and north west towards Abbots Farm.

The walk was longer than she had anticipated, since it took quite a while to reach the river which then meandered along its course. It would have been quicker to go by road, but there was no enjoyment in walking on tarmac and Polly was reluctant to resort to the car. She was young and fit, and unconcerned about the length of the walk unless she arrived so late that coming home would be in the dark. That would necessitate returning by road, but was, she thought, unlikely.

There were no kingfishers in evidence, but she spotted some water voles, two small shoals of fish, and even an otter which quickly slid out of sight beneath the water. And over in the meadows to the west of the river she saw a couple of brown hares cavorting as though it was March, along with the usual rabbits, squirrels, and pheasants.

She hummed to herself as she walked. Even the prospect of facing Jonathan Tunbridge couldn't dampen her mood, until the moment when she realised that the ground beneath her feet was becoming unexpectedly squelchy and the path had all but disappeared. Then, as she felt her feet sinking and rather desperately searched for firmer ground, Polly knew she must have inadvertently discovered the marsh to the south of Abbot's Pond.

At least it meant she was somewhere near the farm, but as a townee with a poorly developed sense of direction, Polly had no idea which way to turn. All she could see were clumps of coarse grass, looking utterly solid but concealing the treacherous, sucking mire beneath. With no time to return the way she had come and therefore no other option, Polly decided she would have to tread from clump to clump as best she could, testing each knot of grass before she trusted her weight to it, and hoping and praying she wouldn't disappear up to the waist in mud in the process.

Her decision paid off, for although it took some considerable time and she ended up with exceedingly muddy feet, eventually the ground began to firm up and in due course she hit a narrow, metalled road. By now thoroughly disorientated, Polly turned left. When she reached a T-junction she mentally tossed a coin which resulted in her turning right, where she was rewarded by the sight of an isolated cluster of farm buildings over to the west. With an overpowering sense of relief, Polly strode along the track, entered the farmyard rather hesitantly, trying to ignore the ferocious barking of unseen farm dogs, and tentatively rang the farmhouse doorbell.

Having stood there for five minutes ringing the doorbell twice more to renewed canine frenzy, Polly was about to write a short note on the back of her business card and stuff it through the letterbox when a skinny youth in Wellington boots

and navy coveralls sauntered across the yard from one of the barns, a black and white border collie at his heels.
He raised dark eyebrows at Polly. "Yes?"
The resemblance to Jonathan Tunbridge was striking. "Um, I just called to see your father."
His brows creased in a frown making him look surly, but his voice was pleasant enough. "Dad? Does he know you're coming? Only he's on the back field. I can get him if you like."
Polly bent to stroke the dog. "No, no, don't disturb him. I just called on the off chance. By the way, I think I upset some of your dogs. They were going crazy."
"No worries; that's Bella and the puppies. She's our house dog at the moment. She had pups eight weeks ago so she's still a bit protective. We keep her in. She's really a gun dog, though. This here's Megan. She's a work dog." The lad stuck out his hand, hard and calloused. "I'm Amos, the youngest. My brother Joe is twenty-four. I'm twenty-one, in case you're wondering. Joe's with Dad now, but I think they've nearly finished. Would you like to come in and wait?"
Polly took his hand, warming to him. "Polly Hewitt. I'm the new rector at Anglesham, Parsondale and the Hartsheads. Just thought I'd call to make your acquaintance."
"Better come round the back then, Reverend. Nobody uses the front door. It's probably why Bella went so crazy. She won't hurt you, though. She's a real softie."
Leaving Megan outside, he guided Polly through the large kitchen which was evidently

where the family spent most of its time by the look of the kettle on kitchen range, the Welsh dresser neatly piled with papers, and the long, pine table. As she passed through she caught a glimpse of a golden retriever—presumably Bella, although quiet now—behind a wire screen dividing the kitchen from the utility room, but to her regret Amos made no suggestion of introducing her to the pups, instead showing her into a spacious lounge.

Despite her protestations that she was content to wait, Amos disappeared to seek his father. Polly took the opportunity to examine her surroundings. The room appeared comfortable enough with the usual armchairs and sofas, but was so spotlessly clean and neat that Polly wondered whether it ever housed the family. It didn't look like a room frequented by two young men. No family photographs adorned the mantelpiece and the walls were devoid of pictures apart from an aerial view of the farm itself. Polly wondered whether the old-fashioned coffee table in highly polished hardwood was an antique. It certainly didn't look used, as there wasn't so much as a magazine on its shiny surface.

Hearing deep male voices, and heavy male footsteps clumping through the kitchen, Polly shot to her feet. A moment later Jonathan Tunbridge, framed by his two sons, stood in the doorway.

Stilling the fluttering of her heart, Polly forced herself to smile. "Just thought I'd call to see how you are, after you left church so abruptly. I thought perhaps you were ill, and I wanted to make sure everything was okay."

JANICE B. SCOTT

It was a speech she had rehearsed on the way here, and she was pleased with it. But Jonathan Tunbridge merely stared at her, his black eyes insolently travelling all the way up from her mud bespattered feet to her face. Then glaring at her until she was forced to drop her gaze, he said, "I wasn't in church on Sunday. I've never seen you before in my life."

CHAPTER FOUR

The man stroked the girl's cheek as she lay passively on her back, her eyes staring and distant. So soft. Such delicate, downy skin. He crushed her fine, blond hair to his face. Like silk to his touch, and carrying him outside to the balmy aroma of fresh woodlands and spring flowers.

His hands travelled down her body, gently unbuttoning her shirt. She made no move, either to assist him or prevent him. He slipped her jeans from her legs and laid his head against the growing mound of her abdomen. Her child—his child! He could feel the faint flutter of movement as the baby kicked. That's my boy!

He would have to be careful now. Women could be funny when their time drew near. He knew that. Perhaps he would have to humour her, allow her more freedom. Then she would know that he wanted only the best for her and the baby. He allowed himself to think of names.

Thomas? James? Perhaps one of those old names, to signify the ancient roots of his family— Nathaniel, Daniel, Enoch?

He could feel himself responding urgently to the warmth of her body, and he tugged off his jeans in readiness, now lying with her on the bed, cradling her in his arms. Still she made no sound, no movement.

"Turn over," he instructed.

She obeyed instantly and lay curled in a foetal position, facing the wall. Did she even realise that he had changed position in order to make it more comfortable for her, being great with child? Did she appreciate his thoughtfulness? She made no sign.

Even as he entered her, it was as though she was elsewhere, far away in some world of her own. She had been a little odd for the four years she had been here, but he loved her just the same, with an abiding, crushing passion.

Afterwards, he dressed himself and pulled up her jeans for her. He always did that.

"Make some tea, there's a love."

She stood without a word and walked in the direction of the kitchen.

***

"We can't stay too long, Oliver; I have to cut the grass tonight. Rain's forecast."

Catriona Waters rolled her eyes. "I don't think Oliver will be cutting ours, and yours is about two inches shorter than ours. Anyway, you haven't been here five minutes and it'll be another hour until the barbie's ready." She appealed to her mother-in-law. "Nina, can't you make him sit down for ten seconds? He makes me feel tired, the way he's always looking for something else to do."

Nina Waters was a quiet, background person. Her mousy hair had lost what little colour it once had and was now dull, prior to turning grey. She had timid hazel eyes behind varifocal glasses with pale frames, and a wan countenance to match. She had kept her slender figure over the years, but paid for it with a prematurely scraggy neck and profusion of facial wrinkles. Her daughter-in-law had long since given up endeavouring to persuade her to wear a little eye-shadow or a touch of lipstick, with result that the sallowness of her skin was accentuated by pallid lips and fading eyes. Dressed in oatmeal linen slacks with a brown polo shirt, she wore sensible sandals protected from the possibility of sweaty feet by sheer knee highs. Catriona despaired over her fashion sense, but when Nina smiled, it was like the sun coming out, and Catriona loved her.

Nina smiled now. "You know Oswald! No one can make him do anything he doesn't want to do. I stopped trying years ago." She called to her husband, who was hovering around the barbecue adding to the discomfort felt by Oliver, already sweltering over the heating coals. "Oswald, why don't you take Emily and Brent for a walk? You know how they love going out with you."

Oswald pulled a face, but with the two children jumping round him shouting, "Can we, Granddad?

Ple-e-e-ze? Can we go fishing?" graciously capitulated.

Since fishing at this age meant a small net attached to a cane, and a jam jar on a piece of string, it was hardly an arduous or lengthy pursuit. Besides, Oswald regarded it as an educational opportunity and delighted in acquainting his grandchildren with the wonders of the natural world.

As he wandered off towards the river with the two children tightly clutching his hands, the three remaining adults visibly relaxed. With the salad already prepared, the rolls buttered, the jelly in the fridge and the ice cream in the freezer, there was nothing more to do until the barbecue had heated sufficiently to begin the cooking.

The two women settled themselves in canvas chairs in the sunshine. Oliver poured out a glass of cold white wine for himself and his wife, and a glass of elderflower cordial for his mother, knowing from past experience that she would be delegated as the homeward driver.

"What did Dad think of Polly?" he asked, sitting down beside his mother.

"Considering she's female and young enough to be his daughter, quite good. But you know your father. Pernickety to a degree, so he found her informality a trifle too friendly. Called it gushing."

"Oh, that's unfair!" Much the same age as Polly, Catriona had taken to her immediately. "I loved her warmth. It felt like she was one of us instead of up on some unreachable pedestal. I think she'll be brilliant. Don't you, Olly?"

Oliver, very much like his father both in looks and temperament and with an almost obsessive need for correctness, was less sure. "You have to maintain some distance, otherwise things can get sloppy. I hope she remembers her position and doesn't get too matey. Cliques can arise so easily, especially cliques around the rector. Then that causes in-fighting, and everything starts to fall apart. Besides, that sort of thing is unfair on everyone else."

Catriona groaned. "For goodness sake, Olly! That was her first service. Bit soon to be talking about cliques, isn't it? Anyway, what do you know about in-fighting round the rector? I don't recall you mentioning any problems with Richard."

"Richard was such a dear. Everyone loved him." Nina invariably acted as peacemaker. "I'm not surprised he's been snapped up by a large city centre parish. He'll be a bishop before he's finished, mark my words."

"Which is more than Polly can ever expect, being female," Catriona grumbled.

With his wife edging towards her favourite topic of feminine equality, Oliver took his glass over to the barbecue. Along with his father's penchant for absolute correctness, he had inherited his mother's dislike of arguments. Much to Catriona's frustration, his usual way of dealing with any potential disagreement was to remove himself.

It was an old-fashioned, charcoal barbecue. Catriona had fancied a gas model, but had subsided when faced with the combined disapproval of Oswald and Oliver. Although she would never admit it, secretly she agreed that the flavour of food cooked on charcoal was superior to that cooked on gas.

Oliver was in his element cooking outdoors, and whistled to himself as he placed ribs and chicken pieces onto the rack. Catriona and Nina left him to it, amicably continuing a conversation as they enjoyed Church House garden. Just across the road from Saint Edmund's church in Lower Hartshead where Oliver was churchwarden, the rear of the Georgian property was laid down to grass, with a number of mature trees providing shade. As well as the grass for their games, the children had a trampoline discreetly out of sight behind a low hedge, close to the kitchen garden that was Catriona's delight. She spent many happy hours producing vegetables for the family, priding herself on the way she was protecting her children's health and keeping an eye on them at the same time.

Oliver had erected a bird table on the upper part of the lawn close to the house, originally to encourage the children to learn about native garden birds, but rather to his surprise, had begun to take a real interest in birds himself. At his children's insistence and following the instructions on television's *Spring Watch*, he had nailed a number of nesting boxes to the trees in the garden and this year had been fascinated to watch the fledglings.

Oliver's parents were often invited to Church House on a Sunday afternoon. Catriona was torn between a genuine desire for her children to have a close and loving relationship with their grandparents, and not wanting to develop a habit which would be difficult to break, so she made sure that the visits were frequent but irregular. She had made it clear from the outset that her in-laws were welcome to visit when invited, but were not welcome to drop in whenever they felt like it. The coolness this had caused with Oswald had been papered over long since, but Catriona was well aware it had never quite disappeared. Consequently she dearly loved her mother-in-law, who to a large extent replaced her own mother hundreds of miles away in Scotland, but was less enamoured of Oswald.

"Here they are, back again," Nina remarked, as the fishing party reappeared from around the front of the house.

As soon as he saw her, Brent snatched his hand from his grandfather and raced to his mother, throwing himself onto her lap.

"Ugh! You're wet," Catriona said.

Brent's lip wobbled and he looked up at her from under lowered lashes. "Grandpa smacked me and I fell in," he whined, choking back a sob.

Catriona's mouth dropped open. She glared at her father-in-law, her eyes flashing dangerously. "He *what?*"

Emily, still holding fast to Oswald's hand, gazed with large, frightened eyes from her mother to her grandfather. Nina went very still. Oliver, happily grilling sausages, was oblivious to the portending drama.

Oswald's face assumed a schoolmaster's expression of righteous justification. "Come now, Brent. Tell your mother the truth, like a big boy.

JANICE B. SCOTT

He went too near the water, Catriona, and refused to come when I called, so I gave him a gentle tap on the behind to remind him of the danger. He then did exactly what I had warned him against, ran off and fell in. I had to fish him out. He's a very naughty boy."

From the safety of Catriona's lap, Brent glared at his grandfather with an expression just like his mother's. Then he stuck out his tongue. Emily slipped her hand out of Oswald's, ran to Nina's side, and stood there, trembling. Nina put an arm round her and held her, but otherwise didn't move or speak.

Oswald's lips compressed and his nostrils pinched. As he went white around his mouth and nose, the colour on his cheeks heightened. "How dare you! I've never met such a rude boy in all my life. You need a jolly good hiding, young man, that's what you need. I'd soon teach you to be polite to your elders. You wouldn't get away with that sort of behaviour in my house."

Catriona jumped up, sending the two children off to play. Her chin jutted as she squared up to her father-in-law. "Just as well he's not in your house then, isn't it? We're no longer in the stone age in the way we treat children, in case you hadn't noticed. It's now illegal to beat children, much as you might have delighted in it in the past."

Oswald's eyes blazed. "Easy to see where the boy learns his manners. He's his mother's son, all right. I know he's my grandson, but frankly, he's a lying little toad and I'd have thought you might have been interested in reaching the truth.

41

VENGEANCE LIES IN WAIT

Doesn't help him in the long run, Catriona, to know that he can get away with anything with his mother. He needs to learn."

"My son doesn't lie," Catriona flashed back, furious at the implication. Then contradicted herself by adding, "Besides, all children lie and I'm not surprised, when people like you threaten them with violence. I'd rather raise a confident child who might occasionally show a healthy spirit than one who's too terrified to open his mouth."

Oswald laughed, a thin, bitter sound. "Violence! You don't know what you're talking about. A smack on the bottom when it was richly deserved never hurt anyone. You know why we've got so many social problems in this country? Because do-gooders like you insist on molly-coddling children so they never learn any respect. No child of mine would ever dare to put his tongue out at his grandfather."

"Oh, for goodness sake! He's five years old. If he has an ASBO at the age of fifteen, I give you full permission to come back and say *"I told you so"*. Meanwhile he's my son, not yours, and Olly and I will bring him up as we choose. We will decide the appropriate level of discipline for our child. I won't have you hitting him for any reason."

"And you think letting him get away with bad manners and bad behaviour is the right way to raise him, do you? Well, I fear for his future, I really do."

"And I fear for his relationship with you. I'm not having him grow up frightened to death of his grandfather, so if you can't keep your hands to yourself you'd better not see him at all."

For a moment, Oswald glared at her. Then he muttered, "I know where all this will lead. History repeating itself. Come on, Nina. I have the grass to cut."

Nina rose immediately, but a troubled expression creased her face. "Perhaps we should just wait until after supper, dear? I think Oliver has nearly finished cooking. It would be such a shame for all that lovely food to go to waste, don't you think? I'm sure Brent didn't mean anything. He's such a good boy usually. He's probably tired and hungry. You know how it is with children."

But Oswald was not about to back down. As he strode from the garden, Nina followed him meekly, but her soul was filled with anguish and her eyes were filled with tears.

CHAPTER FIVE

Polly stood as if she had taken root in the soulless lounge. Had she heard correctly? How could this unbearable man so blatantly deny his presence in church? A plethora of mixed emotions shot through her mind—confusion, dismay, anger, distaste, uncertainty, fear—and were as quickly reflected in her face.

She spotted Amos first. A smile was creeping into his eyes and his mouth was twitching. As she looked from one to the other, Polly noticed that all of them were beginning to grin. Before long, a huge guffaw broke from Jonathan Tunbridge. Soon, all three were rocking with mirth, gasping for breath and wiping the tears from their eyes.

Polly felt more at a disadvantage than ever, although a tiny part of her mind noted that when he smiled, Jonathan's dark disposition lightened almost to pleasantness. If only he hadn't been laughing at her! After her long walk, the filthy mud from the marsh all over her feet and sandals, and her trepidation over the encounter with Jonathan, it was too much. Polly exploded.

"I'm glad all of you find me such an object of merriment; I'm only too well aware of what I must look like. Well, I don't like dishonesty, Mr. Tunbridge. I'm sorry to have troubled you. Next time I see you in church I'll pretend you're not there, shall I?"

Head thrown back, she made to sweep past the three men, but Jonathan stopped her with a burly arm. "Hold you hard there, missy! Not so fast. You're going nowhere."

"Get your hands off me! And get out of my way." More furious than fearful, Polly glared at him.

Amos recovered first. "Please, Reverend. Won't you sit down? There's been a mistake. I'll put the kettle on while Dad tells you about it."

Polly hesitated. Mistake? What mistake? She was torn between satisfying her awakened curiosity and making a memorable exit.

Jonathan seized his opportunity, saying contritely, "I'm sorry, we didn't mean to be rude, but I think you'll understand. Won't you stay for a cup of tea and allow me to explain?" He guided Polly to one of the armchairs, where she sat stiffly on the edge. "This is my son, Joseph. We come from a very religious family, our father was Ezra. Not our mother, she wasn't religious in the same way. Our mother was Maud, Maud Tinstall before she married. She was American—or at least, we were led to believe that her family was. She had no trace of an accent, so I suspect she was really as Norfolk as we are. *Change your name and not your letter, change for worse and not for better, they say, don't they? I wonder.*

"I'm David, my twin brother is Jonathan, and my two sons here are Joseph and Amos. Jonny and I are identical twins; only the family can tell us apart. We thought we might begin to look different as we grew older, but it wasn't to be. We have aged at exactly the same rate, and because we have a similar lifestyle—we're both farmers—similar influences have affected our appearance. So you see the cause of our humour? As soon as Amos fetched me, we all had a pretty good idea what had happened, and we couldn't resist enjoying the moment." He offered his hand. "I apologise. We all do. We weren't laughing at you, but at the situation."

Bemused, Polly took his hand. She still wasn't sure whether he was telling the truth, but he had made her pause. Identical twins? Sounded more like the plot for a novel than real life. "Do you all live together, then? Where's your brother?"

David Tunbridge glanced at her feet. "I see you came over the marsh. That'll be your mistake. You'll have turned left instead of right; most people do since it's the only way off the marsh. Abbot's Farm where my brother lives, is east of here, over the river. This is the family farm, where Jonny and I grew up. I was the elder by twelve minutes, so I inherited the farm, and I'd already married so needed somewhere to live. This is Coot Farm, where I live with Joe and Amos. Jonathan bought the next door farm across the marsh, as soon as he could."

"I see." Polly felt even more foolish to have made such a basic geographic error. If only she had studied the map more carefully before she set out. "So it's just the three of you here?"

A shadow passed over his face. "My wife died four years ago, with cancer."

"Oh dear, that must have been hard for you all."

"It was, but she was ill for years before that. The farm helped our recovery after her death. You're so busy on a farm, there's not much time to sit and mope. We supported each other through it and we've gone on supporting each other since."

Polly took a mug of tea from Amos. "And I expect your brother helped, too. Identical twins are usually very close."

She intercepted a glance between the three men. Then Joe spoke for the first time. "Dad and Uncle Jonny might look the same, but they're totally different in character. Uncle Jonny's not the easiest man to get along with."

"How do you mean?"

Never saying much, Joe shrugged, looking to his father for help. David took up the story. "Take your experience in church. From what you said, I'm guessing my brother walked out of the service before it was finished?"

"I'm afraid he made quite a disturbance coming in late, then he sat at the very front and left as soon as I finished the sermon."

"And you were going to the farm to confront him?"

"Not exactly. But to be honest, he glowered at me so much I thought it might be something I'd said. I was going to pay him a pastoral visit and try and find out what the problem was. I couldn't just leave it like that, could I? I have to sort it before he comes again."

"I shouldn't think it was personal. He—um—wasn't too pleased when he heard there was to be a female rector. He—er—has some difficulty with women."

Polly sipped her tea. "What sort of difficulty?"

As David looked embarrassed, Amos blurted out, "You might as well tell her the whole story, Dad. She'll hear it soon enough and better it comes from us than she hears the village gossip."

Polly said, "If you're about to tell me he's gay, you needn't worry about that. I know loads of gay people. Not a problem for me."

"No, it's nothing like that. I suppose I might as well tell you, since Amos is right. You're bound to hear about it sooner or later. What happened was this.

"Jonny married Isabel a year after I married Theresa. We were both married at your little church in Anglesham, and all the children were christened there, too. Terry and I had Joe a year later, then Amos was born three years after that, but Jonny and Isabel struggled. None of us know what the problem was, but it seemed Isabel couldn't conceive. Then suddenly, when Amos was six, Isabel became pregnant. She produced a daughter, a beautiful little girl, and the first girl to be born into the family for generations. Jonny was over the moon. He idolised that child."

As he fell silent and seemed sunk in reverie, Polly said gently, "Did something happen to her?"

The big man nodded. "She was such a pretty little thing, quite unlike any of the Tunbridges. Small and waif-like with long, flaxen curls, like a little elf, really. Jonny treated her as if she was a princess. We all loved her. She often came over here with her mother, especially when Terry was so ill. Then just after Terry died, Isabel suddenly left. She took Jessica off to France. That was the last anyone saw of either of them."

"What? What happened? Have they stayed there for some reason?"

"So we presume, but nobody really knows. Isabel came from Agen in south west France. She was a student when Jonny met her, over here in the holidays to work on the farm. It was love at first sight for both of them, or so we believed. They married very quickly, but once the novelty wore off, Isabel seemed to be restless and was clearly homesick. She used to talk all the time about her parents' farmhouse—they had a vineyard and produced their own wine—and she always made it sound like a mansion compared to Abbot's Farm. It was approached by a long, winding drive through woodland, or so she said. She went back every year, and stayed for longer and longer periods. After Jessica was born, things improved for a time, and when Terry was ill it was as though Isabel had a purpose in life, helping to care for Terry. But Jessica had never had any Tunbridge characteristics, and you know what it's like in villages. There was increasing gossip, suggesting that Jonny wasn't her father—and considering the length of time it took Isabel to conceive, Jonny himself began to wonder whether the rumours were true, especially as by that stage he and Isabel weren't getting along. They had a huge row one evening, then next day Isabel just took off with the child, and has never been seen or heard of since."

Polly breathed, "That's terrible," recalling the distress felt in her previous parish when a child had disappeared. "Didn't Jonathan follow her?"

"She left a note. Told Jonny she'd had it with him, and begged him not to try to find her."

"Surely he made some effort?"

David shook his head. "Jonny's never had a passport and he couldn't leave the farm."

"Yes, but surely..."

"You don't know Jonny! He has a fierce pride. If Isabel had rejected him, that was that. There was no way he'd demean himself to go crawling after her."

"Perhaps he didn't love her as much as you all thought. True love would conquer pride, wouldn't it?"

David exchanged glances with his sons. They were all looking sombre, and Polly wondered whether she had overstepped some invisible mark.

David said shortly, "We all loved her. She was a breath of fresh air. And young Jessica—well, she was a delight. We still miss her."

Polly said quietly, glancing at the three men, "And it still hurts."

Tears sprang to Amos' eyes and he turned his head away.

David said, "Jonny never got over it. He changed overnight, from the day of their disappearance. He became withdrawn and surly, as if he'd forgotten how to smile. He developed an irrational hatred of women which seems to get deeper as the years go by. Although he'd never admit it, Jonny blames himself. He can't forgive himself, and I reckon he projects all that anger onto women. In his mind, the female sex is responsible for all his woes. So you can see his difficulty when he heard you'd been appointed."

Polly nodded. "Poor man. No wonder he never got over it. So he never contacted her again? Didn't write or anything? And he's never seen his daughter again? No photographs, nothing?"

"If he did write, he never had a reply. No, they've not been heard of from that day to this. It was so sudden, there were all sorts of rumours at the time, most of which continue to this day. Some thought the two of them had been snatched, others that Jonny had killed them both in a fit of rage—although how anybody who had seen him with Jessica could think that is beyond me, since he worshipped the ground she walked on—and yet others that they'd run away with the gypsies. Isabel was so restless. There were some travellers camped in one of Jonny's fields at the time. Jonny questioned them relentlessly and even searched their vans, but neither Isabel nor Jessica were found. The travellers left as soon as they could and have never been back since. They think the farm is cursed. No, I'm afraid Isabel and Jessica disappeared without trace. Poor Jonny took the brunt of it all, and the more morose he became, the thicker the suspicion of him in the mind of the village."

Polly pondered the story as she finished her tea. She couldn't imagine how Jonathan Tunbridge must have felt, losing his wife and child in one go. But why did he make no attempt to find them? "Did nobody offer him counselling or any help?"

David laughed. "I can see you haven't actually met my brother! As I said, we come from a highly religious family. I've rather turned away, myself. Not that I'm against church or anything like that, but I just don't see the need to attend every Sunday. Neither do my boys. They never go, except at Christmas and Easter, and only then because I drag them along. But Jonathan's different. He's much more in the family mould. He's intense about it. Religion was the one thing that got him through. He clung to the church, and the rector was very good to him. Often came and sat with him; did all he could. Even tried to get him down to the pub, but Jonny couldn't take it. Felt they were all pointing at him and whispering. In Jonny's view, religion's his life, but counselling —he would see that as opposition to Christianity, so he'd never consider it."

"So he comes regularly and you three attend church occasionally?"

"I do, and I might even come more often now I've met you! Why, you going to slap my wrist for not coming every week?"

Polly laughed. "As if! No, I was just wondering how the whole congregation knew it was Jonathan in church and not you."

Amos said, "I told you. They're quite different in character. If Uncle Jonny crashed about coming into church, then stomped down the aisle and made a show of leaving early, they'd know immediately who it was. Everyone knows about his temper and he's seen in the village as a loner. Completely unlike Dad."

Polly nodded. "One last question, before I go. Should I visit Jonathan, given all you've told me?"

David shook his head decisively. "Not a good idea. I'll tell him you called, and I'll make sure he behaves himself next time he attends church. We do still manage to communicate, albeit in words of one syllable and only about the farms.

"Come on. I'll give you a lift back to the rectory. Can't have you falling in that marsh all over again. But now you know the way, I do hope you'll visit us often."

CHAPTER SIX

"Tea or coffee? Milk? Sugar?"

Polly smiled at her staff team of two. She wanted the first staff meeting in her new post to run smoothly. She had already discovered an unforeseen difficulty, in that neither Oswald nor Cheryl could manage morning or evening prayers at church.

Since all Church of England clergy are required to recite morning and evening prayer daily, in her previous post, where she had been stipendiary curate to first Henry and then Vernon, Polly had been in the habit of going back to the rectory after morning prayer, for a weekly business meeting. With two non-stipendiary staff members in her new benefice who therefore needed to work outside the church to earn their living, this was impossible. Hence Polly had to give up a precious evening for a staff meeting. As a priest, Oswald presumably said his own prayers at home, and Polly hoped Cheryl too found some time in her day for prayer.

Finding an evening to meet had proven difficult. Both Oswald and Cheryl seemed to have busy lives and were reluctant to spend time discussing the benefice with Polly. Cheryl had opted for five minutes together after a Sunday morning service, but with four different parishes in the benefice the three of them were unlikely to be together on Sunday mornings and Oswald objected that a meeting then would make him late for Sunday lunch, still the most important meal of the week in the Waters' household. Neither could he manage any early evenings, claiming pressure of school work.

Polly had offered several evenings, all of which had been rejected. With her own diary rapidly filling, it was a month before the three of them could get together, hence the need for this evening's meeting to be worthwhile. Otherwise, Polly feared, Cheryl and Oswald would never come again, and she would be left alone to plan the strategy for the parishes and organise the service rota. Not that she minded that—she had already discovered it was quicker in the long run to do things herself—but she wanted to have a genuinely collaborative ministry rather than one that appeared to be collegial on the surface, but actually was her making the decisions and other people acting on them. Anyway, she thought cynically, if more people were involved in the decision making, there would be more to shoulder the inevitable criticisms.

VENGEANCE LIES IN WAIT

"No, thank you." As Oswald refused the cakes, purchased by Polly at considerable expense of time and trouble, he glanced at his watch and sighed. "Is this going to take long, Polly? Only I have a great deal to do in the garden and I don't like to waste fine evenings like this."

"Me neither," Cheryl chimed in, picturing her swimming pool and herself on the lounger.

Polly was irritated. She was doing her best to involve them in the parishes as much as possible, and all they wanted to do was go home. Did they not realise that she too had surrendered her time? Or did they think she wasn't entitled to any time off in the evenings?

"We'd better begin, then, so that we can all enjoy what remains of the evening. We'll start with a prayer. Let us pray."

As the other two obediently bowed their heads, she rattled off a short prayer placing the meeting in God's hands, imploring God's presence and God's input. Then it was down to business.

"I think we should all work right across the benefice rather than you concentrating solely on the Hartsheads, Cheryl, and Oswald only covering Parsondale. That way, everyone will come to know us all and they'll have a variety of preaching methods. It adds richness, don't you think?"

Oswald and Cheryl exchanged glances.

Cheryl said, "That's what we did during the interregnum, but we figured that when you came we'd go back to our own villages. You needn't worry about people getting to know us! The whole area knows us. We like our own patch, don't we, Ozzy?"

Oswald frowned. "I've told you not to call me that. My name is Oswald. I do detest diminutives."

"Ouch! Touchy!" Cheryl smirked, and winked at Polly.

Polly said, "It's all right for you, Cheryl. Your name can hardly be shortened, can it? Anyway, back to business. Are you saying that neither of you wants to take services in Anglesham?"

"I'm not saying that at all." Oswald was still frowning. "I'm very happy to take weddings and baptisms in any parish, and funerals if I can get time off from school, but on Sundays I must confess I do prefer my own area. So much more convenient, don't you think?"

Biting back a retort about worship being somewhat more than personal convenience, Polly nodded. "I understand—I think—but does that mean I have three services every Sunday, since Anglesham has the eight o'clock as well as the nine thirty and someone will have to take an eleven o'clock at Lower Hartshead, while you two just have one service at your own church?"

Cheryl shrugged. "You're paid for it. It's your job. Besides, with two churches in the Hartsheads, Oswald comes over most weeks to take communion in one of them, and in exchange I sometimes go to Parsondale for a matins."

Polly blinked. This was even worse. It sounded as though they had the Hartsheads and Parsondale sewn up between them. "What about me? I'm rector of all four parishes. I need to be seen at all the churches at least once a month."

"We have a Sunday a month off," Cheryl said, inspecting her nails with their latest addition of glittering nail art. "You can come then."

Polly glanced at Oswald, who was regarding her quizzically. Sensing that this was an early challenge to her authority, Polly said, "Well, I think this is a real opportunity for something new, so in future I shall draw up a rota which enables the three of us to work right across the benefice. I'll make sure you two have the majority of services—but not all—in your own patch and have one Sunday a month free. If you need more, you must ask me, and if you feel this isn't working, you must tell me. Please let me know the dates you are unable to manage so I can work around you."

"Haven't brought my diary with me." Cheryl muttered.

Quashing the instinct to scream—why did Cheryl act like an overgrown teenager?—Polly said, "Please email me by tomorrow evening, then. I need to get on with this." She turned to Oswald. "You said you were happy to take occasional offices at any of the churches?"

"Within reason. I'll take the weddings on Saturdays and the baptisms on Sundays, but funerals can be more difficult. I don't mind taking time off for big funerals—I'm senior enough to be able to do that—but I can't justify being away from school for an unimportant occasion."

Polly's eyes widened. Had she interpreted his words correctly? Had he really implied that small funerals were unimportant? And did he expect to take every wedding and baptism anywhere in the benefice? What about her? Wasn't she to be allowed weddings or baptisms?

As if reading her mind, Oswald explained, "Everybody knows me. I've either taught them or their parents, so naturally, when weddings and christenings come along, they ask for me. They want someone they know and like."

"How will they get to know and like me if I never have the opportunity of taking their services for them?"

Oswald shrugged and hunched his shoulders. Not his problem.

Putting aside the annoyance his words had caused, Polly felt a twinge of concern over Oswald. He had been so urbane and charming when they first met, but now he seemed withdrawn, almost morose, as though there was something on his mind.

"Is everything all right, Oswald?"

At this he jerked upright. "Of course. Why do you ask?"

"Nothing. You just seemed a bit—a bit—distracted, that's all."

He snapped, "I'm not in the least distracted and I don't need your concern, thank you."

Stung, Polly said, "I see. Well, I need to become known in the area by the non-churchgoing public, so I shall take the next funeral that presents, no matter who it is. Since you've already arranged the remaining two weddings for this season you can take them, but any that come in for next year will be divided between us, whether they know you or not. As for christenings, we'll share them on a strictly rota basis. As I'm the rector, I shall take two to your one."

She heard an intake of breath from Cheryl, but kept her eyes firmly fixed on Oswald. His lips pursed, setting the thin line of his beard quivering in so comical a fashion that Polly wanted to laugh.

Clearly, he was rattled, but all he said was, "I see. Is that all?"

Wondering whether she had already made a potential enemy, Polly shook her head. She might as well be open about everything she wanted to say, and lay down a few markers while she was at it. "Not quite. The whole benefice needs to be underpinned by prayer. There are no prayer meetings here and neither of you can make morning or evening daily prayer, but I think it's imperative that the three of us meet regularly for prayer. Any suggestions?"

In the silence that followed, Cheryl continued to inspect her nails as though they were in line for the Turner prize, and Oswald stared stonily ahead of him, his mouth still drawn in that thin line. Polly swallowed, but decided to wait it out. Darned if she was going to crack first. Besides, it was clear she had identified a real problem, if these two struggled with prayer. No wonder church attendance in the benefice was less than five per cent of the total population.

Polly reminded herself that five per cent wasn't too bad compared with the national average, but it didn't belay the feeling she had that perhaps things were not quite right in the Anglesham benefice. She put this down to a lack of prayer.

As the silence stretched uncomfortably, the atmosphere sharpened. Cheryl finally capitulated. "What do you mean by regular, Polly? Once a week might be quite difficult."

Polly was pleased to notice that Cheryl's tone had changed. Gone was the bored teenager, and in her place was a glimpse of a sensible woman. For the first time, Polly began to see behind the façade to the professional nurse and the competent reader.

So what is that act about? Polly asked herself. *What is she trying to prove? Or is she just attempting to distance herself from me? Does she see another professional woman as a threat, especially a younger woman?Or does she have something to hide?*

"Personally I think once a month is the minimum. Every fortnight would be preferable, but I recognise that your time is very precious." She wanted to add, *so is mine,* but forestalled herself. "What about you, Oswald? Do you have any observations?"

His jaw was still tight and his eyes coldly angry, but he knew he had been backed into a corner. As a priest he could hardly refuse to meet for prayer, and he had a feeling that Polly Hewitt, young as she was, would not tolerate an endless succession of excuses. That was the trouble with the Church of England. The incumbent—however young and inexperienced—held total power. Polly had to recommend the renewal of Oswald's and Cheryl's licences to the diocesan bishop. It was unthinkable that she might demur. Any suggestion of less than total commitment to him,

Oswald, would do untold damage to his reputation.

He said curtly, "As you wish."

Polly sighed. If it was as hard as this with the staff, what on earth would it be like with the churchwardens and the benefice council?

"Do you have a preferred day and a preferred time? I will do my best to fit in with both of you. Once we've agreed on a regular date, I think all of us should make it a priority. It's no good if one of us decides it's not important and lets other things slip in."

Still with that icy tone Oswald said, "What did you have in mind? Because quite frankly, prayer meetings are not my thing. They usually degenerate into people telling God what to do, or they become gossip shops, peering into everyone else's business. I don't want anything to do with that kind of thing. I'm as anxious as you are to meet regularly for prayer, but before I commit myself, I need to know the proposed format."

And Cheryl, instantly reverting to the teenager, added with a silly grin, "So do I."

Polly's reply was drowned by the urgent ringing of the doorbell, as if a finger was glued to the button.

Throwing an exasperated glance at her two companions, she apologised. "Sorry. I'll have to go. Sounds like there might be trouble of some sort."

CHAPTER SEVEN

The girl sniffed the air appreciatively.

"Glad to be out?" He said it as though he was giving her a particularly special treat, unaware that she'd been in and out for years, whenever she felt like it. There was so much he didn't know.

She shook out her long, blond hair, enjoying the feeling as the wind whipped it around her face. She needed him so much. She loved it when they were together, and dreamed about the day when it would be for ever. "It's nice. The baby will need fresh air, too."

"If you're good, you might come out more often."

"Thank you." She spoke quietly, submissively, but there was a pinprick of anger behind her smile. He said it was still dangerous, but it had been so long. She had been a child when he first rescued her; she was an adult now in everything but the law.

Testing his forbearance, she wandered towards the road.

He was anxious. He couldn't allow her to be seen, that would be disastrous. It would spell the end of everything. Did she realise just how much his happiness depended upon her? Probably not. "Don't stray too far."

Immediately she turned towards him and strolled back, like an obedient puppy. It might earn her another cheap exercise book or some fashionable trinket, for he always rewarded her when she was good.

Hearing voices in the distance, he grabbed her arm and quickly propelled her back. "That's enough for today. But you can come out again tomorrow. How long now do you think? 'Til the baby?"

She shrugged. She was heavy so thought it was maybe another three or four weeks, but how could she tell? She had no mother to help her, no female companionship of any kind. What did she know?

As she sat alone, she worried about the birth. It was her first time, and she had little idea of what would happen. Would there be anyone to assist her? She didn't know.

***

Polly returned a moment later with Jean Bannister in tow. She apologised to her staff. "I'm really sorry, but this is an emergency. We'll have to cut this meeting short, I'm afraid. I know you've given up an evening for it, but I have no option. Perhaps we can reconvene at some other time. Tell them, Jean."

Jean smiled, a quick, nervous smile, unlike her usual relaxed grin. "Hello Oswald, Cheryl. Sorry to barge in like this, but there's some trouble at Anglesham churchyard. I wonder you didn't hear anything from here. I was walking the dog—we often walk to Carley Wood and back along the footpath—when I heard such a racket. A vagrant singing at the top of his voice, clearly high or drunk or both. He started slinging bottles at the gravestones, so there's broken glass everywhere. I would have approached him, but I was anxious about Moses. Fortunately I have him on the lead when I walk through the churchyard, but he wasn't happy. He was barking fit to bust, then when I quietened him, he growled louder than I've ever heard him before, and his hackles were right up. I didn't dare let him loose or we might have been facing a claim for personal damages. Besides, I didn't want him cutting his feet on all that glass. I did call out to the guy, but he was too far gone. Oblivious to me and lurching about all over the place. Only a young chap, too, in his late twenties, I should think. They usually binge drink in a crowd at that age, don't they? At least he was alone, that's something to be thankful for. I ran over the road to Chloe's, but she wasn't there, so I came here. I think we should ring the police."

"No!"

The three women stared at Oswald in surprise.

He added, "I might know him. If he's only a youngster he could be one of my former pupils. I'll come over with you; see if we can't sort this ourselves. Pity to involve the law unnecessarily; such a hassle and so time consuming. Anyway, I doubt they'll want to know about a drunken tramp, especially if there's no real damage. What did he look like, Jean?"

Jean shrugged. "Not sure I took much notice. He looked sort of tattered. He was wearing jeans with huge holes in the knees, I did see that, and a tee shirt which might once have been white. He was young, maybe twenties, thirties, something like that. Brown hair. Thin. Not all that tall. Sorry, that's all I remember. Not much to go on, is it?"

"I'll come too." Cheryl was already gathering her bag. "Just in case our young hobo needs medical attention, or any of you cut yourselves on the broken glass. Besides, I don't want to miss the fun."

Polly couldn't help grinning at this. Her estimation of both her staff members rose a notch. They may not be into prayer quite as much as she would have liked, but it seemed both were more than ready to dive in when practical help was required. Not that she had any idea of what they were going to do when they confronted the vagrant. She didn't fancy offering him a bed in the rectory.

Oswald led the way at a fast trot through the rectory gate into the churchyard. Surprised by his turn of speed, Polly fell back, along with the other two women.

"Wonder what's got into him?" Cheryl grumbled. "I can't hear any singing, Jean. Perhaps he's passed out. That'll make life easier for us."

"It will? What'll we do?" Polly knew she sounded plaintive, but behind her anxiety for the church was a tremor of fear for herself. The rectory adjoined the churchyard and she lived there alone.

When they rounded the corner of the church to the far side of the churchyard, Oswald was already squatting, examining the ground.

He picked up a piece of brown bottle glass. "He's gone. Perhaps he did hear Moses after all, Jean. Anyway, he seems to have scarpered, so I don't think we need worry any further. I'll get this lot cleared up, if you like."

Polly said, "That's nice of you Oswald. I'll help."

She began picking up shards of shattered glass, but Oswald said, "No need for you to do this, Polly. I'll see to it. Look, why don't you three get off home? I've nearly finished clearing up this glass. The rest won't take me five minutes."

"What if he comes back?"

A flicker of some emotion Polly was unable to identify, shot across Oswald's face and was gone. "There's nothing for him here. He won't come back. Go on, now. I'll let you know if there are any problems."

Cheryl said, "You're awfully anxious to get rid of us, Ozzy! Not trying to hide anything, are you?" She nudged Jean and laughed.

Oswald's lips thinned and his nostrils pinched. "This is neither the time nor place for your juvenile humour, Cheryl. Polly, I've already inspected the padlock on the church door. He didn't attempt to get in there. Good thing the church is locked at night. I really don't think there's any need to worry further. I should think he's sleeping it off in a ditch by now. We won't see him again tonight."

Polly shivered, glancing fearfully towards the rectory. "I certainly hope not. Don't know how to deal with drunks. Hope he doesn't come knocking at my door. But will he be safe, if he's in a ditch?"

Oswald glanced at the sky. "No rain forecast for tonight, and it's a warm night. He'll be fine. Don't you worry about it, Polly. Look, if it sets your mind at rest, I'll take a quick scout round when I've finished here, see if I can spot him. I'll make sure he's all right."

"*Would* you, Oswald? You are kind, Thank you so much."

Jean said, "Moses and I will walk back with you, Polly, but I doubt this derelict will come your way. If he'd discovered the rectory, we'd have met him as we came round here. He must have gone in completely the other direction, over towards Carley Wood. You should be okay, but you're welcome to stay the night at mine, if you like."

Polly squeezed her friend's arm. "You're a dear, Jean, but I'll be fine. Come back for a coffee, though. What about you, Cheryl? Fancy another coffee?"

Cheryl's eyes gleamed. "I've a better idea. Let's nip over to the Railway Arms. We can fortify ourselves with something a little stronger than coffee, and at the same time, find out whether our man was in there. Might give us a clue as to who he is and where he's from."

Polly nodded. "Brilliant idea, I fancy a drink. You up for it, Jean? Come on, then, let's go. The Railway Arms it is."

The sight of Polly in her dog collar brought an immediate hush to the pub clientèle. Used to this reaction, Polly grinned and marched up to the bar. The waiting men thronging the bar counter immediately cleared a way for her.

Jean raised her eyebrows at Cheryl. "She seems to have everything nicely in hand. Come on. Let's find a table in the garden."

Polly joined them a moment or two later, bearing a tray with three half pints of cider. "Hope this is okay for you two. I thought it was a bit hot for spirits, but I can go back if you like."

Cheryl, a beer drinker, said, "Can't remember the last time I had a cider. Brings back my youth."

The three women laughed, and touched glasses. Jean said, "If nothing else, our boy has given us a good excuse for girly night out, or part of one at any rate. Did you find out anything, Polly?"

Polly took a long draught and shook her head. "Hasn't been in here. Someone spotted him lurching down the road from Parsondale, so if he walked all that way I should think Oswald's right and he will fall asleep somewhere."

"He might have cut across the footpath behind our place," Cheryl offered. "Did they know anything else, Polly?"

"No one else had seen him, and this guy didn't recognise him. They don't know of any tramps who frequent these parts. Mostly gentlemen of the road follow their own pattern. They may wander the length of Britain, but they usually follow the same routes. I know, because they often stop at rectories for food and cash. In my last parish, we had a slush fund for purposes like that. It's odd, though. Generally you meet vagrants in city centres, where they can beg for money and spend it in the alcohol section of supermarkets. I wonder why he'd come to some out of the way place like this?"

With no plausible answers, the three women fell silent until Cheryl suddenly said, "Hey, I've an idea."

The other two looked at her expectantly.

"Why don't we buy a bottle of cider and a packet of crisps for old Ozzy and take them round to the churchyard? It would be a laugh to see his reaction. Can you imagine him ever eating crisps out of a packet?"

She began to laugh, and the other two couldn't help but join in. Polly said, "You're awful Cheryl! He'll have gone home long since. And you must stop calling him Ozzy. His face goes all sort of white and pinched when you do that."

"I know. That's why I do it. Pompous old git," Cheryl said affectionately. "I feel it's my vocation in life to save him from himself. He's lovely, but he can get a bit above himself. I like to keep him down to earth. You must have noticed how he took over. *"You get off home now, there's good girls. I'll see to this."* Honestly! Typical man. I thought his bubble needed pricking again. So I pricked it."

Laughing, Polly looked at Cheryl with new eyes. Who would have expected such astuteness hidden under the layers of vulgarity? And what else was concealed there? It seemed there was rather more to Cheryl than Polly had realised.

CHAPTER EIGHT

Two messages had been left on Polly's answerphone during her absence. The first was a summons to tea at the manor, home of Sir Giles and Lady Brewster. Polly was to present herself on Wednesday at four o'clock. Since Sir Giles was patron of both Saint Fursey and Saint Edmund churches in Upper and Lower Hartshead respectively, as well as being a long-standing Tory member of parliament for Broadland, she had no alternative but to obey. Not that she minded. She had never been in an MP's house before and had an instant vision of luxurious furniture and priceless antiques. Recalling the expenses scandal of some years previously, she allowed herself a cynical grin as she wondered whether the prestigious manor was his first or second home.

The second message wasn't a message at all, but two minutes of silence before the receiver was replaced with a click. Polly sighed. That was the trouble with an elderly congregation; machinery, even something as commonplace as an answerphone, tended to faze them. Too late now to ring 1471 and find out who had called. She made a mental note to do that in future before ringing the answerphone.

It didn't seem appropriate to turn up at the manor in jeans. Polly fussed over her wardrobe, not knowing how to dress for afternoon tea. In fact, she couldn't remember ever having been invited to afternoon tea before. When she called on elderly parishioners in the afternoons she was usually offered tea which often arrived in the best bone china cups with saucers, on trays daintily covered with lacy cloths, but that was different. In the end she selected her dark green skirt suit, pale green clergy shirt with dog collar, and her black, high heeled shoes which she wore with tights, despite the warmth of the weather.

The door was opened by a smiling, middle-aged, fair haired woman dressed in white shorts and a sky blue tee shirt, with bare feet thrust into shabby, Birkenstock sandals. Polly had met Sir Giles several times since he was patron of the Hartshead churches and therefore instrumental in appointing her, but she had never met Lady Brewster, who had been away visiting her daughter at the daughter's expensive boarding school, at the time of Polly's installation. Surely this couldn't be Lady Brewster?

"Polly! Do come in. So kind of you to visit."

Polly must have looked nonplussed, for the woman added, extending her hand, "I'm so sorry. I'm Maggie. It's lovely to meet you at last. I was sad to miss your installation. How is it going? Are you enjoying Anglesham? Do come through to the garden. Giles is attending to the rose bushes, but he's nearly finished. I'll put the kettle on."

Bemused, Polly followed her into a huge but well kept garden which extended down to the river. She caught a glimpse of Sir Giles in khaki shorts and a blue polo shirt, with an old panama hat protecting his head from the sun. He waved, put down the hose he was using, walked over to the house to turn off the tap, and appeared on the patio beside them. Maggie excused herself and slipped away to produce tea.

"Polly! So good of you to come. I see you've already met my wife. Do sit down. I'll show you round the garden after tea, if you like."

"Thank you, Sir Giles. I'd like that very much," Polly murmured, regretting her high heels and feeling stupidly over-dressed.

"Call me Giles. We don't stand on ceremony, Maggie and I. Get too much of that at Westminster." He laughed. "And Kimberley soon knocks it out of us when she comes home. Kimberley is our daughter. She's away at school at the moment, but she'll be home soon for the holidays." His face darkened for an instant. "She's in what we used to call the sixth form, but what she calls year twelve. A-levels next year, then university."

"What is she going to do? Will she follow in your footsteps?"

He laughed again. "She doesn't have a political bone in her body! We have no idea what she'll do, neither does she. I merely hope she doesn't drift."

Polly said, "Perhaps she'll take a year out," just as the tea arrived.

Maggie said, "I hope you don't mind mugs, Polly? Have one of these sandwiches, they're smoked salmon and cucumber. Here's a piece of lemon for you. I think it's so much nicer squeezed over the bread, don't you?

"I've been saying exactly that to Giles. He worries too much. Kimberley will sort herself out when she's ready, and a gap year may be just what she needs. A few months in sub-Saharan Africa seeing how the other half live might prove a timely shock to the system."

Polly helped herself to a sandwich, dutifully squeezing lemon juice over it. "What is she taking at A-level?"

Giles answered. "English, French, and history, with German at AS. She'll need A-stars to get into Oxbridge, though. She may have to settle for one of the redbrick universities."

Polly said, "Well, Durham or Exeter, or even Norwich are very good, aren't they?"

"Quite right, Polly. That's what I keep telling Giles. He is rather stuck in the past, you know." Maggie smiled affectionately at her husband. "We need to let Kimberley find her own way. I'm sure she will, if we don't pressurise her too much."

"Teenage years can be difficult, can't they?" Polly took another sandwich. They were delicious.

Giles spoke with feeling. "You can say that again! She's a clever girl, too. I just don't want to see all that education wasted, to say nothing of the cost. Still, as you say, I expect she'll settle down in due course. Not that I imagine she'll want to come home, so I doubt the University of East Anglia will be high on her list."

Polly laughed. "She sounds as if she enjoys life."

"And so she should at her age," Maggie said. "Polly, will you have another cake? No? How about the garden now, then I'll show you round the house if you like."

Polly's eyes gleamed. She would most definitely like. She glanced down at her feet.

Maggie intercepted her glance. "What size are you? Are you six, the same as me? I thought so. I've a pair of sandals you can borrow. Hang on a minute."

She returned from the house with a pair of beautiful sandals. Polly gasped. "Oh, they're much too nice for the garden! Are they hand-made?"

Maggie nodded. "From Morocco. Best quality leather, although I doubt the jewels are genuine! Don't worry, Polly. There's been no rain for several weeks, so there won't be any mud. You can't hurt them, and they're more practical than your heels."

Polly grinned, ruefully. "To be honest, I didn't know what to wear, so thought I'd dress up rather than down. I feel such a fool."

"No, you mustn't feel that! Our fault entirely. We should have made it clear on the message that we're laid back types. Still, no harm done. You'll know next time."

Polly brightened. She liked the Brewsters, who, despite the title, were some of the most down-to-earth people she had met.

"Talking of mud," she said, "I got caught on the marsh up near Abbot's Farm. I can't imagine what it must be like after rain."

"Best avoided." Giles frowned. "You wouldn't want to venture up there in the winter. As far as I know, nobody has yet lost their life there, but it's been a near thing once or twice. They look harmless enough, but they contain hidden depths. Like Norfolk people, really."

Polly and Maggie both laughed, and Polly slipped the sandals onto her feet. Thank goodness she was wearing tights. It would have been too embarrassing to stick sweaty feet into such pristine footwear.

The three of them sauntered around the garden with Giles proudly pointing out his healthy vegetables and his delightful flower beds ("Attended by a gardener," Maggie whispered), then down to the river, where the Brewsters had a rowing boat attached to a small staithe.

Giles said, "Fancy a row? Come on, we'll take you upriver to the marsh and back. I know the footpath runs along the river, but things look quite different from the water. We might spot a marsh harrier, too. They're tend to be about in the early evening."

Both Giles and Maggie proved to be competent rowers. Polly, who had never rowed before, took a turn at the oars only to discover that rowing was more of a skill than she had appreciated, especially in a tight skirt. They passed a pleasant hour meandering up the river as far as Abbot's Farm. Polly craned her neck for a good look, but the farm buildings were too far from the river bank for more than a cursory glance.

Giles said drily, "I see you've met our resident Norfolk ingrate."

"Excuse me?"

"Jonathan Tunbridge. Ancient family hereabouts, the Tunbridges. They go back years. The twins stayed, but none of the girls has ever returned."

"The girls?"

"The twins had three older sisters. According to my father, they used to be known as the three graces—Faith, Hope and Charity. Don't know if those were their real names, but it was such an oppressively religious family that that's how they were always known in the village. Each one of them was off the moment she reached sixteen, and as far as I know, has never been back since."

"Not even to visit their brothers?"

Giles grinned. "Have you *met* Jonny Tunbridge?"

"Don't mind Giles," Maggie laid a hand on Polly's arm. "He says things he's no right to say. Darling, Jonny Tunbridge is a constituent of yours, whatever you may think of him."

"More's the pity," muttered Giles.

Maggie leaned towards Polly, "Giles has fielded a few complaints from that direction, that's all."

"Oh?"

But they refused to be drawn and nothing more was said on the subject of Jonathan Tunbridge, although Polly wondered whether any of the complaints had been over the appointment of a female priest.

As Polly checked her watch, Giles turned for home. Polly had already missed evening prayers, but decided it hardly mattered since no one else attended. She would say her own prayers later. This was much more fun.

Maggie noticed the glance. "I'm afraid we've kept you rather a long time, Polly. If you've nothing else on, why don't you stay to supper?"

"Oh, I couldn't! You've both been so kind. I've had a great afternoon. I mustn't trouble you any further."

"It's no trouble," Maggie insisted. "Nothing special. We're light eaters, but we'd love you to join us, wouldn't we, Giles?"

At Giles' enthusiastic nod, Polly capitulated. While Maggie disappeared into the kitchen, Giles escorted Polly around the house. It was, as she had expected, tastefully and expensively furnished, but felt very homely.

She picked up from the grand piano a framed photograph of a blond, teenage girl with long hair flowing in the wind, holding the reins of a pony. "Is this Kimberley?"

Giles nodded. "Our only child. We would have liked more, but it wasn't to be. Beautiful, isn't she?"

"She takes after her mother." Then, realising what she had said, Polly stammered, "I didn't mean—I—um, she resembles Maggie, doesn't she?"

To her relief, Giles roared with laughter. "I shall have to remember that! Maggie will love it! But you're right, of course. Maggie was just like that when I first knew her."

Polly picked up another photograph of a much younger Giles and Maggie. "Neither of you have changed very much. No wonder Kimberley is so gorgeous." Then she wondered whether she sounded sycophantic.

Giles didn't seem to notice. "A few more wrinkles, the odd grey hair or two, that's all. We try to keep active and restrict those boring business dinners that are filled with cholesterol, and I suppose it pays off."

"Supper's ready," Maggie called out, and to Polly's surprise, Giles ushered her into the large, farmhouse style kitchen where supper was laid out on the table. Somehow, Polly hadn't thought of the gentry eating in the kitchen, but it added to the comfortable feel of the house.

After a simple meal of cold meats and salad washed down with Chablis and followed by a variety of cheeses, the three of them repaired to the lounge for coffee. By now, Polly felt as if they were old friends. This was the best time she had had since arriving in Anglesham, and she looked forward to seeing a lot more of Giles and Maggie Brewster.

CHAPTER NINE

Extract from the girl's diary:
I can never forgive my father. I go over and over it in my mind, but all I can see is him standing there with the shotgun in his hand. I don't know what happened after that. I can't remember anything more until they brought me here. They were so kind, looking after me.

I told them I couldn't go to the police, and they understood. They didn't make me. They are my family now and I love them. At least, I think I do. Sometimes I long to live a normal life like other people, like my life used to be before that terrible time, but it's too dangerous. Most of the time I understand that.

What about my baby, though? Why should she have to suffer this narrow existence, shut away from society? Perhaps I should give her up for

adoption. There are plenty of couples longing for a baby of their own, she'd have a good life.
   Except—except that I don't think I will be able to do that. When she's born, I don't think I will be able to part with her. Already I feel this fierce intensity of love which I've never felt before, not even for him, and I love him. I need him. He provides for me. I never go short. I owe him a debt of gratitude that I can never repay. Perhaps he will take us both away from here, abroad where we can't be traced. Then we can be a proper family together. That would be so good.
   When will she be born? I hope it's soon, and I hope it doesn't hurt too much.

***

   Clearing out the vestry at Anglesham church proved to be a herculean task. Unearthing old receipts dating back thirty years, Polly doubted if anything at all had been done during Richard's incumbency. She pushed to one side everything she thought could be ditched, and to the other side, in neat piles, everything she thought should be saved for posterity. There were some interesting old service registers and PCC minute books, and hidden away at the back of the safe, a marriage register dating back to 1860. It made fascinating reading. Back in those days almost all brides and grooms signed their names with a wavering cross, and the groom's occupation was usually farm labourer. In later years when the bride's occupation was added, it tended to be housemaid or scullery maid. As Polly carefully turned the pages of the register, around 1894 the crosses gradually became replaced by proper signatures after the introduction of compulsory education for all children, finally implemented in rural areas in 1880. Some names were still around in the village. One of the earliest recorded weddings was a Tunbridge from Abbot's Farm, and Tunbridges continued to feature at roughly twenty year intervals throughout the register. There were also Talbots in 1910. Polly wondered whether they were relations of the brothers Alan and Ralph, at Parsondale. It seemed that in those days, Norfolk country folk often moved only to the next village.

Having spent far too long musing over the register, Polly regretfully returned it to the safe. She was amazed that it was still kept in the church, and wondered whether the archdeacon knew of its existence. Probably not, since he would have demanded that it be deposited with the Norfolk Records Office for safe keeping and storage under the correct conditions. Ink was already beginning to fade on some of the pages, and several pages had been spoiled by water. Around the 1960s a number of pages had been filled in illegally with ballpoint pen rather than the required recording ink, resulting in entries that were already beginning to disappear.

As she moved the bag containing last Sunday's offering to one side, and rummaged in the safe to ascertain whether there were any more hidden treasures, Polly heard a noise in the church. She wasn't alarmed, since the church was left open during daylight hours for anyone to drop in, but thought she ought to greet whoever was there. Debating with herself over whether or not to lock the safe for the few moments she was likely to be away, in the end she closed the door without locking it, hid the key in its usual place at the back of the drawer, and sauntered out of the vestry into the church.

At first she couldn't see anyone, but when the noise she had heard—a kind of rustling or tearing sound—was repeated, she quietly tiptoed towards the east end of the church, not wanting to disturb anyone at prayer.

Crouched down in the front pew, hidden from the view of anyone entering the church, was a ragged, unkempt man, feverishly tearing out pages from the pew bible and rolling them around some sort of tobacco. Polly suspected it was at the very least, cannabis.

Shocked and angry, Polly tried to make her voice non-judgemental, but it came out sharply. "What are you doing?"

The man's head shot up, his eyes wide, guilty and fearful. He shrank back against the pew, edging away from her.

"Smoke. Just a smoke." His voice, barely above a mutter, nonetheless contained an element of culture in the rounded vowels.

Doing her best to be as welcoming as she was sure Jesus would have been, Polly squatted down until she was at his height. "Who are you?"

"Dizzy. I'm dizzy."

"I'm not surprised, smoking that stuff! What's your name?"

Immediately he drew back. Polly could have kicked herself, although a large part of her was still cautious. She wasn't sure quite how far she wanted to follow Jesus in welcoming this man, but speaking as gently as she could, she said, "Would you like a drink? Something to eat? The rectory's only next door. I won't bite you," she added, with a poor attempt at humour.

He gazed at her with frightened eyes, but nodded almost imperceptibly. Since squatting was inordinately uncomfortable, Polly stood up, glad to stretch her back, but despite his malnourished appearance, the man was quick. In one bound he was up, tossing the damaged pew bible at her. Snatching up a handful of torn pages, he darted out of the pew, crashing past her and making for the door.

Taken by surprise, Polly fell back against the pew. When she had recovered her breath, she called, "Come back. I won't hurt you," knowing even as she did so, that it was futile.

He reached the door, muttering and mumbling to himself. Polly caught the words, "Women's church", then he turned suddenly, shouted, "Monstrous regiment of women!" and was gone.

Polly didn't know whether to laugh or cry. If she was honest, she was greatly relieved he had gone, having no desire at all to entertain him at the rectory, but she was annoyed at the wanton damage to the bible and wondered whether she ought to lock the church. Then she decided she needed to consult the churchwardens first, so after glancing around the church to make sure there was no further damage, and looking round the churchyard to ensure he had gone, she walked over to Jean's cottage by the railway.

Jean was concerned for her. "You shouldn't have been there alone with him. Why didn't you ring?"

Polly grinned, sheepishly. "Forgot my mobile phone. Anyway, didn't think I'd need it. Don't worry, Jean, I'll make sure to take it with me in future."

"I presume it was the same man, the one I saw?"

"About five ten, really skinny, longish brown hair, quite thin and straggly, dirty old jeans and a filthy tee shirt?"

Jean nodded. "That's him."

"I asked him his name, but all he would say was that he was dizzy. Anyway, Jean, what do you think? Should we lock the church for the time being, until he disappears again? I don't like doing it 'cos I think a locked church gives entirely the wrong message, but it might be safer just for now."

"I think we might have to, don't you? And we should definitely tell Chloe. Not much point in having a police officer as churchwarden if you don't use them. As a matter of fact, I've a feeling she's off today. Hang on, Polly, I'll give her a ring. Perhaps we could go round and bring her up to speed with what's been happening."

Chloe was at home. The two women walked to the Old Police House where Chloe lived, opposite the church. Perhaps she had seen something.

After listening to Polly's story, Chloe had no doubts as to the course of action they should take. "Of course we must lock the church. If you remember, Jean, I argued strongly against keeping it open in the first place. This is exactly the sort of thing I could foresee happening."

"He hasn't done any real damage," Polly objected. "Just the one bible."

"What about his down-and-out friends? He may be alone at the moment, but the news that there's a good, free store of thin paper for roll-ups plus a quiet, undisturbed place to smoke them, will soon spread. Anyway, it sounds as if he might be escalating. First the churchyard, now the church. Are you sure he didn't do any more damage, Polly?"

Polly shook her head, feeling a little nervous. For all her slight build and her deceptively sweet face framed by the loosely curling dark hair, Chloe Fortnum had a centre of steel. Polly always had the feeling that Chloe could see right through her. She had a moment's fleeting sympathy for any criminal facing DI Chloe Fortnum.

Jean suggested, "Let's go over to the church and check. Then we can decided whether or not he's enough of a threat to lock the church for a few weeks, until he disappears again."

Ignoring a sniff from Chloe, Polly nodded enthusiastically. "Good idea. If the worst comes to the worst, we could always consider installing CCTV. Not that I like the idea of spying on people who only want a time of quiet prayer, but it might be a better solution than denying them access altogether."

As they walked across the road Chloe said, "The trouble with you two is that you're too trusting by half. You think that because this is a quiet village in the heart of rural Norfolk, nothing will ever happen here. You couldn't be more wrong. This is exactly the sort of area targeted by ruthless criminals to set up their drug farms or money laundering enterprises. You can't be too careful."

As Polly bit back a laugh, Jean retorted, "And the trouble with you, Chloe, is that you're too suspicious by half. Because you work every day with the criminal fraternity, you think everyone has evil intentions. I hardly think our vagrant fits into the hardened villain category. Much more likely to be a young man down on his luck."

Chloe muttered, "We'll see," as they entered the churchyard.

Chloe spent some time examining the area of the churchyard where the vagrant had been digging the first time he was disturbed, before she would allow them to enter the church. She refused to share any conclusions with the other two. As their eyes grew accustomed to the gloom inside the medieval building with its stained glass windows cutting out most of the light, the three of them stood just inside the west door, looking around. Everything seemed to be in order.

Polly felt relief wash over her. "There you are! He's gone, perhaps for good."

Jean agreed. "It doesn't look as though he's damaged anything else in here. That's good. I vote we keep the church open."

"Don't be so hasty." Chloe was crossing to the vestry. "Let's take a look in here first."

The other two were close behind her when she pushed open the door. Polly gasped, and Jean drew in her breath. Only Chloe seemed unsurprised, her forehead creasing in a slight frown. The contents of the safe were strewn all over the floor.

"Stay there," she ordered as she began to pick her way carefully across the floor. "Let's see if the lock is damaged. There may be fingerprints. Polly, do you know whether there was any money in the safe?"

Polly nodded, slowly. "He hasn't picked the lock. I'm so sorry; I was working in here when I heard him in the church. I forgot to lock the safe. This is all my fault."

"Was there any money? Last Sunday's collection?"

Jean said, "Yes. Bagged up and counted. There should be a record of how much, written in the service register. Jim was away this week. We usually leave it for him to collect next time he comes. If I remember rightly, it was in the region of a hundred and fifty pounds."

"Well, it's not here now. Polly, has anything else been taken?"

"The nineteenth century marriage register," Polly looked around the floor. "Is that here? Thank goodness! We must take it to the records office in Norwich. Especially now, after this. It's an important historical document. It needs to be in safe keeping." She repeated, "I'm so sorry. This is all my fault."

Chloe looked impatient. "Not the point. Come on, if nothing else is missing, let's get this lot tidied up. Then we're going to lock the church whatever you two say, and I'm going back to the station to check the database. We might have met this guy before."

Jean asked timidly, "What about fingerprints?"

Chloe laughed. "For a hundred and fifty quid? It would cost well over that to set up. No, ladies. I can report it and give you a crime number—we'll need that if we want to claim on the insurance—but I can't justify sending any of my staff to deal with this. I'm afraid we just have to bite it and learn our lesson. Never leave the church unlocked."

CHAPTER TEN

Polly sent an emergency email to all eight churchwardens, warning them of the theft from Anglesham church, suggesting they lock the churches as a temporary measure, and inviting them to an emergency benefice council meeting at the rectory to discuss the situation.

The rectory was a large, square, 1950s building, set in an acre of land which was mostly laid down to grass and shrubs, with a small orchard of plum and apple trees at the bottom of the garden. Polly's study was just inside the front door on the left, so that the rest of the rectory could remain relatively private. It was big enough to accommodate the eight churchwardens plus Cheryl, Oswald and Polly herself, although there was only one settee and two armchairs. The rest would have to sit on upright, dining room chairs, but at least they had cushions. Polly had a swivel, high backed typist's chair, which she used at the computer and which could rock gently. She loved it and was determined no one else would sit there. Besides, it held sway over the room.

As this was the first benefice council in her new post, Polly decided to provide wine, strawberries and cream, making it a social event as well as a meeting.

Oswald was the first to arrive. Stroking his peculiar beard with his right hand he surveyed the room, then made a beeline for Polly's swivel chair.

With a sinking heart she wondered whether it was worth fighting over, but she was tired. Even as she thought it, she heard herself saying, "Sorry, Oswald. I'm afraid that's mine."

She smiled at him to soften the words, but saw his lips form into that thin, pinched line. "Of course. An armchair, then? Would that be permissible?"

Ignoring his sarcasm, she offered him a glass of wine. "Help yourself to nibbles. Strawberries to follow."

"I'm allergic to strawberries."

"Oh. That's a shame; I'll try and remember to provide raspberries as well, next time."

Fortunately, the others began to arrive quite quickly. The Talbot brothers took the sofa, and everybody politely avoided the remaining armchair so that it was left for the final arrival, Chloe Fortnum. One or two refused wine, going for soft drinks instead, but all except Oswald had strawberries and cream, and there was soon a healthy buzz of conversation. Oliver Waters nodded to his father across the room, but sat down next to Maureen Bagshott, his fellow churchwarden at Lower Hartshead.

When the cutlery and crockery had been removed to the kitchen, Polly opened the meeting with prayer before starting the business. She gave a brief résumé of the two events which had precipitated the meeting, then handed over to Chloe for her observations.

Chloe had no new information. "We have hundreds like him on our database, and there must be hundreds more who haven't appeared on our radar. My advice is to keep all the churches locked unless someone is in attendance, until we're sure this threat is past. Even then, it's a risk, leaving open churches unattended. I advise you to close them permanently, except when in use, of course."

Ralph Talbot objected, "But don't Ecclesiastical Insurance prefer churches to be left open? They say it's actually less risk. If the churches are locked, a determined thief will damage the lock and the door in order to gain entry."

Chloe was impatient. "That's as may be. I'm giving you my professional advice. Take it or leave it. Besides, only a criminal gang who are targeting churches would bother to cut off locks or hacksaw their way through those huge, oak doors, and I don't think any of our churches have anything sufficiently valuable to warrant the attention of a criminal gang. Open doors on the other hand, simply invite precisely the sort of person we're trying to prevent; drug addicts, loners, drunks and so on."

"Surely we should be inviting in vulnerable people like that, not trying to prevent them, shouldn't we?"

Chloe glared at Elizabeth Braconridge. "No matter how Christian you may be at Upper Hartshead, Elizabeth, I would suggest you need to be practical. This guy trashed the vestry at Anglesham, nicked over a hundred quid in cash, and used the pages of a bible for his weed. If that's the sort of thing you want happening at Upper Hartshead, be my guest."

Elizabeth flushed, and subsided.

Polly looked around at the serious faces. "But Elizabeth does have a point, doesn't she? Surely our churches are for the whole parish, not just for churchgoers. We might be surprised at the number of people who like to drop in for a quiet moment, or just to absorb the historicity. What's more, they often slip a couple of quid into the wall safe. And aren't we in the business of supporting the weak and vulnerable?"

There were several nods, and a few mutters of agreement, ignoring Chloe's snort. The Talbot brothers began a conversation between themselves, which irritated Polly, especially as she couldn't hear what they were saying.

She waited for someone else to contribute, but when nobody did, pointedly asked, "What do you think, Oswald?"

Oswald sounded bored. "I think we should move on. Obviously we have to strike the right balance between keeping the churches closed and welcoming in all the local riff-raff. I suggest each church needs to think about being open at specific times, and drawing up a rota to man the church. Polly, you spoke to this vagrant, didn't you? What exactly did he say?"

Blanching at the reference to *riff-raff*, but deciding it was politic to say nothing, Polly shrugged. "Not a lot. I asked him who he was, but he'd been smoking weed and he only said he was dizzy. Nothing much else."

The effect of this innocuous statement on the two Waters was electrifying. Oswald and Oliver exchanged an alarmed glance; Oliver began to shake and Oswald turned ashen.

"What?" Chloe was naturally observant, and not about to allow any significant glances go unchallenged.

Oliver was the first to recover. "Um—dad hasn't been feeling too well, lately. Are you okay, Dad?"

Oswald swallowed, his Adam's apple bobbing nervously in his thin throat. "Er—yes, thank you, Oliver. It's a little warm in here with so many of us."

"What's been wrong, then, Oswald? I didn't know you were ill. We could open a window, or the patio doors behind Ralph and Alan, if you like." Polly nodded to the Talbots, and Ralph obediently rose.

Oswald said hastily, "No, it's all right. I'm fine now. Just been a little off-colour. A momentary blip, nothing to be alarmed about. Perhaps we could have one of the small windows open at the top, though?"

Jim Miles, churchwarden of Upper Hartshead, obliged. Polly offered Oswald another glass of wine, or some water, both of which he refused. He could have done with another shot of alcohol, but was mindful of Chloe's watchful eye, since he was driving.

Oliver drew the attention away from his father by asking, "Did the guy say anything else, Polly?"

"Only some rubbish about women. What was it now?" She frowned in an effort of concentration. "Oh yes, I remember. He said Anglesham was a women's church, whatever that might mean. Then just as he was going he shouted something about a monstrous regiment of women." She shrugged. "Clearly under the influence!"

Nobody laughed. Again there was that quick exchange of glances between Oswald and Oliver, but others were looking embarrassed.

Polly said, "What?"

There was a silence until Alan Talbot, the gentler of the two brothers, said, "There's been some talk, Polly. Because both churchwardens at Anglesham are female, then with you coming, some folk reckon it's a church run by women and therefore only women will attend. We all know that's rubbish, but folks can be strange, especially where religion is concerned."

Polly sighed. "And were there any problems at Parsondale when Richard was here with you two as churchwardens? Did anyone mention that it was a church only for men, run by men? No, I thought not."

Oswald had recovered his usual, superior style. "No need to get upset, Polly. All those opposed to women priests left before you came. It's not a problem now." But he looked uneasy and refused to meet Polly's eyes.

She frowned. "Is there something I should know?"

Oswald sat up straighter in the chair and looked down his nose at her. "Indeed not! I don't know what you mean. Unless anyone else has something to say?" He glanced round. "If we've said all we want to say, we should declare the meeting closed."

Polly could feel steam rising. She fought to control it. "I don't think we're quite finished yet, thank you, Oswald. There are several people here who haven't had a chance to speak, and I'd like to know what they think. Jim? Maureen? Cheryl?"

Cheryl came to her rescue. "What about, Polly? About the intruder or about keeping the churches open? I vote we keep them open but that all of us develop a habit of popping in from time to time, whenever we pass. That way, our visits will be irregular. It should discourage any would-be petty thieves, and as Chloe says, we're hardly in a position to do anything about deliberately targeted attacks. By the way, I assume we've all had our roofs and non-metal valuables marked with SafeWater? If you haven't it's free from Ecclesiastical Insurance, and well worth doing."

Maureen Bagshott added, "You can get a pen thing too, with kind of invisible ink, to mark all church items. Once they're marked, it shows up under ultra-violet light, so that if anything is stolen, the police can return it to its rightful owner." She turned to Polly. "I agree with Cheryl. People need to feel they can enter a church when they like, at least during daylight hours. If you go up to a church and see it all chained and padlocked, it just puts you off for ever."

Polly nodded, pleased with the support. "Obviously it's down to you as churchwardens to make the final decision for your particular church, but it would be good if we could come to a benefice decision, even if we can only agree on restricted opening hours. That's better than nothing." She smiled at Chloe. "I know that's going against police advice, Chloe, but churches are in a slightly different category from other buildings, aren't they? Our work has to be more about people than buildings, doesn't it?"

Chloe shrugged exaggeratedly, but she winked surreptitiously at Polly, who grinned.

Oswald was still rattled. "You're wrong, all of you. We are responsible for national treasures. We are the guardians of our nation's heritage. There's nowhere else in the world with as many medieval church buildings as Norwich diocese. It's our duty to preserve them to the best of our ability and to safeguard their important historical contents. "

Cheryl affected a yawn. "Come off it, Ozzy. Enough of the lecture. Polly's right. We're in the people and God business, not the buildings business."

Polly hid a smile.

Jim Miles suddenly said, "That's a point. None of us has mentioned God. Where's our faith? Let's put our money where our mouth is, and pray about our churches. Let's ask God to protect them. That should do the trick."

It was a comment which effectively ended the discussion, so Polly soon drew the meeting to a close, finishing with everyone reciting the grace. As she said farewell and saw people out, she reflected that it had been a useful meeting in a number of regards. The atmosphere, on the whole, had been good, and she felt they were beginning to pull together as a team. But what on earth had got into the Waters, father and son? What was it that had upset them so much?

CHAPTER ELEVEN

She slipped into the darkness like a shadow, even though her bulk prevented her moving as quickly as usual.

He had gone to bed. She knew his routine. He would often visit her during the day when he had a spare minute or two, and most days he would sit with her for the evening until he retired for the night. But he never stayed with her, and after his evening visit he never returned before next day.

Left to herself for the rest of the time, long ago she had worked out how to escape the confines of her prison to go out into the fresh air. It couldn't be dangerous at night, could it? No one would see her after dark, for she knew how to keep herself hidden. The exit was cleverly concealed so that none of them had ever suspected. Not that he ever explored her place that far. He trusted her and he never ventured too far past the bed.

She revelled in the warmth of the summer night, breathing in great lungfuls of air and formulating a plan to persuade him to allow her outside during daylight hours. The baby would need fresh air and sunshine. She would work on that, as he had shown he cared about the baby, his son, so he thought. Huh! Much he knew. It was a girl, she had no doubt about that.

Meanwhile, she wandered farther than she had ever done before, acquainting herself with the topography so that when the time was right she would know exactly where she was going. She knew herself to be a creature of the night. The velvety darkness was a friend to her. She located the church and the rectory, and she was satisfied. She sat for a while in the churchyard, feeling a kinship with those other entombed bodies, and knowing that like them, one day she too would rise again. But the time was not yet right. She would need him when the baby was born, but after that, who knew what she might achieve?

***

Tired even before the meeting and exhausted afterwards, Polly picked up the phone. "Tom? Hi, Babes. How's it going? Any chance of you popping up this weekend?"

There was a staccato reply, interrupted by sounds of static and long silences. Polly sighed. "I see you're on your mobile; you're breaking up. Look, I can't hear you, give me a ring when you get a better signal, will you? Love you."

Disappointed, she replaced the receiver. She and Tom rang each other most evenings, unless

Polly's meetings went on for so long that she didn't like to disturb him. Tom, her solicitor boyfriend for nearly five years, had started a new job at Oxford over a year ago. He had pleaded with Polly to join him there, and Polly had gone so far as to look at all the clergy vacancies in the Oxford diocese, but somehow it hadn't happened. She had experienced a strange reluctance to move away from Norfolk, and had jokingly reminded Tom that most Norfolk people return to the county in due time. He had retorted that she wasn't really Norfolk—which was true, as she had been born and grew up in Streatham—but she felt such strong bonds with the county that she regarded herself as an adopted daughter. Anyway, she disliked being reminded of her humble origins. Although she was in occasional contact with her mother and her half-brother Toby, Polly seldom saw either of them, especially as Toby was now well into his teens and more interested in clubbing, drinking, girls, gangs and possibly drugs (to Polly's chagrin) than in his big sister. Polly worried about him from time to time as their alcoholic mother wasn't a good influence on anyone growing up, but since Polly had left home long before Toby was born, she knew very little about him, and he seemed to prefer it that way.

When the bishop had mentioned Anglesham benefice to her, Polly had felt indifferent towards the proposal, but had agreed to meet some of the people and look around. Something had happened at that meeting. She was never able to identify quite what, but it had resulted in a strong pull for Polly and a growing conviction that for some inexplicable reason, God wanted her at Anglesham.

Tom, a convinced atheist, had been hurt. They had spent a year apart, and it had not occurred to him that Polly would look anywhere other than Oxford for her next post. Since that had proved to be erroneous, he assumed immediately that it was because she wanted to dump him. They had gone through a sticky few months, during which Polly had tried and failed to persuade Tom that her choice of new parish was a calling from God. Polly was torn between the desire to be with Tom and the compelling need to go where she felt God was drawing her. It was a difficult claim for Polly to justify, since she had no idea why she felt so strongly about Anglesham and district, had no future plans for it, and could no more describe God's apparent call than fly. Tom, who was into five and ten year plans through his work, was unable to understand how anyone could take on a new post based not on empirical reasoning, but merely on feelings.

"It's all emotion with you," he had said, "but if you don't engage brain you'll come a cropper. Bound to. No one can run their life based entirely on what *feels* right."

Polly had protested, "You don't understand. That's how God talks to me. God puts ideas into my mind and I have to follow them. With God, sometimes your brain gets in the way."

Tom couldn't cope with a religion in which Polly appeared happy to bypass her brain, and had jeered. "How do you know it's God? Why couldn't it be some daft, brain-addled idea of your own?"

Unable to answer satisfactorily, Polly had snapped, "I just know, that's all. I wouldn't expect you to understand," which hadn't helped.

They had patched things up over the past year, and because her stubbornness was actually one of the things he loved about her, Tom had reluctantly accepted Polly's decision, making up his mind to run with it as best he could. Although he would never have admitted it, he had a sneaking admiration that she was able to follow so completely what could only be a whim, without any real regard for her own future. There was never much chance of promotion within the Church of England especially for women, but in a tucked away rural backwater like Anglesham, as far as Tom could see, there was no hope whatsoever. Still, that might work in his favour. He had thought vaguely that they would be married some time after Polly settled in Oxford, but was honest enough to admit some relief that marriage was not on the cards yet. Although he was now in his late thirties, Tom still didn't feel ready for such a drastic step, and Polly obstinately refused to consider anything less. But after a few years in a dead end job, who knows what Polly might feel? The dreaming spires and busy, city centre churches with plenty of young people might begin to appear very enticing indeed.

So the relationship continued at a distance. The two of them rang each other most days and texted regularly, and Tom drove back to Norfolk whenever he could at weekends. It was less than satisfactory because Polly had only Fridays off and had to work on Saturdays and Sundays, but she managed to fit in enough free time to make him feel his visits were worthwhile. Even after a year in Oxford, meeting all sorts of attractive and high-flying women, no one had measured up to Polly. Tom was unable to pinpoint exactly what it was about her that so enchanted him. He loved her wild, frizzy blond hair, her ample curves, her sky blue eyes, her laughing mouth, but perhaps most of all, he loved her dedication and her unexpectedness. He had seen her in all moods. He had been there when she lost her temper, railing in colourful language against the church and everyone in it. He had seen the depth of compassion she showed when dealing with those Tom considered to be irritating in the extreme. He had shared in her tears and her laughter, and had grinned at her irreverence. Perhaps, Tom thought, what he really loved was that she was one of the few people he had met who was thoroughly real. Polly wore no façade. She was so certain in God's acceptance of her and forgiveness for her just as she was, that unlike so many Christians Tom knew, she had no need of any kind of mask. Polly was able to be herself with no pretence, and had little time for the self-righteous attitude of those who tried constantly to be good. Since Tom spent much of his life endeavouring to measure up to standards set by other people, to wear the right clothes and move in the right circles, he envied Polly's freedom even while a small part of him wondered how she would be accepted by those who mattered, if she ever became his wife.

Although Polly had failed to hear his reply from his mobile, Tom had heard her end of the conversation perfectly, and had detected a wistful note. He had been visiting an important client in the client's large and impressive home surrounded by electronic surveillance wizardry which had played havoc with the call, and now on his way home, wondered whether he should ring back. He glanced at the clock on his dashboard. Already past eleven, and he had another three quarters of an hour before reaching home. Rather than chance a rushed call which wouldn't help either of them, Tom decided to wait until morning before ringing Polly. By then she might be feeling bouncy again, and if not, he would have time to talk her through whatever was troubling her.

Tom had been more concerned than he had admitted when Polly moved into Anglesham rectory. The house was both bigger and more isolated than Polly's former curate house in Mundenford, and Polly was naturally gregarious. How would she cope with the change, rattling around in that great place by herself, with no one to to act as a sounding-board for her? Tom was aware that although curates were universally loved, this was seldom the case with incumbents. There was always somebody to carp and criticise whatever the rector did or failed to do, and most people strongly resisted change. Polly had enjoyed introducing new ideas, playing at being rector both in Henry's absence, and later in Vernon's absence, in her previous post as curate in Thorpemunden and district, but Tom suspected she had little idea how different life would be now that she had sole responsibility for four parishes and nearly three thousand people.

As it happened, Tom was called away unexpectedly next morning, to see a client who had been arrested. A solicitor now dealing mainly with criminal cases, Tom had trained himself to work only with the facts, putting aside his own opinions as to innocence or guilt. Polly had been unable to understand this.

"You must know," she had argued, "whether or not your client is guilty. Doesn't it trouble you that you may be allowing back onto the streets someone who is a danger to other people?"

Tom had shrugged. "It's not my decision. I don't allow anything. The jury decide on innocence or guilt on the basis of the facts. All I do is help to present the facts to them. Besides, I'm only the back room guy. I'm not a lawyer or a barrister."

Polly had been less than satisfied with his answer, and as he drove to the Thames Valley police headquarters in Kidlington, Tom allowed himself to ponder about his client, a small-time crook whom he detested. It put all thoughts of ringing Polly from his mind, so that it wasn't until the evening that he made the call.

"Sweet Pea! So sorry, got caught up in an unexpected case. The way it goes, I'm afraid, when you're dealing with the criminal fraternity. They get picked up at the most unexpected times, and I have to drop everything to go immediately. A bit like deaths in your field, I suppose. You have no choice; you just have to go."

There was a gulp on the other end of the line. Then, to his dismay, he heard the unmistakeable sound of weeping.

Tom, uneasy with tears at the best of times, felt his heart plummeting. "Polly! Whatever's the matter? Is it me not coming last weekend? I'm so sorry; I'm definitely coming this weekend whatever happens, honestly I am. Hey, Polly love, please, don't cry. Tell me what it's about. Please, Polly."

After further strangled sobbing, Polly managed to articulate, "Oh Tom! It's not you, Babes. Something's happened. Something awful. Tom, this is really scary. I'm so afraid, I hardly dare sleep at night."

"*What?* What on earth is it? Have you told the police? Are you safe there? Polly, listen to me. Go and stay with a friend—how about Jean Bannister? She'd have you, wouldn't she? Polly, what's happened? Tell me, please tell me."

CHAPTER TWELVE

"Oswald, do stop pacing. Why don't you sit down and turn on the television? I'll bring you a cup of tea."

Oswald snarled, "I suppose you think that will help, do you? A nice cuppa to solve every problem. It might surprise you to learn that there are problems which are too deep to be solved even by the English infatuation with a nice cup of tea."

Nina flinched. Oswald could be irritatingly superior and a stickler for correctness at all costs, but he was seldom nasty.

She said quietly, "Haven't you patched things up with Oliver and Catriona yet?"

He turned at that, his face angry and his nose pinched and white. "Me? Exactly why do you think it's up to me to make amends? Anyway, it's not Oliver. He knows how to behave. It's that abominable wife of his. He should never have married her. I knew she'd be trouble."

"Oswald." Nina's voice was reproachful. "Catriona has a lot of good points. Oliver could have done far worse, as I'm sure you know in your heart of hearts. I just wonder whether that incident was worth alienating them over? It was such a small matter and it seems to have blown up out of all proportion. I just thought—you're so good at pastoral work. I always think it takes a great man to be magnanimous when he knows he's in the right, don't you?"

Oswald began to subside. His wife always had that effect on him, but it wasn't really the row with Catriona which was bothering him.

"Oliver was all right with me the last time I saw him. I expect we'll get another invitation to lunch soon, but I suppose I could make an excuse to go and see Oliver on church business, if you really think it's necessary. Goes against the grain, but no doubt Catriona and I would be polite enough to each other. Would that satisfy you?"

Nina's face broke into one of her beaming smiles. "You're such a good priest, Oswald. You live it, and the whole parish sees that. You're a wonderful role model for them to follow."

"Hm. Well, I don't know about that..." Oswald was susceptible to flattery. He felt his wife's usual soothing touch on his life and began to relax a little. Then he added, "Nina, there's something else. Something I must tell you."

Nina's eyebrows rose. "Problems at school? Why didn't you say? I'll be so glad when you retire from that place, Oswald. Conditions for teaching are so much worse than they were when you started."

"Not entirely, Nina. The money is much better, for a start. No, this has nothing to do with school. Nina, I want you to make absolutely sure you lock and bolt all doors and windows when you go out, and don't let anybody into the house. Do you understand me?"

"I'm not quite sure I do, dear. I usually lock the door when I go out, you know that. What do you mean, don't let anyone in the house? What if one of my friends comes to call?"

Oswald said testily, "I don't mean them. I mean..." he hesitated. "I mean, no strangers or—or anyone who *might* be a stranger."

Nina was puzzled. "I still don't understand. How can there be someone who might be a stranger? Either I know them or I don't, surely? What's been going on, Oswald? Is there something I should know?"

To her dismay he sank into a chair and put his head in his hands. "I didn't want to tell you this. Oliver knows, but neither of us wanted to worry you. I wouldn't tell you now if I wasn't so worried. There's been a vagrant hanging about Anglesham church. A tramp. A *young* tramp, Nina."

"So?"

Oswald sighed heavily. "He told Polly he was dizzy."

Nina sat down heavily. Her hand flew to her mouth, which opened in consternation. "Oh Oswald! You don't think—? You're not saying—?"

Oswald nodded. "I'm afraid that's exactly what I'm saying. So you see the need to bar all the doors and windows. We can't have him here, we simply can't."

Nina's face was full of anguish. She clasped her hands in front of her. "But Oswald—"

"—no, Nina. I'm sorry, I know how you feel, but no. We can't have it. Absolutely not."

***

Polly gulped back her sobs. It was the sound of Tom's voice which had nearly broken her. Until he rang, she had managed to keep an unconcerned face no matter what her private turmoil, but the concern she heard from him had temporarily unravelled her.

She took a deep breath. "It started a while ago, Babes, but I didn't pay any attention at first. I thought it was an elderly parishioner who couldn't cope with the new technology. You know how it is."

Tom didn't know. He was confused. "Technology? What, computers? Email?"

"Nothing so complicated. Phone. Some weeks ago. My answerphone showed a message, but when I checked it there was only silence. I thought nothing of it. But since then, it's happened several times. The phone rings, but when I answer it there's just silence at the other end. Or sometimes it's the answerphone showing a string of messages, but they're all silent. I thought at first it had gone wrong, but it hasn't. It's fine."

"Might have been one of those advertising firms. You know—they ring a load of numbers all at once, then only speak to the first one to answer. All the rest get silence. Although I was under the impression that had been outlawed some time ago. Trouble is, you can't report them because if you ring 1471 it's always number withheld."

"That's exactly what I thought, advertising. But it's recently got worse. I think the calls have now started happening at night, so unless they're coming from India or somewhere, it's not an advertising agency."

Tom was alarmed. "At *night?* What do you mean, at night? During the evening, you mean?"

"I wish! No, Babes. Last night when I was fast asleep, I woke up suddenly to the sound of the phone ringing. It was two o'clock in the morning. I felt sure it was a parishioner in some sort of awful trouble, so I shot out of bed to answer it, only to find complete silence. Then I heard the click as the phone was replaced. It'll be heavy breathing next," she added, with an attempt at jocularity.

Tom heard the underlying fear in her voice. "You must tell the police, Polly. They can put a trace on your phone. Either that, or change the number and go ex-directory."

"Can't do that, can I? I'm public property, remember. People have to know my number. I can just imagine that the one time I refused to answer, it would be someone dying who needed me. Anyway, that's not all."

"There's *more?*" Tom could feel his stomach churning. "What more?"

"Inadvertently, I left my robes in Parsondale church on Sunday. I'd been taking the morning service there, and as it's an eleven o'clock service, I didn't have to go on anywhere else. I got chatting—you know how it is—and the Talbot brothers were waiting to lock the church. We've had this tramp hanging around—he caused a bit of damage in Anglesham church and stole some money, so we're keeping all the churches locked unless there's someone to man them. You know what they're like, these hobos. They come and go. Anyway, I forgot the robes. It didn't matter, but I had a mid-week Eucharist at Anglesham this morning, so I went to Parsondale first to collect my white cassock-alb and my stole, both of which were hanging in the vestry, only to find that some miserable so-and-so had poured recording ink all down my cassock-alb. It's indelible—used for marriage registers—so I'll never get it out. It's completely ruined my cassock-alb."

There was an audible intake of breath from Tom. "What did you do?"

"Not much I could do. I relocked the vestry and the church, went home and collected my choir robes—the black cassock and white surplice—and wore them. Didn't have much choice, and nobody noticed. It is a bit scary, though, Tom. I keep wondering what's going to happen next, and who hates me so much that they'd do something like that. Makes me feel a bit like jelly."

"You think they're linked? You think the same person is responsible for the phone calls and the damage to your robes?"

"Come on, Babes! Don't tell me you think there's more than one! It's enough with one unknown person hating my guts. I don't want any more."

"Do you think it's this tramp, then? Why would he do something like that? Would he have access to a phone? I suppose he might, these days. And I suppose he could be drunk enough to ring a number in the middle of the night. Sounds a bit unlikely, though. You'd expect raucous singing from a drunk, not silence. Anyway, how did he get into Parsondale church if it was locked?"

Polly sighed. "I've been asking myself those same questions over and over again, but I haven't come up with any answers, except he apparently dislikes women priests, for some reason. Something he said when I caught him at Anglesham. I suppose it's just conceivable that he found—or stole—a phone which had my number programmed in, and then just idly rang the number. Unlikely, I know, but just possible. Doesn't explain all the other phone calls, though. Anyway, how could he get into the church? You need two keys for that great west door, a huge key from way back when, and a small modern key which fits a newish, modern lock on the door. Could somebody pick both locks? I have no idea. Then he'd have to pick the lock to the vestry as well. Mind you, if he's basing his movements on Anglesham church, he'd realise that the safe is kept in the vestry. So he could have been after money again."

"Was the safe damaged?"

"No, that's the funny part about it. The safe was completely untouched. There's no sign of any effort to tamper with it. It looks very much as though I was deliberately targeted, but I really don't know why and it's all making me feel very nervous."

"I'm not surprised! Listen, Polly, you must tell the police. Promise me you'll do that?"

Polly was moved by the concern in his voice. "Don't worry, Babes. I've already rung Chloe, and I'm going to see her tomorrow. She'll know what to do."

Tom said, "Who has keys to the church? Just the churchwardens?"

Polly laughed. "I can see you don't know much about churches, Tom! Quite a lot of people have one of the small keys. Me, Oswald as the local priest at Parsondale, then Ralph and Alan the churchwardens, Minnie—she's the flower lady and she passes her key on to whoever is doing the flowers for the week—then there's one shared between the cleaners—again, people take it in turns on a rota basis to clean the church—I think Cheryl might have one too, although I'm not sure. So any number of people have access to the key, and any of them could have had it copied for their own convenience, so the truth is, we don't know how many keys are out there."

"What about the big key? You said both were needed to get into the church. No one could have copied that, surely?"

"There's only two of those. Ralph keeps one, and the other..." she hesitated.

"What?"

"Well, it's hidden in the churchyard. Hangs on a nail on the back of one of those big, rectangular stone tombs. Everyone needs it, see," she added in a rush, "so it has to be accessible."

Tom sighed. "So there's no security whatsoever. Anyone could gain access to the church. All you have to do is get hold of one of the small keys and know where the big one is hidden, and the whole world knows that! Hm, wonder what Chloe will think about those arrangements?"

CHAPTER THIRTEEN

Chloe Fortnum, used to dealing with all manner of serious crimes, was bracing rather than sympathetic. She listened to Polly in silence, but it was clear she thought all the incidents Polly related to her, were trivial.

"I'm afraid this might be the sort of territory you priests have to inhabit," she said briskly, "especially you, Polly. You're very young for this post, you're single, and you're female. Almost all members of your congregations are more than thirty years older than you and have a lot more experience of life. You'll have to work hard to win their respect. We've not had a woman priest anywhere near here before, so you're a new phenomenon for all of them. We had some discussion about whether we wanted to have a female priest before you came, and the majority stoutly declared that it made no difference. For most of them, that was their head talking. They all want to be seen as politically correct, especially as the bishop had assured us there were no longer any theological grounds on which to bar women from the priesthood. I'm not so sure everyone felt quite the same in their hearts, though. You need to understand that for many of them, the church is their life. They've grown up in these villages and lived here all their lives. They're used to having a man in charge. This is a big change for them."

Polly sipped her coffee and regarded her churchwarden thoughtfully. "Are you telling me you think this harassment is something to do with some feeling against women priests, then? I thought all that had died out years ago. Woman have been priests in England since 1994."

"But not round here. That's the point I'm trying to make. You're not only the first woman priest to be seen in the Anglesham area, you're also the first female rector in the deanery. So for folk around here, it's as though it was 1994, with all the attendant fears and emotions. It won't last, and already most people fully support you. Anyway, all this unpleasantness you've been experiencing isn't personal, you know. I would think it's much more about your office of priest."

"Huh! You try being woken up in the middle of the night by a silent phone call and then tell me it's not personal," Polly retorted, and then wished she hadn't, as a shadow passed over Chloe's face and her eyes became distant.

"Sorry," Polly added. "You must get loads of middle-of-the-night phone calls which are much worse than a few moments of silence. Of course you do. Murders and rapes and awful things like that."

Chloe acknowledged her words with a tilt of her head and a slight smile. "We can put a trace on your phone, if you like. That way we could check your incoming calls and find out where they're coming from, as long as your unknown caller isn't using a succession of pay-as-you-go mobiles, or public call boxes. Not that there are many of those around here, but then, he or she may not live round here."

"She? You don't think it could be a woman, do you? What about the tramp, the one who stole the money from Anglesham? I thought it must be him. He didn't seem to think much of women priests."

Chloe lifted her shoulders in a slight shrug. "Unlikely, I think. He was too far gone to know what he was saying, wasn't he? I suspect he was only after money to finance his habit. Nasty, I know, but common enough. I don't think we'll have much more trouble from him. He saw an opportunity and took it. Your silent phone calls and the staining of your robes are more likely to be a member of one of your congregations who, I'm sorry to say, would like to chase you out. Both types of incident are a kind of message, aren't they? *I'm not speaking to you* and *you have no right to be wearing these robes*, wouldn't you say?"

Polly sighed. "Nice! So now I'll be peering at everyone, wondering who it is who hates me so much simply because I happen to be female. Not much I can do about that, is there? Brilliant way to start a new job. Not."

"Well, you have your churchwardens and your staff. We're all behind you. And it's only one person. Don't let it get out of proportion. As I've already said, the other hundred-odd all support you, and would be horrified if they knew you were being targeted. Have you told anyone else, by the way?"

Polly shook her head. "Only Tom, and he's down in Oxford so he doesn't count. I didn't want to spread anxiety about. What do you think? Should I keep quiet about it all, or should I let people know what's going on?"

"I think the fewer who know the better, just at the moment. But you must tell me. I want to know every detail of every event, so that when we eventually catch him or her, we'll have plenty of evidence to prosecute."

A small pucker appeared between Polly's eyebrows. "You make it sound as if you expect more. Is it going to get worse?"

"Oh, I shouldn't think so. We'll get that trace on your phone and I'll keep my eyes open. Keep the churches locked for the time being, make sure you keep your robes and any personal possessions with you, and be sure to lock all your doors and windows whenever you leave the rectory. You'll be fine, Polly. Don't worry about it."

Hm, Polly thought. *Easy to say, and all right for you, but not sure I fancy living in a prison. Lord, I thought this post was going to be so good, but now I'm not sure I want to be here at all. When will it all end?*

She smiled at Chloe, thanked her for her help, and promised to let her know if anything else occurred. But it was a forlorn Polly that made her way home.

As Polly walked back across the road to the rectory garden, which she entered via Anglesham churchyard, out of the corner of her eye she caught a glimpse of movement. Her heart began to pound and her pace quickened. Her immediate instinct was to pretend that she'd seen nothing, keep her head down and scuttle into the safety of the rectory as fast as she could, but in view of Chloe's attitude, she told herself sternly not to be such a wimp. It was probably someone laying flowers on the grave of a loved one. It was her duty as rector to greet them pleasantly and make them feel at home. Polly's philosophy was that the church should welcome all those who never attended services just as warmly as it welcomed its own members. Besides, a warm smile and a kind word to those struggling with the aftermath of bereavement might give them hope and encouragement, and might even lead to them attending church one day.

Accordingly, she marched deliberately into the churchyard and began to search around amidst the graves. When someone was bent double attending to flowers, it wasn't necessarily easy to see them. But the churchyard appeared to be empty, which was odd, since Polly was sure she had detected movement. It was an extensive churchyard, having received the deceased of Anglesham since at least the seventeenth century and possibly earlier, so Polly strolled methodically up and down all the lines of graves and round the corner into the new part, which had been used since 1970, when the older part had been declared full and had been officially closed to new burials.

Still nothing. Determined to prove to herself that despite her pounding heart she had nothing to fear, Polly turned her attention to the church. It was securely padlocked, so no chance of anyone entering there. Beginning to think that perhaps her taut mind was playing tricks on her, she wondered whether to give up, but decided to walk all round the church just in case someone was loitering out of sight.

It was as she turned the second corner, convinced by now that she was wasting her time, that she came upon Byron Henderson, furtively huddled against the wall.

"Byron! What on earth are you doing? You're not ill, are you?"

Self-consciously, he straightened up. With an attempt at joviality he said, "Oh! Hello, Polly. How are you? Lovely day don't you think? I was just— er—checking the walls for—er—signs of damp. Yes, that was it. Signs of damp. Can badly damage the stonework of these medieval buildings. You need to get your churchwardens to dig out round the footage of the walls here and make sure the guttering is free of leaves. Otherwise you could have an expensive repair bill on your hands."

"And you're doing all this checking at Anglesham church, why? You don't even attend church here. You go to Upper Hartshead. To a disinterested observer, you might be thought to be hiding from me. So come on. Give me something marginally more plausible. What's this all about?"

Byron laughed, his florid face turning a darker shade of purple and his eyes all but disappearing into the folds of flesh. "Hiding from you, Polly?

That's ridiculous. Why would I want to do that? Lovely lady like you." His eyes raked her from top to toe lasciviously, but he added, "I sometimes wander about in the churchyards. I like the sense of peace they give me."

When Polly continued to look at him, her head tilted to one side, her eyebrows lifted and her face clearly revealing her scepticism, he heaved a sigh. "Well, I suppose I'd better come clean. Cheryl sent me. She's been a bit worried about you ever since that vagrant appeared. She wanted me to check the church and keep an eye on you, but I saw you coming and I had an inkling you wouldn't appreciate anyone checking up on you, so I made myself scarce. Didn't think you'd spotted me."

Polly's face softened. She certainly didn't need Byron of all people following her around, but couldn't help feeling it was thoughtful of Cheryl to be so concerned.

"That's nice of Cheryl, but as you see, I'm perfectly all right. What's more, I've checked the church and the churchyard and there's nothing untoward. So why don't you go home now and tell Cheryl that?"

Byron had regained his natural swagger. As if in response to her words, he sidled up to Polly and slid an arm around her shoulders. Polly stiffened. There were some men, she reflected, who could give you a hug without causing any offence whatsoever. Byron Henderson was not one of them. Hating his perspiring touch upon her and his hot breath fanning her cheek, she twisted out of his grasp as inconspicuously as she could. To Polly's mind, the one thing worse than an unknown intruder was being caught alone in an isolated spot with Byron Henderson, so it was a tricky situation. She didn't want to upset Byron by making him feel small or rejected, and she certainly didn't want any disagreement with Cheryl over him. He wasn't worth it.

Keeping her voice light, she said, "See you around, Byron. Give my love to Cheryl," and sauntered back towards her garden as quickly as she could, without fleeing too obviously. She turned back just once to see what effect this had on Byron, but he was still standing where she had left him. He had a strange expression on his face, though. What was it? Bewildered, Polly shook her head as she wondered whether she had identified his expression correctly. Was his face really full of relief, and if so, why?

CHAPTER FOURTEEN

Extract from the girl's diary:

Although I can never forgive my father, I did love him once. I remember those stories he told me, so full of life and colour. I loved them when I was little. Stories of the woods and the trees, of the Green Man, and of Old Shuck, that terrifying dog. Tales of his family too, of his parents and his brother and sisters and his granddad, and the place where they lived. I like to remember all those yarns when I'm lonely. They keep me going.

I wanted to know more about his family, but his face kind of closed up when I asked and he always changed the subject. He was the youngest, so I suppose he doesn't remember too much about his older siblings. He said the girls went away when he was small, but I don't know. Something about the way he said it. He wouldn't tell me why he grew up in fear, either, but he once let slip that his own father was afraid too. Perhaps the old granddad ruled the roost like some kind of Victorian patriarch.

It always sounded like the women of the family were scared too, although not his brother. He wasn't afraid of anything. I don't know why, but I remember my father telling me the girls sometimes stayed here, where I live. I like to think my unknown aunts might have been here, like me. Perhaps I'll name my baby after my aunts. I feel a kinship with them, even though I never met any of them. It would be a fitting tribute to them, I think.

***

The phone was ringing when Polly let herself into the rectory. She was seized with a dread which she felt in the pit of her stomach. It had been no idle rhetoric when she had told Tom that she felt like jelly; she had to sit down as she lifted the receiver, and again her heart was thumping uncomfortably.

With a sudden idea, she held the phone to her ear but said nothing. She counted slowly to ten—ten seconds was surely long enough for anyone to speak if they were going to—then she quietly replaced the receiver. Perhaps that would deter her unwelcome caller.

She had just gone into the kitchen to prepare a cheese sandwich for lunch when the phone rang again. With a smothered exclamation, Polly hurried out into the hall and repeated her previous procedure. By refusing to speak, she felt it gave her back a certain control over the situation. Darned if this pervert was going to detect any fear in her voice. She wondered who would get fed up first, and determined that it wouldn't be her.

When the phone rang for a third time, a grim smile played around Polly's lips. But to her dismay, a stuttering voice began to speak before she had time to replace the receiver.

"Um, is that the Reverend Polly Hewitt?"

Embarrassed by her unnecessary and foolish actions, Polly said shortly, "Yes?"

"Oh good. I think there must be a fault on the line. I rang twice before, but although it sounded as if the telephone was lifted, no one answered."

"Oh?" was all Polly could think of to say.

"Well, never mind. I'll report it for you if you like. Reverend Hewitt, this is Francis Bancroft of Williams and Bancroft, funeral directors. We have a funeral coming up; service in church followed by burial in Anglesham churchyard."

"Oh! Just a minute, Mr. Bancroft. I'll get a pen and notepad and take some details from you."

He said hastily, "No need to trouble yourself, Reverend. The family are friends of Reverend Waters, so they've asked if he might take the funeral. The son went to school at Riversmead High, so he knows Reverend Waters quite well. The deceased is his father. Mother is still alive, but the son—John—is arranging the funeral."

Polly took a deep breath. She had known this moment would come, and was aware that she was about to make herself unpopular, probably with the whole village.

As easily as she could, she said, "I'll take the funeral, Mr. Bancroft. Oswald is working full time, you know."

There was a pause on the other end of the line. "He has taken many funerals for us in the past, Reverend. I think he's able to get time off without too much difficulty, and the family have specifically requested him. In fact, they haven't agreed a date yet. They were perfectly willing to wait to see when Reverend Waters is available."

"Mr. Bancroft, I can assure you that Oswald will not be available for this funeral."

"Yes, actually he is, Reverend. He suggested Friday week in the afternoon and he says if that's no good, he can fit in more or less any time."

Polly felt hot anger shoot to the surface and boil over. "Do I hear you correctly, Mr. Bancroft? Are you telling me that you consulted my OLM before you consulted me?"

"Oh, well I—um—the last incumbent was happy for me to go straight to Oswald. Richard always said there was no point in bothering him; I might as well approach Oswald direct if the family requested him."

"Richard has left. I am incumbent here now and I require the proper protocols to be observed," Polly said coldly, "and as you very well know, that means you always approach me in the first instant. I, as incumbent, will decide who takes funerals, not you, not the family and certainly not my OLM." But her anger subsided as quickly as it had arisen, and she added in a gentler voice, "Look, Mr. Bancroft. I need to get to know my parishioners, and funerals are one of the best means of doing that, especially a village funeral where most of the village will be present. I have to start taking funerals here, no matter what the family want. I'm afraid they only buy into the funeral service. They can't dictate who they want to take it; that's up to my discretion."

"Yes, I do see, Reverend Hewitt." There was a pause, in which Polly imagined the funeral director searching for the right words. "Um, this is quite a prominent family in Anglesham—the Davidsons—perhaps you've come across them?"

"I've heard the name mentioned. Wasn't he chair of the parish council?"

"That's right, and I'm afraid it was an unexpected death, so the family are very emotional. He was only sixty-two. Dropped dead on the sixteenth tee at the golf course. His golfing partners called the air ambulance, but I'm afraid it was too late."

Thirty-four year old Polly said, "Oh dear, I'm sorry to hear that. Must have been traumatic for all concerned," but mentally she shrugged. The death couldn't have been totally unexpected, if he was that old. She added, "Perhaps you could explain to the family that I will be taking the funeral. Friday week, you said? No problem. Can you give me a phone number and the details? I'll ring tonight."

Mr. Bancroft had become smoothly professional. "Of course, Reverend Hewitt. Leave it with me. I'll post a confirmation to you. There is a slight chance that the funeral will have to be postponed as an inquest will be held, but that's scheduled for Wednesday week and I don't foresee any difficulties. Mr. Davidson had a previous heart attack some years ago, so I expect the inquest will be a formality. I will keep you informed. Will you book the organist and the verger and let me know their fees, please?"

"I will. Thank you, Mr. Bancroft. I look forward to working with you."

With a sinking feeling as she replaced the phone, Polly realised that not only had she made a fool of herself over the silence issue, but she had just talked herself into working on her day off, and it was too late to rescind now. She had made such a fuss that she was bound to carry it through. She hoped it wouldn't result in funerals every Friday, because Williams and Bancroft would find it odd if she started to refuse all Friday funerals when she had held out so vehemently for this one. And what if Oswald refused to take Friday funerals just to spite her? Part of her wondered whether Oswald had suggested a Friday deliberately because he knew it was her day off, which would, in theory, leave him to take the funeral. Polly began to wonder how stupid she had been, and resolved to go round to the Waters that evening. She owed it to Oswald to talk this through with him. Hopefully he would see her point of view.

***

Nina was in the kitchen, busily preparing dinner when the doorbell rang. She was partly relieved and partly disappointed when, moving with alacrity as he always did these days when there was someone at the door, Oswald reached it ahead of her. On hearing Polly's voice, Nina's turbulent emotions subsided and she returned her task, burying herself in the comfortable and familiar routine.

"Polly!" Oswald glanced at his watch. Twenty minutes until dinner. "Do come in." Escorting her into the lounge—magnolia walls and paintwork, dark blue velvet curtains stretching to the floor, comfortable but elegant suite in a lighter blue, checked fabric, large flat screen television in one corner, and family photos on the mantelpiece, including a graduate one of Oliver—he indicated an armchair for her. Polly sat down, but Oswald remained standing.

"To what do we owe the pleasure, Polly?"

Polly perched on the edge of her chair. She felt uncomfortable with Oswald towering over her, and was aware of the unmistakeable piquancy of roast beef. Recollecting that mealtimes were important to Oswald, she felt at an immediate disadvantage.

Oh well, best get it over with. "I had a call from Williams and Bancroft this afternoon."

Oswald's eyes narrowed. He knew perfectly well what was coming since Francis Bancroft had rung him with the bad news, but he had no intention of helping Polly out. "Oh?"

Polly nodded. "Mr. Jack Davidson—chairman of the council—has died. The family want the funeral in Anglesham church. I believe you once knew the son, John?"

"I know John, yes. He was one of my students, and a very able student, too. We're still in touch."

"Oswald, you remember how we discussed funerals some time ago?"

"*Did* we?" Oswald feigned surprise.

Polly said pointedly, "As I think you know, the family have asked for you to take the funeral, but when you and I discussed the issue of funerals, you'll remember, I'm sure, that we agreed I would take the next funeral, whoever it was."

"*Did* we? I don't remember agreeing to anything."

Polly glared at him. "You know we did. Anyway, I'm sorry, I know they're friends of yours, but I feel it's only right for a prominent figure in the community that I take this funeral myself. Not because it's me, but because the rector must be seen to be involved in the service for the chairman of the parish council. It sends the right message."

"Oh, I *see!*" Oswald smirked.

Flushing, Polly dropped her eyes. She stood up. "I just wanted to tell you myself."

"So you came all the way out here to Parsondale! That *was* kind of you."

Suddenly irritated by his sarcasm and the way he made her feel like a schoolgirl again, Polly turned. "Oswald, is there anything wrong? When I started here we seemed to get on all right, but just lately you've been—I don't know—kind of hostile. I don't know what I've done to upset you, but I am aware you don't like me. Whatever your personal feelings, we have to make this relationship between us work. I'm asking for your support, for the good of the benefice."

As she gazed at him with those clear, yet vulnerable blue eyes, Oswald's denial came automatically. "My dear girl, I don't know what you're talking about, and I don't think you do, either. Hostile towards you? What nonsense." But he couldn't help adding, "I always knew emotionalism would be a problem with you women priests. I'm afraid you're showing that rather clearly, my dear. Now I certainly don't want to be accused of telling you what to do, but perhaps you should take a step back and review your facts. I think you'll find I have supported you admirably."

Polly swallowed back a sharp retort and the urge to kick him. She muttered, "I'll just say goodbye to Nina, then I'll get out of your way. Oswald, whatever your problem is, may God be with you."

Had she waited, she might have spotted the perturbed expression that fleetingly crossed Oswald's face, but she left, her bearing haughty. Popping her head round the kitchen door on her way out, Polly exchanged pleasantries with Nina, but inhaling the gorgeous aroma of roast beef and gazing longingly at the Yorkshire puddings which Nina had just lifted from the oven, made her suddenly aware of her own hunger.

Polly smiled, said her farewells, and set off home to a lonely supper of baked beans, a jacket potato and cold meat, and the even lonelier prospect of an evening on her own with the possibility of more disturbing phone calls. As she went, she wondered for the first time whether Oswald was a closet opponent of women priests, because if he was, life here in Anglesham benefice could prove to be very tricky indeed.

CHAPTER FIFTEEN

It was after one of her night-time excursions, when she awoke late next morning, that the girl discovered her bed was wet. She had no idea why, and was aware of a feeling of shame. It was many years since she had wet the bed in her sleep.

Rising quickly, she stripped the soiled sheets from her bed and dragged them to the bathroom, where she left them to soak in the bath. She washed and dressed herself, then set to remaking her bed, grimacing as she thought of what would happen there yet again, what he would do to her. Although she loved him, she had never enjoyed what he told her was love-making. It had been terrifying the first time, but he had told her it would make her into a woman. Over the years she had learned to tolerate it because that was what he wanted, so she supposed she must be a woman now, especially as she was expecting his baby. To be truthful, he hadn't molested her quite so much lately. As she grew bigger with the baby, his evening visits had diminished in number, affording her considerable relief. She loved sitting on the sofa with him, cuddling and chatting, but it was the other. If only she could be heavily pregnant all the time!

She stopped and bent double as a sharp pain seized her belly, but it was gone almost as soon as it came, and she carried on with her task. She had more pains at sporadic intervals throughout the day, but they seemed to disappear quickly. Perhaps she had caught a bug. Even here, isolated and alone, she became ill from time to time. It was not entirely unwelcome. He was solicitous towards her when she was ill, with little acts of kindness like bringing her drinks and preparing meals for her. It made a nice change from the constant preparation of meals for them and all the housework she was expected to do.

She had little idea of how long she had been here. She knew only that she had been quite small when she came, but now was grown. She didn't know how old she was because she had no means of measuring the passage of time, but occasionally he brought her a cake with a candle on it and told her that it was her birthday. She liked those days. He was so nice to her, even though it always ended in the same way, in her bed.

She was an avid reader even when he had brought her here, and he kept her supplied with books. That, and writing in her notebooks—which she kept hidden in a secret place known only to her—were her only form of entertainment, except on those rare occasions when they allowed her to *watch television in the big house. She read copiously and lost herself in books. And she had acquired considerable knowledge, more than she ever let on to him. He thought he knew all about her, but he knew nothing. She felt so ambiguous about him, loving him one minute but wanting to push him away the next. She knew one thing. She probably couldn't survive without him, for she relied on him for everything.*

As the pain came again, stronger now and more frequent, she cried out and curled up on the bed. Was this it, then? Was the baby on its way?

***

Polly rang the Davidson family as soon as she was home, arranging to visit them in a week's time. Evelyn Davidson was cool and clipped on the phone, answering in monosyllables and refusing Polly's offer to visit sooner. Polly detected an undertone of hostility in her voice, and she heard out Polly's expressions of sympathy in silence.

"I'll make sure my son John is here when you come," she said, and Polly was unsure whether that was a veiled threat or the common sense need to have support when discussing the funeral service.

Adding the date to her diary, the phone rang again almost immediately. Curbing the now familiar dread, Polly picked it up.

The voice at the other end of the line launched in immediately. "Polly, I just felt I must ring you about last Sunday's hymns. You're still new here so you may not be aware of it, but none of us knew them. We like hymns we know. None of us like those newfangled ones we had on Sunday. I just thought you'd want to know."

Polly sighed. "Good morning to you, Hilary. I'm sorry you didn't like the hymns, but if you say you like hymns you know, perhaps you'll grow to like these when you know them better."

Hilary snorted. "We can't sing them. The rhythm's all funny. People will leave, Polly, if we get rubbish like that every week. They're all grumbling. What's wrong with the good old traditional hymns we've sung since we were at school? We like them."

"Nothing's wrong with them, Hilary, but we need to begin to learn a few modern hymns, enlarge our repertoire. Children don't sing the old hymns in school any more, so we're in danger of losing touch with the modern generations."

"But we don't have any children in church. I mean, if they came, we'd be pleased to sing their hymns, but what's the point of us having to sing hymns we don't like when the children don't come?"

Biting back the obvious retort, Polly argued, "If you go to another church on holiday, say, or even the cathedral, you'll be bound to come across some of these so-called new hymns. Actually, even the newest I introduced is at least thirty years old. I really think we need to make an effort to become familiar with some of them."

Hilary Frazer sounded horrified. Polly could picture her pushing back the straying strands of grey hair into her bun, and adjusting her glasses. "I'm sorry you feel like that, Polly. We don't hold with all these changes. I don't know what's happening to the Church of England these days. We love our church and we don't want it to change. We like it the way it is. We're too old to start changing things now."

Polly sighed. "All right, Hilary. I'll try to make sure that we have a reasonable mixture of old and new. How would that suit? Maybe one or two new ones a week."

"I don't think we can cope with more than one, Polly. Doris doesn't like playing them, you know."

"Doris hasn't said a word to me, but all right. We'll learn one new hymn a week. I hope that satisfies you."

"I'm only trying to help. I didn't mean to upset you. We all think the same."

"Thank you, Hilary," Polly said, wearily. "I appreciate your honesty in bringing this to my attention. Now if you'll excuse me, I must get on."

"Oh yes, of course. You rectors are so busy, and with four parishes, too. It's such a lot for a young girl like you. I don't know how you manage. It never used to be like this. When I was a girl we had our own rector at Upper Hartshead, dear old Canon Carruthers. That was before we joined with Lower Hartshead, and years before we had to join up with Anglesham and Parsondale as well. He was lovely. Strict, mind, but lovely. We children had to do as we were told and sit quietly in church. I don't know why children today can't do that. I blame the parents. They don't—"

"—goodbye, Hilary, and thank you so much for ringing." Polly replaced the phone, despairing over ever bringing any newcomers into Upper Hartshead church when even the introduction of new hymns was met with opposition. No wonder there were no children or young people. The place was dying on its feet. When the present generation of churchgoers ended, there would be no congregation at all at Upper Hartshead.

Making herself a mug of hot chocolate, Polly settled down to watch an hour of television before retiring for the night. Perhaps it would induce sufficient depth of sleep to stop her worrying about sad old people who didn't like the hymns, and more importantly, make her oblivious to any midnight phone calls.

***

After an blessedly undisturbed night's sleep Polly was jaunty again next morning, but the phone started ringing at eight fifteen, before she had thought about breakfast and before she had left for morning prayers.

"Hello?"

"Polly? It's Ralph. I don't want to worry you, but I think we've had a break-in at Parsondale. The flower money has gone missing."

Polly's shoulders sagged. "Oh no! How much? When did it happen?"

"Not much. They only keep about fifty quid in hand since most of the flower arrangers provide their own flowers, so it isn't a lot. They have a float for special occasions like Easter, or for anyone who can't afford to give the flowers. Church flowers are very expensive these days, so it's quite an outlay for anyone who doesn't grow their own."

"Yes, of course. Still, fifty quid is fifty quid, especially in the church where we're always strapped for cash. Every penny counts. Who discovered it was missing?"

"Minnie Reynolds. She's in charge of the flower arrangers; she does the rota and organises a flower festival every other year. She doesn't usually check the money, but for some reason she checked it yesterday and found the bag was empty."

"When was it last checked?"

Ralph said ruefully, "That's the problem. She can't remember. She thinks it may have been a month or so ago. They don't need to check it every week, so it's a bit random."

"So it could have gone missing any time during the last month?"

"I'm afraid so."

"Just out of interest, Ralph, where is it kept?"

"In the vestry. Not in the safe, because they need to be able to get at it, but in a drawer in the table. They push it to the back so that it's not immediately obvious."

"So it could have gone when ink was poured down my robes," Polly mused, thinking aloud.

"What?"

"Oh, sorry Ralph, you didn't know; I've kept it quiet. Recording ink was poured down my cassock-alb. I discovered it last Wednesday. I told Chloe, but she advised me to keep it quiet. She said the fewer who knew about it, the better. I didn't know there'd been a theft; everything else seemed to be in order. Might be an idea to change the lock on the vestry door, though."

"I wish you'd told me about this, Polly. Do Alan or Oswald know?"

"No, only Chloe. I'm sorry, Ralph," Polly repeated. "I didn't want to make a fuss, especially as it seemed to be directed at me rather than the church."

"We are your churchwardens, Polly. We're here to support you. How can we do that if keep us out of the loop? Besides, we need to know what's going on inside our own church. We're legally responsible for it."

"Yes, I know. Well, you can tell Alan, but please keep it to yourselves, Ralph. I don't want Oswald or anyone else knowing. It's very personal, and I don't want to be the object of pitying glances. Nor do I want it to spread by other people thinking it's a good idea and jumping on the bandwagon."

"Polly!" Ralph sounded reproachful. "No one else would do a thing like that. This was the work of a narrow minded obsessive, surely. Some evil person with too much time on his hands. I hope you don't think we're all mental?"

"No, of course not. Look, Ralph. Who knew where the money was kept? A lot of people seem to have access to the keys, but how many of them knew money was kept in the drawer? I didn't."

"Well, the flower arrangers, obviously. There's a dozen of them on the flower rota, although they're not all churchgoers. Some just do the flowers, but don't come to services. Alan and me, Oswald, possibly the treasurer, although he doesn't deal with the flower money, only the Sunday offerings, and those are removed from church after the service. We never keep any money in the safe—just as well, isn't it?"

"And that's been the pattern for how long?"

"Years. Ever since I remember, even when I was a lad. There's never been any trouble before, so we never thought about it as a security issue."

"So any number of people not only had access, but also knew money was kept in the drawer?"

"I suppose so, but as I said, we've never had any trouble before. It can't have been any of our regulars. They've all been here for years. None of them would dream of stealing money."

"I'm sure you're right. I expect it was that young tramp who's been hanging around and stole money from Anglesham. Actually Ralph, this makes me feel better. I was afraid someone from the congregation who didn't like me, ruined my gown. If it was a stranger, especially one who's off his head with dope, I don't feel nearly so bad. Still, you need to tell the police about the theft; get a crime number. Why don't you ring Chloe?"

"Good idea. I'll do that."

With no time left for breakfast or even a cup of tea, Polly snatched a glass of water and a couple of biscuits, collected her book of daily prayer, and set off through the garden for morning prayers at Anglesham church. The day hadn't started well and she felt unsettled—a familiar feeling to her lately—but all was not yet lost. Half an hour's quiet prayer might be just what she needed.

No one disturbed Polly in Anglesham church. She knelt at the altar rail and opened her heart to God.

God, what's going on here? Is it me? Am I somehow attracting evil? What am I doing wrong? And what about introducing change? How am I going to do that when they're so opposed to anything I suggest? And how am I going to get new people in—younger people, families—when everyone is so old? Dear God, I feel as though everything is beginning to weigh me down and I don't know what to do. I've got so many ideas, but I can't implement them. I need help, but even Oswald is against me. If I can't get Oswald and

Cheryl on side, I haven't a hope in hell. God, what should I do? Why did you send me here? Why won't you help me? Why is it that people seemed to love me when I was a curate, but now I'm a rector so many seem to dislike me or even hate me? God, I don't understand. I'm no different. Why won't they help me? Why do they try to kibosh every change I suggest? How can I lead them if they never agree with me? How can I move the church forward when all I meet is opposition?

There was no reply, but Polly felt better for having voiced her concerns. She sat in a pew and turned up the bible reading for the day, Joshua chapter one, verses one to nine.

Oh great! All about battles and war and the walls of Jericho falling down at a trumpet blast. If only life were that easy! Just what I don't need at the moment.

But when she read verse nine; *I hereby command you: Be strong and courageous; do not be frightened or dismayed, for the Lord your God is with you wherever you go,* Polly felt as though the verse was aimed directly at her, and her spirits soared. Maybe this was God's way of answering her prayer. God was with her after all; what she had to do was to trust God.

Polly skipped home after prayers with a lighter heart. It was going to be all right. Whatever happened, God would see her through. Wouldn't he? As if to encourage her positive mood, there was a parcel waiting for her on the rectory doorstep.

Polly took it indoors, turning it over curiously in her hands. It was the size and shape of a shoe box, and she felt quite excited as she stripped off the brown paper wrapping with her name printed in felt-tip. At least somebody loved her enough to leave an unexpected gift for her. Inside the box were layers of tissue paper, which Polly drew out and placed to one side. There was no note, and she wondered who her unknown benefactor might be.

In the bottom of the box was a Barbie doll with curling blond hair and wearing a black shirt, dog collar, and white cassock-alb. It was Polly to a tee. Polly was thrilled, until she noticed the smear of ink down the front of the cassock-alb. Then her hands began to tremble, for as she lifted the doll from the box, Polly saw that it was full of pins stuck through the heart, the head, the kidneys, the limbs, everywhere. With a cry of horror she dropped the doll back into its box, where it lay, gazing up at her with unblinking blue eyes.

CHAPTER SIXTEEN

The girl's breath was coming now in ragged, panting gasps. As the pain burst over her in waves, she screamed, although without any real expectation that any of them would hear. The place was thoroughly soundproofed. Besides, she only wanted him.

She had been though a lot in her short life, but never anything like this. She had no idea what to do. With limited access to the outside world, she had never witnessed a birth. She had experienced plenty of inner terror and pain though, and she had learned how to deal with those.

She gritted her teeth and forced herself to breathe deeply. When the contraction came again, this time more strongly, she imagined herself riding on the crest of a wave, and instinctively went with the contraction, panting to roll over the top of it. She found it was just about bearable that way.

He came in some hours later, as she found herself pushing with all her strength. She didn't know why she was pushing, it didn't seem to be of her own volition. She couldn't help herself.

He rushed to her, directing her hands to the bed rail. "Grip this. It'll be better. I'll ease him out. There's his head!" His voice held a tone of wonder that she had never heard before. "Come on. You're doing fine. One more push."

She couldn't help but obey him, and felt the instant relief as the baby emerged. She ordered,"Give her to me."

It was the first time she had spoken to him in such terms, but he did as she said, turning puzzled eyes upon her. "How did you know it's girl?"

"I knew."

"She's beautiful. My daughter." His voice was full of reverence. Then he added, "Come on, you need to push again. I know you're tired, but it's the afterbirth. You need to expel it. There. Good girl. I'll tie the cord."

He seemed to know exactly what to do. She wondered whether he had delivered other babies, but realised he knew everything. He had been her saviour before, now he was her saviour all over again. Expertly he tied the cord, wrapped the baby in a towel and handed the baby to her. "I'll wash her in a minute. Just need to bury this first."

He washed them both, gently and with love. He changed the bed linen again and made sure the place was clean and neat. She loved him then, but she knew she would have to fight him for the sake of her baby.

As she cradled her new baby, she was suffused with an overwhelming love like nothing she had ever experienced before, and with an overwhelming, protective fierceness. She knew without any shadow of doubt that she would do anything to protect this baby, her brand new daughter.

***

Unable to still the trembling of her arms and legs, Polly collapsed onto a kitchen chair. She hated the doll staring up at her like that, but she couldn't bring herself to touch the box again. With a hand clapped over her mouth, Polly felt slightly sick. What should she do? Ring the archdeacon or the rural dean? Would either of them understand, or would they dismiss her worries and note her down as an hysterical female who was unable to take a joke?

Some joke, she told herself grimly. *Whoever did this has a very sick sense of humour indeed. They've made it abundantly clear I'm not welcome here. Perhaps I should go now, move to Oxford and settle down with Tom.*

At the moment that sounded like paradise, to be with Tom, cared for, loved, looked after, wanted, respected. Everything that was lacking here at Anglesham. Even as she tried to tell herself that this was the work of just one demented person, an insistent voice in her brain whispered that you only needed one as evil as this. There could be three hundred people supporting her, but they wouldn't be able to wipe out this terrifying abhorrence.

Then she fell to thinking about voodoo, and despite her Christianity, wondering whether there was any truth in voodoo. She had seen on television well-documented cases of people who had died because a voodoo curse had been put on them with pins stuck through an effigy of them. Polly shuddered. Was this how it would end —in her death if she stayed at Anglesham? Would she gradually notice an increased lethargy until she faded away altogether, while the doctors shook their heads over her mystery illness and declared it to be the result of female hysteria?

The loud and repeated ringing of the doorbell jerked Polly from her reverie. Instinctively inclined to ignore it and pretend she wasn't in, the shaking of her hands increased. What if it was the perpetrator of this terrible threat come to finish her off? If she stayed low and ignored it, perhaps whoever it was would go away. She didn't feel like facing anyone at the moment, least of all some parishioner come to pile their problems upon her, but the pealing was followed by the rattling of the letterbox and Cheryl's voice loudly calling through.

"Polly? I know you're there. Open the door, I want to talk to you. Polly? Polly? Where are you?"

Groaning, Polly reluctantly crossed to the front door and opened it.

Without pausing for a greeting, Cheryl rudely pushed past her into the house, observing, "What's wrong with you? I was out there for ages, you might have opened the door. I knew you were in. For God's sake cheer up, Polly. You look like a smacked arse. Come on misery guts, I need a coffee."

Before Polly could respond or waylay her, she had marched into the kitchen. "What's this? Oh, dear God!"

Even Cheryl fell silent as she viewed the doll in its wrappings. Then she turned to Polly, her brashness forgotten as she asked quietly, "May I?"

At a nod from Polly she lifted the doll from the box and peered at it closely. "Let's take these out."

Without waiting for assent she began to remove the pins, placing them in a little heap on the kitchen table. "There. That's better. Now, let's see what we can do with this cassock-alb."

She stripped the doll and carried the miniature cassock-alb to the sink, where she turned on the cold water tap. "Ah, I thought so. See, I think this dirty mark is water-based felt-tip. It's coming out. We'll use your hair drier to dry this tiny robe, and it'll be perfect. Quite a keepsake when the unpleasantness is removed."

Polly found her voice. "Horrible thing. It's hateful. I don't want to keep it, I don't want to touch it and I never want to see it again."

"What rubbish! Of course you want it! If nothing else, you could sell it on Ebay. Any woman priest would be delighted to own this, especially a curly-haired blond. But I think it's brilliant without the pins and the stain. It looks just like you, Polly—you should be proud of it."

"*Proud?* You're insane. How can you say that? Someone wants me dead or gone and I should be *proud?* I'm not staying here. I'm going to pack up and leave Anglesham benefice. It's clear I'm not wanted here. I've no wish to stay where I'm not wanted."

Cheryl taunted, "Oh my! Feeling a little sorry for ourself, are we? I didn't have you down as quite such a wimp."

"Well, maybe you should have," Polly muttered.

Cheryl turned the hair drier on full blast. "So you're just going to sit back and let them win, are you? No fight in you? No backbone? Perhaps you'd better go, then. Better give up ministry too. As I understand it, ministry is full of niggles and nastiness. I'm told you get at least one enemy in every parish, so it's no good running away and thinking the grass will be any greener elsewhere. It won't be. The problems might be different, but they'll be there, just the same. So if you can't handle the first hurdle, you'd best give up altogether."

Feeling anger rise inside her, Polly glared at her. "It's all very well for you to talk. You're not on the receiving end. How do you imagine I felt when I opened this box?"

"Gave you quite a turn, of course it did. But it's only a doll. It can't hurt you—unless you let it get inside your head. I may not have been on the receiving end of this, but I can tell you I've had plenty of problems to deal with in my time. You don't know anything, Polly, you haven't been around long enough. Show a bit of spunk, for God's sake."

"And how, exactly, do you suggest I do that?"

"Chuck these pins away and sit the doll on your desk, so that everyone who comes in can admire it. Tell them how thrilled you are to receive it. Tell them it inspires you and look happy. That'll turn the tables on whoever did this. Word will get around about how delighted you are with your gift."

"Won't that encourage escalation?"

Having dressed the doll in its clean cassock-alb, Cheryl was busy with the kettle. She lifted her shoulders. "So what? You can take it. What can they do if you refuse to be terrorised? Whatever the motive behind this, they don't want you dead. I think they're just trying to frighten you, and yes, maybe it is someone trying to get rid of you. All the more reason to stay, in my book."

"Frighten me? They're succeeding," Polly muttered.

"Only if you let them. It's up to you. Anyway, what are you doing keeping this to yourself? This is exactly the sort of thing you need to share. A problem shared, and all that. By the way, have you got any brandy?"

"What? Er, yes, I suppose so. In the cupboard in the lounge; there's a bottle of Baileys. Is that brandy?"

"That'll do. Back in a minute."

Cheryl returned a moment later brandishing the bottle. Pouring a generous measure into each mug of coffee, she handed one to Polly. "Drink that."

Polly took the mug and sipped. As the hot liquid coursed through her, the shaking began to ease and she started to feel more human. "This is delicious, Cheryl. Why have I never tried this before?"

Cheryl regarded her approvingly. "That's better. Brought a bit of colour to your cheeks, and I do believe, the hint of a smile to your lips. About time."

Polly couldn't help grinning. "You're impossible, Cheryl, but you do make me feel better. Do you really think I can outsmart whoever is doing this?"

"Of course you can! And for your information, I don't make you feel anything. No one can make you feel. You're responsible for your own feelings. You may react in certain ways to certain stimuli, but other people can only press buttons. They can't make you react. Only you can do that."

"Cheryl, is this a touch of counselling for me? First the pep talk, then the counselling?"

A slow smile spread across Cheryl's face until the scarlet slash of her mouth seemed wider than ever. "At least you're coming back to life. Beginning to think again." She indicated Polly's empty mug. "Want another?"

"Not coffee, but I wouldn't mind another Baileys. How about you? Going to join me?"

"Need you ask? Of course I am. Look, handle this doll so you get the feel of her. I don't want you too terrified to touch her after I've gone. Here, take her."

She thrust the doll into Polly's hands. Squeamish at first, Polly soon realised that Cheryl had spoken sense. The doll had no power to harm her. It was just a doll—and beautifully dressed as a female priest.

"Perhaps I do like her after all," she murmured. "Quite flattering to have my own image in a Barbie. I will keep it, Cheryl. I'll sit her on my desk as my own special mascot. And Cheryl—thank you.

"By the way, did you just happen by and decide to drop in, or was there something you wanted to talk about? I thought you said you needed to ask me something?"

"I'd nearly forgotten in all the drama! Yes, we need to start planning for harvest festival."

"What? It's months away, isn't it?"

Cheryl nodded. "It is, but with the summer holidays coming up September will be here before you can blink. We always have a benefice harvest supper on the Saturday night, followed by a harvest festival service in each of the churches on the Sunday morning, and it's always the last weekend of September."

"Sounds cool. Where is the supper held?"

"That's why I'm here. Traditionally—and I mean for years now—we've held it in Jonathan Tunbridge's barn. Whichever parish is organising the evening—we take it in turns—decides on the entertainment, and we quite often have an old-fashioned barn dance. It's Upper Hartshead's turn this year, so I've been delegated to ask you whether you have any ideas or preferences."

Polly lifted her eyebrows and made a deprecating face. "Not at the moment. How about you and the churchwardens? Have you thought of anything?"

"We quite fancy the idea of a masked ball. Well, not a ball, exactly. More of a dance. We'd have the usual harvest supper—cold meats and salad followed by a variety of sweets—then put on our masks for the dance. Could be fun. We'd run a competition for the most original mask, and one for the church with the best masks over all. What do you think?"

Polly nodded. "Sounds great. Will it happen automatically, or do I have to approach Jonathan? Couldn't we have it in David's barn instead?"

"Put it like this. It does happen automatically, but Jonathan would be very put out if you failed to approach him officially, and steaming if you approached David instead of him. After all, it's Jonathan who's the churchgoer. So I'm afraid that's your next task, Polly. Approaching Jonathan Tunbridge to ask if we can use his barn for this year's harvest supper."

CHAPTER SEVENTEEN

On the Sunday morning, Polly climbed the steps to the pulpit, holding up the skirt of her long robe in one hand. She had tripped over the hem too often to want to repeat the experience. Starting her sermon with the usual short prayer, she waited until the congregation had sat down and ceased to shuffle. When the sea of faces was gazing at her expectantly, she began.

"For my text this morning I have deviated from the set readings for the day. Something interesting—I might even say exciting—happened to me this week. It made me think. I want to reflect upon the event theologically with you, so I've chosen for my text, Matthew chapter seven, verse eleven. If you then, who are evil, know how to give good gifts to your children, how much more will your Father in heaven give good things to those who ask him.

"I had a good gift given to me this week. Well, not exactly given to me, but left anonymously on my doorstep. I have it here with me."

She reached down onto the floor of the pulpit where she had hidden the doll, and brought it out with a flourish. "This beautiful doll was left for me in a shoe box, carefully packed around with tissue paper. As you see, it has been made entirely in my image, complete with cassock-alb, dog collar and stole. I don't know who so lovingly made this for me, clearly spending hours getting all the details exact, but I want to thank whoever it was from the bottom of my heart. This little doll is now my mascot and will sit on my desk and guard me. It has really brought home to me the truth of those words of Jesus in Matthew's gospel, *If you then, who are evil,*" she paused significantly, "*know how to give good gifts to your children, how much more will your Father in heaven give good things to those who ask him.*"

As she went on to talk about God's gift of himself to any who believed in him, she covertly scanned the congregation for any signs of discomfort. Was anyone feeling twitchy? Was the guilty party a member of St. Peter and St. Paul's congregation, or from one of the other churches? Polly intended to repeat the sermon in each of the four churches in the benefice, in the hope of flushing out her enemy, although she was aware that the element of surprise would be lacking at the other churches, who would certainly have heard about her sermon long before she preached it there. Apparently the doll had not been given by anyone from Anglesham church, for the whole congregation appeared to be riveted by her words. Jonathan Tunbridge was the only person not looking at her, but that was normal.

Since that first abortive service, Jonathan Tunbridge had been attending St. Peter and St. Paul's church at Anglesham regularly. Still withdrawn and morose, otherwise he behaved impeccably, while somehow managing to avoid any contact with Polly whatsoever. He never raised his eyes during the service and when she stood at the great west door at the close of the service, waiting with a smile on her face to say farewell to departing members of the congregation, Jonathan invariably slipped past her without making eye contact and without shaking hands.

Polly wondered whether she should deliberately waylay him after church on that particular Sunday morning, risking some sort of public showdown with him if he was the perpetrator of the doll episode, or whether she would be better to visit the farm one evening. Better still, perhaps she could ring, hoping he would be out so that she could leave a message on his answerphone without having to face him. On the whole she thought it was unlikely that he had left the doll, even though he was the only avowed detester of women priests in the benefice. He had large, spade-like farmer's hands, which looked to be quite unsuitable for the fine work required for fashioning dolls' clothes.

In the end, events were taken out of her hands by her own natural impulsiveness. As she spotted Jonathan edging behind her at the door after the service, she interrupted Maisie Faulkner's account of her rising blood pressure and increasing number of daily tablets, to call after him.

"Jonathan!"

He turned at the sound of his name, but scowled when he realised who had called him. "What?"

Ignoring the blatant rudeness, Polly called, "Just need a quick word with you. I'll pop over one evening this week if that's all right?"

Jonathan grunted, turned on his heel and continued on his way.

"Ill take that as a yes, then," Polly murmured.

Maisie Faulkner, who had been watching this encounter wide-eyed, made excuses for him. "Of course, he's never been the same since he lost his wife and daughter." She peered eagerly at Polly. "You did know the story, did you?"

"Yes, I have heard it, thank you Maisie. Several times, actually."

"Oh!" Maisie's face fell. "Well, as I was saying, I have to see the doctor again next week to check my blood pressure. He may need to adjust the tablets. Then I go to the hospital in a fortnight for tests."

She waited hopefully for Polly to enquire further into the nature of the forthcoming tests, but by now there was a queue behind her, all patiently waiting to say goodbye to Polly and shake her hand, so Polly merely promised, "I shall keep you very much in my prayers, Maisie. Be sure to let me know how you get on."

It was sufficient for a broad smile to spread across Maisie's careworn features, and she departed relieved and happy. Polly made a mental note to visit her prior to her hospital visit, just to encourage and reassure her. As a widow living alone with only her small, white Yorkshire terrier for company, Maisie was one of a number of lonely people whose only relief was the church.

When she had finished the second round of goodbyes at the door, saying farewell to those who had stayed for coffee, Polly strolled back into the church. With just the one service this morning, she had plenty of time to spare while Cheryl and Oswald between them took the services at the other three churches. Polly liked to linger every four weeks or so, to give more time to the important pastoral task of chatting to her parishioners, a part of her work which tended to be rushed when she had to go on to one of the other churches for the later service.

By the time Polly had passed the time of day with everyone, the two churchwardens, Jean and Chloe, were the only people remaining in church. They were clearing up the last vestiges of empty coffee cups, replacing hymn books, and generally tidying the church, but it was clear they had been chatting.

Chloe, as usual, came straight to the point. "That was an interesting text, Polly."

Polly glanced sharply at her. "It was an interesting gift."

"I'm sure it was. The part of the text which particularly caught my attention was the reference to evil people. You could have chosen a text about love and gifts, but you didn't, you linked it with evil. Why was that?"

Polly's eyes slid away as she struggled to come up with a plausible reason for her choice. "I—um —I didn't know who had given it. It was the first text which occurred to me," she finished lamely.

"Now tell us what really happened."

Polly sat down heavily in the pew. She sighed. "I know you'll wheedle it out of me, Chloe, so I suppose I'd better come clean. But I really don't want it to go any further. Cheryl knows because she happened to call soon after I picked up the box, but nobody else does and I think we should keep it that way."

As she related the episode, the two women listened intently. Jean looked horrified, but Chloe was deep in thought.

"Cheryl persuaded you it was just mischief? Someone out to upset you?" she asked.

Polly nodded. "She thought I should brazen it out; turn the tables on them. Hence this morning's sermon, which I shall take to the other churches next week."

Jean was full of a motherly concern. "Are you safe, in that rectory all by yourself? Why don't you come and stay with me? Or if you won't do that, how about borrowing Moses for a while?"

Chloe agreed. "That's not a bad idea, Polly. You could consider investing in a dog. That or a couple of geese. They make brilliant guard dogs. I don't think you'd be troubled again with a gander around."

Laughing, Polly reassured her friends. "I'll be fine. As Cheryl said, I don't think anyone's out to do me any real damage. They're trying to frighten me, but when they realise I refuse to be intimidated, perhaps they'll leave me alone."

Chloe nodded, but Jean said firmly, "I'm coming home with you anyway, Polly. And I shall call in at least once a day to make sure you're all right. You'll get sick of the sight of me, but indulge me in this. By the way, have you any idea who's doing this?"

"None at all. I had wondered about Jonny Tunbridge, but he's so openly antagonistic that I can't think why he'd need to bother with anything so underhand. It must be someone who pretends to approve of me, but who's a closet opponent. Anyway, I have to visit Jonathan this week, so I may well ask him outright."

There was a sharp intake of breath from Jean. "Do you want me to come with you?"

As Polly shook her head, Jean added, "Do be careful, Polly. Please don't go courting trouble."

Polly said lightly, "You remind me of my friend Sue. She has a parish in London and she looks after me from a distance. She always telling me to be careful and keep out of trouble. Don't worry, Jean. I'll be fine. You'll see."

***

In view of her previous disaster when attempting to visit Jonathan Tunbridge, Polly rang him on the Wednesday morning to alert him to her proposed visit that evening. She left a message on his answerphone, assuming that he would be in for lunch and would pick up his messages. That evening, she drove to the isolated Abbot's Farm.

As she made her way through the rusting machinery that littered the yard, and waited on the doorstep, Polly tried to still the beating of her heart and slow her short, rapid breathing, but hearing Jonathan's footsteps approaching the door nearly caused her to turn tail and flee. She forced herself to keep still and held her head high, with a fixed smile on her face.

Jonathan opened the door, not speaking but indicating with a flick of his head that she should follow him. Polly carefully closed the front door behind her, wondering as she did so whether she might not have been wiser to leave it open. She hurried after her host, following him into the kitchen where he stood, waiting.

Polly thrust out her chin, determined to wait him out. Darned if she was going to do all the running. It was time he spoke to her.

When the silence threatened to become uncomfortable, Jonathan growled, "Well?"

Suddenly irritated by this uncouth display, Polly said, "Good evening, Jonathan. It's very good to see you, too."

He raised his eyes to glare at her. "What do you want?"

"Two things. May we hold the Harvest Festival celebrations in your barn again, please? It's the last Saturday evening in September, as usual. Upper Hartshead are planning the entertainment this year, and I understand they'd like to have a masked dance after the supper. Would that be all right with you?"

She half expected an outburst or a downright refusal, but he merely nodded. When she said nothing more, he asked, "What else?"

Polly swallowed, feeling less sure of herself now. She wished she hadn't mentioned two things. Why couldn't she keep her mouth shut? But he was waiting.

Polly said, "Sunday's sermon. Do you know anything about the doll that was left on my doorstep?"

He was either an excellent actor, or genuinely astonished. "Me? Why would I be giving you presents?"

"This particular gift had pins stuck in it. I think it was intended to frighten me—or worse. Was it your handiwork, Jonathan?"

CHAPTER EIGHTEEN

For a moment, Jonathan Tunbridge stood as if turned to stone. Only his eyes, black and glowering, seemed alive, and they were flashing dangerously. Polly caught her breath, wishing her words unsaid. She felt like a cornered animal, but instead of the urge to attack, found herself fearful, shrinking inside. As Jonathan's head lowered and his shoulders hunched, Polly slowly edged away, but the back of her knees caught the rim of a kitchen chair and she fell onto it in an embarrassing heap.

With the added humiliation of the ungainly fall, Polly flushed uncomfortably and lowered her eyes, but to her surprise, Jonathan's posture had relaxed. As if nothing untoward had happened, he walked to the other side of the kitchen table, pulled out a chair and sat opposite her. Having swept aside a pile of newspapers to provide a little space on the pine surface, he rested his elbows, steepled his hands and stared at her. Polly swivelled in her seat to face him, but unwilling to share his proximity too closely or to succumb to the unspoken pressure to explain, leaned back to observe her surroundings.

Very similar to his twin brother's farmhouse in furnishings and layout, Abbot's Farm had one big difference. Whereas David's home was pristine in its neatness, Jonathan's was one of the untidiest and dirtiest places Polly had encountered. Apart from the mess on the table, the surface of the kitchen dresser was piled high with old bills, letters, magazines and sundry papers. Crockery was drying on the draining board, but the sink could barely be seen under a huge accumulation of greasy pots and pans. Grime encrusted the skirting board and encroached over the tiled floor, and it didn't take too much imagination to picture various rodents sharing the kitchen. With the faint smell of stale food in the air and bringing to mind the haphazard farmyard outside, full of rusting farm machinery, car parts and heaps of old wood, Polly wondered what the rest of the house was like. She was unable to repress a small shudder. She hoped he wouldn't offer her tea, and then couldn't help smiling at such an incongruous thought. Jonathan Tunbridge would never offer her anything.

A muscle twitched at the corner of Jonathan's mouth and his eyes took on a sardonic gleam, almost as if he could read her thoughts. "Gypsies."

"Excuse me?" Polly's brow creased in bewilderment, as she wondered whether she had missed part of the conversation.

"Gypsies. They're back."

"Gypsies? Where? On your land? I haven't seen any, and no one's mentioned them. It's usually the first thing I hear, if travellers have arrived."

"Sly lot. Keep themselves hidden. On the common, just south of the marsh. Up to no good."

"Are you sure? How would they get there? There's no road across the common, only round the edge."

He gave a snort of humourless laughter. "Think you know it 'cos you once walked a footpath which dumped you in the marsh? There's acres of untouched land. They drive their vans straight over it. Don't need no roads."

Polly's lips pinched. Clearly his brother had told him of her hapless visit. No doubt they'd had a good laugh together. "How come you've seen them, then?"

The scornful glint in his eyes deepened. "I know every inch of the common, the marsh, and all the land round here for a twenty mile radius. Grew up here, remember. Just 'cos I work for a living don't mean I haven't time to go walking now and again."

Polly shivered at the thought of suddenly coming across the sinister Jonathan Tunbridge while out for a pleasant afternoon stroll. "How long have they been there?"

He shrugged. "Week or so. Maybe more."

"So why haven't they been into the village for supplies? How come nobody else but you knows about them?"

"Reckon you've had a visit or two at the church, from what I hear."

Polly's mind shot to the vagrant who had been the cause of so much trouble. Could he be a gypsy? He hadn't looked like a gypsy. Then she realised she was thinking only of a stereotype. But why would a stranger—gypsy or not—target her with silent phone calls and voodoo dolls? It didn't make any sense. "What he stole wouldn't take him far. How many are there?"

"Couple of vans. One family, I should think. They do that sometimes. Split up and head out on their own."

"What do they do for food? They can't live on nothing, and the Anglesham Stores haven't reported any strangers."

"Wouldn't shop there. Too small. More likely use a supermarket where they're anonymous. Besides, they poach. Shoot rabbits and game. Plenty of pheasants around here. And steal milk from my brother's dairy herd."

There was an odd expression on his face as he added this last titbit, almost, Polly thought, as if he found a strange satisfaction in the idea that David's produce was being pilfered.

"And your precious grain, I suppose!" Angered by his apparent pleasure in his brother's misfortune, the sarcastic words were out before Polly could bite them back.

His eyes hardened and his voice became cold. "They won't set foot on this farm. Never. Not ever."

"I—I'm sorry. I heard about your wife and daughter."

"Save your pity for them that need it," he said roughly. Adding, "So what are you going to do about it?"

"About what?"

"Them gypsies. You've gotta get them moved."

"*Me?* Why me? What do you mean? Why do I have to get them moved? And how would I do that, always supposing I wanted to?"

"You're the rector. Your job to lead. You'd best get up the council and tell them."

"I'll do no such thing," Polly retorted. "Besides, I don't necessarily agree with you that travellers should be moved on. They're God's children too, you know, and it's common land. They have to live somewhere, and if they're doing no harm, why shouldn't they stay a while on the common?"

Again, he snorted with humourless mirth. "No harm? Huh! Leaving litter and filth, stealing from the locals, corrupting our kids. That what you call no harm?"

"That's pure prejudice. Just because some travellers might do some of those things, it doesn't mean all of them do."

At that, he laughed out loud and his voice took on a sneering quality. "Never come across gypsies before, have you? Soon change your tune if you had. Keep your do-gooding for your own flock, unless you want to empty the church. I'm as God-fearing as the next man, and I can tell you, none of them churchgoers want any gypsies around here. You'll see."

"Perhaps *you're* the one that'll see," Polly replied, tartly. "The church folk around here may possess more Christian love than you realise." Then her voice took on a softer note, and despite herself, she leaned towards him. "Look, Jonathan. I understand that you've had bad experiences in the past, but don't let them colour your whole life. If you could only open up and allow Jesus to take control, I'm sure things would be better for you."

Jonathan jerked away from her as if she had struck him, and stood up, glaring. His eyes hardened and his mouth narrowed to a thin line. "Keep your evangelical clap-trap for those that need it. I'm old church, myself. Don't hold with none of this newfangled nonsense and I'll thank you to keep your bible-bashing away from me. Got that? And got all you came for? Harvest supper and your barn dance. Nothing else to keep you here, then."

Polly moistened her lips, angry at being so summarily dismissed, feeling foolish and aware that she'd inadvertently overstepped some mark, but unsure what. Her voice was coolly formal. "I apologise if I've said anything to upset you. Thank you for the use of your barn."

She nodded at him without smiling and followed him to the back door. He opened it for her, but just as she was passing into what looked more like a scrapyard than a farmyard, he grabbed her arm in a vice-like grip. Polly caught her breath.

"Keep away from them gypsies, you hear? No place for a kid like you. Get up the council about them."

Polly tossed her head. She said coldly, "Thank you for your concern, Jonathan. Noted. You may be sure I shall think and pray carefully about the situation before taking any action."

Then she marched to her car, head held high. Not daring to look back to see how he had taken her words, it wasn't until she was well on the road home that she found she could begin to relax and mull over his unexpected news.

Polly drove slowly, craning her neck as she passed the common, but was unable to detect any indication of the presence of caravans. She was half tempted to park the car and explore on foot simply because Jonathan had forbidden her to do so, but it was a dark evening with rain promised, and dusk was already threatening. In the end, she decided to call on Jean instead. She might have heard something.

After Abbot's Farm, it was a relief to enter the cleanliness of the old Crossing-Keeper's Cottage, which was always neat and cared for properly, although never so perfect that Polly was afraid to sit down. She plumped up a cushion and settled herself on the sofa in the lounge while Jean repaired to the kitchen to make tea.

When they were both engaged in sipping their drinks, Jean spoke. Her voice was full of concern. "Are you okay, Polly? I know these recent incidents have really upset you. You seem to have lost something of your bounce."

Polly grimaced. "Maybe that's because I've just spent half an hour in the delightful company of Jonathan Tunbridge."

"Oh goodness! I knew you were planning to see him, but I didn't think you'd go there alone, at night. I thought David had told you to keep away from him?"

"And I had kept away from him, but I needed to ask his permission to use his barn for the harvest supper, apparently. So I really had no choice. Well, I suppose I could have caught him after church, but it seemed like a good opportunity to try and break the ice a bit. Not that it worked. He despises me. Thinks I'm young and stupid as well as committing the cardinal sin of being female. Made that abundantly clear."

"Do you think so? Perhaps he's not quite as awful as he appears. I suspect there's some showmanship going on there. He's one of those bark worse than bite types. I know he's scary, but he's always been a loyal member of the church."

"Could do without his sort of loyalty," Polly muttered. Then added, "Sorry. I shouldn't have said that. He's part of the flock and I have to deal with that. Don't think I'll visit too often, though. Have you ever been there? The place is filthy, revolting."

Jean grinned. "Needs a good woman to take him in hand."

"Well, I'm not offering! By the way, Jean, have you heard anything about any gypsies around here? Jonathan reckons there's a family on the common. He's no time for them, of course—not surprising, given his past history—but if it's true, I thought I might try and make contact."

Jean looked worried, increasing the lines on her forehead. "Do you think that's wise? They don't have a very good reputation and you don't want to put yourself at odds with the congregation."

"That's exactly what Jonathan said! But I can't allow prejudice to prevent me from doing God's work, can I? Perhaps the congregation needs to change its attitude."

"If you're sure that befriending travellers really is God's work. I thought you were here to look after your congregations. Oh! That reminds me. Maggie Brewster was looking for you. She came over to the church earlier this evening, while I was checking that all was well. Looked quite worried, I thought."

"Maggie? I wonder what she wants? I'll ring her." Polly stretched, and stood up. "Thanks for the tea, Jean. I'd like to stay and chat, but I'd better get along or it'll be too late to phone her tonight. I don't like to ring after nine o'clock, and it's already a quarter to. See you whenever."

CHAPTER NINETEEN

"We need to have a normal life, just you me and the baby. Like other people. Our daughter needs that. We can't live here for ever, her and me."

He stared at her with his mouth hanging open, as if she had gone insane. "What about the danger? What if you're recognised?"

"We could go abroad. America, or Brazil. Somewhere warm. You'd get a job. I could work, too."

"Sorry." He was abrupt, as he always was when refusing her requests. "I have to go. I don't want you to talk about this any more. Forget it. She'll be all right here, just like you."

She knew then that it was hopeless. And she knew what she must do to save her baby from a fate like her own.

When he had gone, as the baby slept peacefully, she held a pillow over the baby's face, pressing down gently so as not to hurt her daughter. The baby's legs kicked, once, twice, then were still.

When she was sure the baby had stopped breathing, the girl wept.

***

Polly was glad to reach home before it was fully dark. Not normally a nervous person, she glanced round anxiously, peering into the undergrowth between the mature trees in the rectory garden, the hairs on the back of her neck pricking uncomfortably, for she was half afraid some unknown enemy was concealed there. Then mentally scolding herself for being stupidly paranoid, she took a deep breath, inserted her key, opened the front door and stepped boldly into her home. But she was unable to relax fully until she had flooded the rectory with light, swiftly opened every door to check that nothing was untoward, and drawn the curtains over exposed ground floor windows.

Only when this routine was completed did she calm down sufficiently to pick up the phone. "Maggie? Hi, it's me, Polly. How are you? Everything okay? Jean said you were trying to contact me. I'm sorry it's so late, but I've only just come in."

"Polly!" The relief in Maggie's voice was almost palpable. "Thank you so much for ringing. I—I don't know where else to turn. I'm so worried, Polly. Look, I can't really talk about it on the phone. Could I come round tomorrow?"

"Yes, of course. Come tomorrow morning." In her mind, Polly swiftly reorganised her day. The funeral visit to Evelyn and John Davidson wasn't scheduled until the afternoon so that should be all right, but she would have to fit in Maisie Faulkner, prior to Maisie's hospital appointment, later than planned. "Um, Maggie, could you give me any indication of what this is about? Might help you to sleep better if you've shared some of it."

"Sleep! I haven't slept properly for days, Polly. You're going to know anyway, so I don't suppose it will hurt if I tell you now. It's Kimberley, our daughter. She's been sacked."

"Sacked? I don't quite understand..."

Maggie heaved a sigh. "Expelled, then. From her very expensive and high class boarding school. Not that I care about the money, or the disgrace, come to that. But Giles had to collect her. It was so embarrassing for him. I just hope the press don't get hold of it, you know what they're like. They'd use anything to ruin his political career. Giles brought her home from school a week ago. Naturally he was very angry, but I talked to him and persuaded him to calm down. We planned to sit down together as a family and discuss the situation in an adult fashion. No recriminations, just asking what she was going to do with her life and whether she wanted to pick up the A-levels at a local college, but we didn't get the chance. As soon as she was home, she slammed up to her bedroom and refused to come out. I was so worried, Polly. I took up food on a tray and left it outside the door, but it wasn't touched. It's not as though she can afford to lose weight, either. She's as thin as a stick, now. I don't know where all the pounds have gone. She was never large, but now she's painfully thin. I don't know why. Hope it's not that anorexia disease.

"Anyway, I stuck it as long as I could—Giles had gone back to London, he was needed for an important division in the House and you can't miss those even if you're on your deathbed—I kept banging on Kimberley's door, but she refused to answer. After a day of this, I called a locksmith from Norwich. He took the lock off Kimberley's door and I went in, but she wasn't there. She must have slammed upstairs for our benefit, locked her bedroom door from the outside, then immediately crept down again and slipped out of the back door. Polly, I have no idea where she is, and I'm worried sick."

"How old is Kimberley, Maggie?"

"Seventeen. She's more or less finished her first year of A-levels. That's why we were less upset than we might have been when the school contacted us. It's nearly the end of the academic year, and we thought she could could start the final year at one of the sixth form colleges, or at City College in Norwich. She was never particularly happy at boarding school, but we wanted her to have the best possible education. Is that so very wrong?"

"Of course not! You wanted the best for your child—and still do. Maggie, have you contacted the police?"

"Not yet. To tell you the truth, Polly, I'm rather afraid to do so. After all, she wasn't abducted or anything like that. She went of her own accord, and she's over sixteen. I'm not sure the police would be very interested, and if I go down that route, the media is certain to get wind of it. Besides, Kimberley would kill me if she thought I'd put the police onto her."

"What does Giles say?"

There was a pause, then Maggie admitted, "He doesn't think we should do anything. He's seething, Polly, and this has made him worse. He's more or less washed his hands of her. Of course," she added in a rush, "it's only temporary. The problem is, we only had the one child, so Kimberley is very special to him. She was always his little girl. He's never been able to allow her to grow up, still expects her to want to do all those father-daughter things she used to do when she was about ten. Ponies and fishing and long country walks, stuff like that. But she stopped all that when she entered adolescence, and inevitably the teenage moods started. And the rows. Giles simply couldn't cope with it, so he spent more and more time in London while Kimberley was home for the holidays. That way, he was able to kid himself that nothing had changed. And he's away from it all now. I don't mean he has his head stuck in the sand, but it's not the same for him. He's working in London, miles away, immersed in great affairs of state. It's not the same as being here on the ground, worrying yourself sick every minute of every day."

"No, I can see that. Maggie," Polly chose her words carefully. "What made the school sack Kimberley? Was it a one-off event, or an accumulation?"

Maggie sighed again. "Both. Kimberley has presented behavioural problems ever since she went to that school. She attended the local Church of England primary school here, and did well there with no problems whatsoever, but they all change schools at the age of eleven so it seemed like the ideal time to move her forward and develop her gifts. Of course, we knew it would mean leaving her childhood friends behind, but at that age, they make new friends quickly enough—or so we thought. All her primary school friends went to Riversmead High, where Oswald Waters teaches. As a matter of fact, his son used to babysit for Kimberley when she was younger. In retrospect, I think she'd have been happier living at home, keeping the friends she'd grown up with and attending the local comprehensive where she knew one of the teachers, but it's easy to be wise after the event, isn't it? We wanted her to have the best education money can buy, to give her a good start in life. And to be fair, although we both realised the behavioural problems were because she was homesick, we thought she'd soon settle down, once she made friends. But she made the wrong sort of friends, and I suspect that the bad behaviour became a habit. You know what it's like. Once the teachers label you as a troublemaker, you never lose the epithet."

"What sort of behavioural problems did she have? Attention deficit, something like that?"

"That was part of it, certainly. But not as a medical condition. She's far from incapable of paying attention. Actually, I think that was part of the problem. Kimberley is exceptionally bright. She has a very high IQ—it was measured when she was eight and was way up in the hundred and forties, which was partly why we both wanted her to make the most of it in a top class school—but I think she was bored. She counteracted her boredom by disrupting her classes and playing truant. And the more disruptive she was, the more kudos she acquired in the eyes of her classmates—you know what teenage girls are like. A small gang of them used to go out after lights out, led—according to the school—by Kimberley, drive to the nearest town and visit night clubs. They all became seventeen this last year, so they all have driving licences, and four of them have their own cars at school. Kimberley wanted one too, but Giles did put his foot down over that. Promised her one when she passed A-levels and got into Cambridge. Not that it had much effect. She drives her friends' cars. Anyway, on the final escapade they were stopped by the police for speeding, the driver was breathalysed and found to be way over the limit. It wasn't Kimberley driving on that occasion, thank God, but according to the other girls, she had been the perpetrator of the whole incident and had kept plying them with alcohol, although why they didn't have the wit to refuse, I can't imagine. Still, Kimberley got all the blame, hence she is no longer associated with the school."

Polly suppressed an urge to laugh. Drink driving, with the loss of life it so often entailed, was not a laughing matter, but Kimberley sounded like such a feisty girl. "Maggie, clearly Kimberley is a very lively young woman with huge leadership potential. Once she settles down, she'll go far in life, like her dad."

"Hardly the point at the moment, is it? She's missing, Polly, and I don't know where she is. I don't want her to ruin her life almost before it's begun, but how can I help her if I can't find her?"

Polly offered, "Would you like me to come round now?"

"No, of course not. I don't think either of us can do much tonight. But maybe in the morning we could discuss strategies for finding her—and I do need your prayers, Polly."

"Definitely. You'll all be very much in my thoughts and prayers. Maggie, just so that I can get an early start on this tomorrow, have you had any wind of Kimberley since she left? Has anybody caught sight of her? Did she keep in touch with any primary school friends? Or has she a boyfriend back near her boarding school?"

Maggie hesitated. "I—I'm not sure, to be honest. I have no idea whether or not she has a boyfriend. She's never mentioned anyone. Neither has she mentioned any of her former friends, and since mostly we kept her with us in the holidays, she didn't have much opportunity to renew old friendships. Besides, you grow away from people in time, don't you? I haven't contacted any of them, and I'm not sure I can even remember any names, so I don't think we can go down that route just yet."

"Oh." Polly felt some sympathy for Kimberley beginning to stir. "And there's nothing else? No other avenues we can explore around here?"

"Lizzie Braconridge, the churchwarden at Upper Hartshead, did mention in passing that she thought she'd seen her. Said how nice it must be to have Kimberley home early for the holidays. I'm afraid I just muttered something innocuous. Didn't want all this trouble getting about. It's family business, and we don't want anyone else to know. Except you, of course."

"I understand that. Anything that passes between us is completely confidential, Maggie. Did Elizabeth mention where she'd seen Kimberley?"

"I think she only glimpsed her in passing. Wasn't even certain it was her. Lizzie was driving back home from Parsondale and thought she spotted Kimberley on the footpath behind our house. That was the day before yesterday, so to be honest, I think it's unlikely. Could have been anyone. How many fair-haired teenage girls wearing jeans do you know? Every other girl you see has long blond hair and they all look the same in jeans and tee shirts. She probably only thought it was Kimberley because of the location. I should think Kimberley's miles away from here by now. She never wanted to come and live at home. And where would she be staying around here? We'd soon get to hear about it. No, I reckon London or one of the bigger cities. I suppose it could be Norwich, but that would risk being seen by someone who knows her and thus being tracked down by us. I'm afraid she's made it abundantly clear she wants nothing to do with us, but I just can't let her go like that without making some effort to patch things up. And the worst thing is, I don't even know what we're supposed to have done wrong. Why is she taking it out on us?"

"Have you checked Norwich rail station? Or the local bus routes?"

"Not yet. I wanted to talk to you first. Oh Polly, do you think I'll ever see my daughter again?"

"Of course you will! Don't be so silly. Come round first thing and we'll look at possibilities together. The internet for one. It has loads of websites for finding missing people. I know it's silly to tell you not to worry, Maggie, but you'll see. This is where your faith becomes so important. Trust God, Maggie. Everything will be all right. Try and get some sleep, now, and we'll get to work tomorrow. Okay?"

Maggie said tremulously, "Okay. And thanks, Polly. You are a dear."

But Polly was less sure than she had sounded. She felt as though another weight had landed on her shoulders. What were the chances of finding Kimberley Brewster? If they did find her, would she want to come home? And how long before the press discovered that local MP Sir Giles Brewster's daughter was a runaway?

CHAPTER TWENTY

Having slept much better than she had anticipated given the disturbing news she had received from Maggie Brewster, Polly awoke to overcast skies, a sure sign that the warm, summer weather was about to break. But never one to let a grey day depress her, Polly sang as she thrust two slices of bread into the toaster and spooned instant coffee into a mug.

Just before eight thirty she opened the door of the rectory for her usual walk through the rectory garden to the church next door for morning prayers, but her bright mood vanished like snow in summer as a sudden shock sent her heart plummeting. On the doorstep was a wicker Moses basket. Her heart beating loudly, Polly reached a trembling hand towards the basket, but then drew back. What now? Dare she approach it? What threat would she find this time? Another doll with pins stuck in it? And more to the point, how long could she go on like this, in dread of opening her own front door for fear of what she might find outside, and dread of silent phone calls while she was inside?

To steady herself, she closed her eyes momentarily and drew in a deep breath, silently pleading with God for help. Suppose—terror of terrors—the basket contained something really dangerous, like a live snake? Was anybody evil enough to do that? Was she really hated to that extent? Polly shuddered. Reaching back into the hall she grabbed an umbrella. Gritting her teeth, she forced herself to propel the basket with the umbrella, turning it round to face her, keeping it at arm's length for safety and ready to leap back if anything at all slid out of it.

As soon as she saw the basket's contents, her pent-up breath exhaled in a long sigh. Tossing aside the umbrella, she reached down, picked up the basket, cradled it close to her and returned indoors.

Carrying the basket through into the kitchen, she placed it carefully on the kitchen table. Murmuring, "You little darling," Polly lifted out a tiny, new-born baby, securely wrapped in a warm shawl with a pale pink edging, underneath which were exquisitely made, snowy white baby clothes. Packed around the baby was a soft blanket. But the baby was unmoving, not even whimpering. As she made to gently cuddle the baby, Polly gasped, for despite the coverings, the baby's skin was ice-cold and her perfect little face was faintly waxy. With a cry of horror, Polly replaced the child in the basket, feeling her neck for a pulse. There was none. The baby girl was dead.

Deeply shocked, Polly sank onto a chair, her hand covering her mouth. Who could do such a thing? A doll with pins was bad enough, but a dead baby! This was an action too far.

How long has this poor little baby been dead? How did she die? Who did this?

The thoughts precipitated Polly into action. She had to do something, but what? Call an ambulance? Too late for that, surely. A doctor, then. Presumably someone would have to certify the death. The police. Yes, that was it. Call the police. Let them deal with everything. This latest atrocity was way out of Polly's league.

Please God, let Chloe be in. Please. I can't cope with this.

Polly lifted the receiver with trembling hands and dialled Chloe's number, praying that Chloe was there. To Polly's relief, the phone was answered before the answer machine cut in.

"Yes?" Chloe's clipped tones sounded breathless.

"Chloe! Thank God! Something awful has happened and I—I—" To her dismay, Polly began to weep, silently at first but more noisily as the tears took hold. "I—I'm sorry," she managed to splutter between sobs, "c—can you come over? I need you."

Trying to avoid looking at the dead baby lying in the basket on her kitchen table, Polly crossed to the sink to dry her tears and splash cold water on her face. She took deep breaths to steady herself and kept repeating over and over again, Help me God. Help me, God. Help me, God.

Then she filled the kettle, dropped a couple of teabags into the pot, fished two mugs from the cupboard and poured a little milk into each. As the kettle boiled, she began to think more rationally. Who had done this? Had the baby been murdered, or died of natural causes? Was this the same perpetrator, the one who had made the silent phone calls and sent the doll? Was it the same person who had damaged her cassock-alb and stolen the money? Although Polly's head was in a whirl, she felt instinctively that this was different.

The baby looked as if she had been cared for extremely well. Her clothes were beautifully handmade. She was warmly dressed in a hand stitched, white babygro and hand knitted, white cardigan with pink edging, with a little knitted cap on her head and matching mittens on her hands, and as tightly bound in the crocheted shawl as if she was swaddled. The basket was well padded and the baby had been tucked around with the blanket. This looked like a much loved baby, not an unwanted nuisance which had been discarded like so much rubbish.

Thoughtfully, Polly crossed to the basket once again. Carefully, she lifted out the baby, laying her gently on the table. Then she rummaged around in the basket, to see whether any clues had been left. Her search was rewarded by the rustle of paper. Pinned to the underside of the blanket was a note. Polly unpinned it and spread it out on the kitchen table. A message was scrawled in a rounded, childish hand, on cheap, lined paper torn from a notebook.

Please look after my baby and give her a Christian burial. Her name is Mary Elizabeth Madison.

Polly felt compassion fill her. This was no cruel joke. This was a young, teenage mother, distraught at the death of her child. Perhaps the baby had been stillborn. Perhaps the pregnancy had been somehow kept secret. Perhaps—

Polly's musings were interrupted by the insistent ringing of the doorbell. Chloe. Polly folded the note, slipped it into her pocket and replaced the baby in the basket, making the sign of the cross on the baby's forehead, murmuring a prayer for her soul and dropping a kiss on her forehead, before she answered the door.

Chloe's tousled hair was still wet from a shower, and her normally immaculate clothes had been discarded in favour of grey jogging pants and a sweatshirt.

Polly was immediately contrite. "It's your day off! I'm so sorry, Chloe, I didn't know."

"Never mind that. I'm used to emergencies, day off or not. What's the trouble?"

"You'd better come in." Polly led the way into the kitchen and poured out the tea. Silently, she handed a mug to Chloe, who was staring open-mouthed at the baby in the basket.

"What in the world?" Even as she spoke, Chloe placed two fingers delicately on the baby's neck. She looked at Polly. "It's dead."

"I know. I found her on the doorstep. Felt a bit panicky when I rang you. Sorry about all that."

Without answering, Chloe took Polly's phone off the rest and dialled the station. She gave a terse set of instructions, replaced the phone, and turned to Polly. "What time?"

"Excuse me?"

"What time did you find the baby?"

Polly glanced at her watch. "I was just going out for morning prayers—they've gone by the board again—so it must have been about fifteen minutes ago, around half past eight. But I have no idea how long she'd been there."

"Have you touched her?"

"Well, yes. I lifted her out. Didn't know she was dead until then."

"How do you know it's a girl?"

Polly shrugged. "I just assumed, because of the pink edging. I haven't looked, if that's what you mean."

"Did you notice anything unusual last night or early this morning?"

Polly wrinkled her brow in an effort at remembrance. "I don't think so. What sort of thing? Oh, only that—" She tailed off.

"Only what? Everything you can remember is important. We need to find the mother. She may be in need of medical attention. We don't know yet what we're dealing with. It could be murder. Forensics will tell us how it died."

"Mary Elizabeth Madison," Polly automatically supplied.

"What?"

Polly blushed. "Not it, she. It's a girl, Mary Elizabeth Madison. That's her name. The baby."

"How do you know?"

Polly fished the note out of her pocket and handed it over.

Chloe quickly scanned it. "And you didn't think this was important? Anything else you haven't told me?"

"No, of course not! I'm sorry, Chloe, I just forgot. I could see she'd been well cared for, so I wondered whether there was any clue to her identity. This was pinned to the underside of the blanket."

"Where's the pin?"

"What? Oh. I put it in here, I think."

As Polly went to rummage in the jar on the kitchen dresser containing rubber bands, varieties of pens and assorted paper clips, Chloe stopped her. "I'll take it. You've added quite enough fingerprints already, thank you."

Using a clean tissue, she fished out the large safety pin, wrapped it carefully in the tissue and placed it on the surface of the dresser. "Forensics will need this."

"What for? Surely you just need to find a Madison from the telephone directory to locate the mother? Isn't that what will happen next?"

"Of course, but it may not be quite that simple. I'm afraid forensics will be all over this place like a rash. The pathologist will examine the baby to ascertain the cause of death. We'll do our best to locate the mother, and take it from there."

"You mean a post mortem? What about the burial? The mother—presumably the mother, although I suppose it could conceivably have been the father—particularly requested a Christian burial. That's why Mary Elizabeth was left on my doorstep, so that I could perform the necessary Christian rites. This was a mother who really loved her daughter."

"Hm." Chloe raised an eyebrow. "I'll reserve judgement over that until we find out exactly how this poor little mite met her end. Yes, of course there'll be a post mortem, but I see no reason why you shouldn't bury her eventually. Might be a long time, though. Depends on whether we find any relatives. Obviously our first priority is to find the mother. Polly, my folks will need to question you again, but it's purely routine. Is that okay with you?"

Polly nodded. "I have to go out later this morning, and I'll be out all afternoon. Got a funeral visit."

"No problem. Polly, just now when I asked you if you could recall anything unusual, you hesitated. Did you remember something?"

"Not really. It was just silly. I don't think it was anything—just a feeling. Nothing you'd call evidence."

"Come on, tell me. The most trivial details can be important, never mind how silly they may seem."

"Well, it was last night in the garden. I'd been out until about a quarter to nine, so it wasn't quite dark. I just had this eerie feeling, as though someone was watching me. You know how you can kind of feel it when someone's eyes are boring into you? It felt like that. I glanced around, but I couldn't see anything. Mind you, dusk was falling and it was a bit scary, so to be honest, I shot indoors as quickly as I could."

Chloe looked thoughtful. "Could be significant. We'll know more when the pathologist tells us the time of death, but if the baby was placed on your doorstep last night, she must have been dead before then. Otherwise, why ask for a burial? Why not a christening?"

"Phew!" Polly blew out her cheeks. "Just for a moment I thought you were going to say she'd died from hypothermia during the night. I'm already beginning to feel guilty that I didn't notice anything concrete and didn't have the nerve to properly investigate the grounds. Don't want Mary Elizabeth's death on my conscience as well. Chloe, you don't think this has anything to do with the other incidents, do you?"

Chloe shook her head. "Not a chance. We won't know anything definite until all the reports are in, but at first glance, I'd say it was a stillbirth, probably premature by the size, left by someone who wanted your help, not to harm you or frighten you."

"Thank goodness. That's what I thought." Adding, as the doorbell rang loudly, "That must be your people."

Together, the two of them went to the front door. But it wasn't the police team. Maggie stood on the doorstep. Polly had forgotten all about her.

CHAPTER TWENTY-ONE

"Maggie!"

Maggie's eyebrows lifted at Polly's surprised tone. Then, spotting Chloe, she frowned. "Chloe! I didn't expect to see you here." She glanced from one to the other. "Polly, I thought it was just you and I meeting. I thought I spoke to you in confidence."

Polly ushered her in. "Maggie, Chloe is here because something terrible has happened. At the moment nobody else knows about it, but since you're here, we might as well tell you. Anyway, there'll be no keeping this quiet. I should think the whole of East Anglia will know before too long. You'd better be prepared though. It isn't very nice. Chloe, can she come into the kitchen?"

"No, better use your study or the lounge. No offence, Maggie, but Polly's kitchen is virtually a crime scene, so we need to preserve it as much as possible. I'll bring in another tea, Polly."

Maggie's eyes widened. "A crime scene? What on earth is going on?"

The two of them settled into the armchairs in the study, while Chloe disappeared to find another mug of tea. "I had a shock this morning, Maggie. Someone left a baby on my doorstep during the night."

"A baby? What, a real one? A newborn baby, you mean? Out there all night by itself? Is it all right?"

"I'm afraid not. It's a little girl, Mary Elizabeth, but I'm afraid she's dead."

"Dead? It's criminal, leaving a small baby out in the open all night; at that age they can get hypothermia however warm the night. Even if she couldn't look after her, you'd think the mother would realise, wouldn't you? These young people, they have no sense."

"It didn't happen during the night, thank goodness. I'd never have been able to live with myself if it had. I'd have been wondering whether I heard some slight sound and ignored it, or whether I could have saved her if only I'd got to her sooner. But she was already dead when she was left on the doorstep. There was a note, giving her name and requesting a Christian burial for her. We don't know any more than that. I rang Chloe immediately and she's waiting for her guys to come and take over. They have to locate the mother in case she needs help, and they need to gather all the information they can from both the crib and the surroundings—mainly my door posts, I suppose."

Chloe came in with a mug of tea for Maggie, but quickly left to supervise her team.

Maggie cradled the mug in her hands. "Does Chloe have any ideas? Any clues as to the mother?"

"She's going to fingerprint the Moses basket and the safety pin which was used for the note, as well as the front door and the step. And I suppose they'll be checking the paper and ink, and looking for other forensic evidence—hairs, fibres, that sort of thing. They have to do a post mortem on the baby too, so they'll soon have her DNA. I suppose they'll try and match it up."

"But they can only do that if the mother is on the DNA database, can't they?"

"Or some other close relative. They can trace people through the DNA of relatives now. They've solved a few cold cases that way recently, I believe. There have been huge advances in DNA techniques, so I understand. There was a programme on Horizon a while back."

Maggie nodded. "I saw that, come to think of it. But if no one in the family is known to the police, and the mother hasn't had any medical attention —as seems likely—I can't see how they'll ever find out the child's identity." Her brow furrowed. "Polly, you don't think..."

"What?"

Maggie looked worried. "You don't think Kimberley could be the mother, do you?"

"Do you?"

"No, not really. It just seems such a coincidence, her not communicating with us and then suddenly disappearing. A baby could account for that, couldn't it? But come to think of it, Kimberley was too thin. Still, if she'd already had the baby, and had it hidden in a bag or something when she came home..."

Polly leaned forward. "Listen, Maggie. Her name is Mary Elizabeth Madison and she was in a Moses basket. Kimberley is a Brewster, not a Madison. The baby was dressed exquisitely in hand made baby clothes. Can Kimberley knit or sew? No, I thought not—it's a dying art. Oops! Wish I hadn't said that! You told me Giles collected Kimberley. Could she have secreted a Moses basket and a baby without one of you knowing?"

Relief flooded Maggie's face. "No, of course not. Nothing to do with Kimberley's disappearance, then. Merely a coincidence."

"I think so," Polly said, gently, "which brings us to the purpose of your visit. How about if I contact Major Allen? I met him once at the cathedral when the Salvation Army band was playing. He's based in Norwich, but he seemed very nice. Easy to talk to and a genuinely concerned with social awareness. I'm sure he'd point us in the right direction, and he's very discreet. No one need know."

Maggie nodded, her fair hair falling over her forehead. She pushed it back with a distracted gesture. "You said something about websites, too."

"There are masses of websites featuring missing people. Let's have a go on the computer. I'll type missing people into Google... there, a hundred and seventy four million results! Where would you like to start?"

Maggie leaned over her shoulder. "We can get rid of all the foreign sites, for a start. She can't have gone abroad, we have her passport. Stick UK onto the end of missing people, Polly. That's better. Look, that's reduced it to a mere sixteen million, nine hundred thousand! Shall we start from the top? The most popular sites appear first, don't they? I suppose you have to be careful of the unscrupulous who are only after the names and addresses of vulnerable people, but this first one, www.missingpeople.org.uk looks bona fide. Try that one for starters."

Polly stood up. "Why don't you sit down here, Maggie, and take a look? See, there's a form you can fill in. Can't do any harm, and who knows what it might bring? Then just work your way through as many of the other websites as you want. I think you're right about the police. It looks as though they only deal with people at risk and under the age of sixteen or over sixty-five, so Kimberley probably doesn't qualify.

"Listen, I have to go out for a bit. Why don't you stay here and work on my computer? I'll only be a couple of hours and I'll take the key, so if you're the last to go, just slam the door. It's a Yale, so it'll lock itself. I'll just pop through and tell Chloe. Stay as long as you want."

Polly was glad to get out of the house. There was something claustrophobic about all the activity going on around her, and with the police teams taking over, it didn't feel like home at all. She glanced at her watch. Not yet half past ten, so plenty of time to visit Maisie Faulkner. Driving towards the old oak tree, she parked just behind it out of sight of the road, and fished out her phone.

"Tom? Hi Babes. Can you talk? Haven't caught you at a bad moment in the middle of something, have I?"

"Sweet Pea! Delighted to hear you, as always. How are tricks in your part of the world?"

"That's partly why I'm ringing you. Some really awful things have happened, which may or may not be connected. The police are coping with the worst part of it, but I think I'm going to have to solve the rest myself. Either that, or I move from these parishes, and that doesn't feel quite right. Feels like running away, and I'm darned if I'm going to let some malignant parishioner chase me out."

There was a sharp intake of breath from Tom. "You're not planning on doing anything stupid, are you? I know you, Polly! Act first and think afterwards. Please don't do anything without talking it over with me first."

"As I said, that's why I'm ringing you. Tom, can you come over this weekend?"

"I'd already planned to, Sweet Pea, and I have half a day owing to me so I'll be with you early Friday evening. Will that do?"

"That's brilliant. Haven't time to do much before then, anyway. See you on Friday then, ready for a spot of amateur sleuthing on Saturday. Love you. 'Bye for now."

Tom was about to urge her, "Promise me you won't do anything until I get there," but Polly had already rung off. Knowing her as he did, he was left feeling uneasy. Polly never waited for anyone. Once the thought was in her mind, it was as good as done. Tom sent her a quick text, dont do anything til me there. Xxx.

But there was no reply.

It was just after eleven when Polly kept her finger pressed to Maisie Faulkner's doorbell. Maisie being elderly and a little deaf, it was always necessary to give her time to hear the bell and get to the door. Perhaps today Polly had made her rush, for she opened the door with a frown which expanded into a broad, gummy smile when she saw who was standing on the doorstep.

"Come in, dear, come in." She ushered Polly into the small back lounge, where her little white terrier was playing with something on the rug. Startled, Polly just had time to register that it was a set of dentures, when Maisie drew her attention to the back garden. Polly crossed to the French windows.

"It's lovely, Maisie. Do you do it all yourself?" Turning back to her hostess, she was stunned to see that Maisie now had a full set of teeth, while the little dog had no toys at all. Had her eyes deceived her? That was the speed of lightning. Who would have thought the old lady could move so fast? And yuk! Double yuk! Polly was disconcerted. "Um—I—I just called to wish you well for tomorrow, Maisie. What time do you have to be at the hospital?"

"Half past eleven. That nice Mr. Henderson is taking me. You know, the one who's so friendly with our Cheryl."

Polly was surprised. Perhaps there was something to be said for Byron Henderson after all. "That is kind of him."

"He's a driver," Maisie explained. "Of course, he gets paid for it, but not very much. I think they only pay enough to cover the petrol and wear and tear on the car. It's a village thing for people without transport. There's a rota of people willing to drive. With just the one bus a day, it's impossible to get to the hospital if you don't have your own car. I like having Mr. Henderson, though. He's so nice, not like some of them who just sit and wait in the car park. He comes in with me and waits with me, and then he goes off somewhere while I see the consultant, and comes back later. He's nearly always back when I've finished."

"Where does he go?" Polly asked, idly.

Maisie leaned towards her, wearing what Polly was learning to recognise as her conspiratorial face. "I think he knows one of the nurses. He always goes off towards the pharmacy department, and he looks very happy when he comes back. I expect they have coffee together. I wouldn't tell Cheryl, though," she added, in a burst of self-righteousness. "Men have to have their little secrets, don't they?"

Trying to keep a straight face, Polly murmured, "Mm, I suppose so. Maisie, may I say a prayer with you before I go? I'd like to ask God's special blessing on you for tomorrow."

The old lady's eyes filled. "Thank you so much, Rector. If truth be told, I am a little worried. I'm afraid it may be cancer. My sister died of it a year ago, and I'm the last of my generation. I would be grateful for your prayers."

CHAPTER TWENTY-TWO

Reluctant to return home until the rectory was free of police and deceased babies, Polly drove to the Woodcutter's Arms in the coastal town of Riversmead for lunch. A small town, but considerably larger than any of the four villages in the Anglesham benefice, Riversmead boasted a high school serving all the nearby areas, and a street of shops, as well as the usual tourist attractions of ice-cream kiosks, a promenade and seafront cafés. Polly reckoned she had time to buy in supplies for the weekend, thus sparing Tom a trip to the supermarket on Saturday morning.

Mindful that a decent midday meal would spare her having to cook in the evening, she ordered the house speciality, Yorkshire pudding filled with mince and gravy and served with new potatoes, carrots and peas, washed down with diet lemonade. It was a mammoth plateful when it arrived, but removed the necessity for a dessert and would suffice until a late-night sandwich. Fortunately, there was no one she recognised in the pub, so she was able to sit in a quiet corner, musing while she ate her lunch and fortified herself for the afternoon funeral visit, which threatened to be difficult.

She flipped open her reporter's notebook to confirm the details of the forthcoming funeral.

Deceased—Jack Farley Davidson.

Age—62 years. Died very suddenly on 16th tee at golf course. Air ambulance called. Unable to revive him.

Address—The Gables, 4 Norwich Road, Anglesham.

Next Of Kin—wife, Evelyn. (Also a son, John.)

Date, Time, Place of funeral—Tuesday 23rd, 2.00pm, Anglesham church, followed by burial in churchyard.

Satisfied that she had all the details correct, Polly turned to the events uppermost in her mind. Opening the notebook from the back, she jotted down all the episodes of the last few weeks in what she hoped was chronological order— intimidating telephone calls, vagrant, theft from safe, ink down cassock-alb, theft of flower money, doll on doorstep, baby on doorstep—then she began to write down random thoughts.

Are all—or any—of the above events linked? If so, which ones?

What is aimed at me, and why? All of them? Is it personal, against the office I hold, or to frighten me for some other reason?

Assuming the vagrant is connected to the theft, is he also connected to the doll? To Mary Elizabeth Madison? Why did he suddenly appear?

Does Kimberley Brewster somehow fit into all this, or is that a completely separate issue?

Who left the baby on my doorstep? Is there any connection between her and the doll? Is the baby an escalation of events, or again, completely separate?

Is the arrival of the gypsies (N.B. Confirm truth of this) a coincidence or linked to any of the above? (N.B.2. Find the gypsies first!!)

Why is Oswald Waters so off? Is it me (if so, what have I done?) or something else? (N.B. Ask him again!!)

Considering how wrong I've been in the past, should I trust my gut instinct re. Byron Henderson and Jonny Tunbridge?

She was none too happy when she had finished, since writing it down intensified her confusion by throwing up more questions with no answers, but at least she felt she had somewhere to start. Two lines of enquiry—Oswald and the diddicoys. Feeling there wasn't much else to accomplish at the moment, she paid her bill, and set off for the supermarket.

It was while Polly was browsing in the pasta section, wondering what exotic dish she could cook for Tom without too much effort, that a bright voice behind her greeted her. "Rector! What are you doing out here? Day off?"

Stifling her irritation at the assumption that she was entitled to do her grocery shopping only on her one free day, Polly pasted on a smile. But when she recognised the speaker, the smile broadened into a grin. "David! Or is it Jonathan, perchance?"

David Tunbridge laughed. "I see you're learning to tell us apart without too much difficulty! It must be my gleaming smile. Fancy a coffee?"

Polly hesitated. "I've just had one actually, but hey, why not? How are the boys? Haven't seen either of them for ages."

"Grown up men, now, Polly. They do their own thing, don't involve their poor old dad much. Spend most of their spare time in Norwich these days, and come home long after I'm asleep. Don't know how they keep going, since they're up at dawn for the farm."

"Ah! You were young once, David! Dancing the night away is par for the course, isn't it? Anyway, young or not, you're just the man I wanted to see. I've something to ask you."

"In that case... Let's use the café here. Cappuccino?"

Polly waited until they were seated at a corner table before tackling David. "Tell me about the gypsies."

"Gypsies? What gypsies?"

"Well, diddicoys, travellers, hobos, whatever you want to call them."

A small frown appeared, drawing his black brows together and immediately making him appear as sinister as his brother. "Where are these gypsies?"

"I was told they were on Anglesham Common, and were stealing milk from you."

David threw back his head and roared with laughter, causing startled looks from several tables. "You don't mean those hippie kids in a couple of vans, do you? They're not gypsies, nor travellers, neither. For your information, they aren't stealing anything. They have milk in exchange for work on the farm. They're harmless enough. Who's been filling your head with tales?" He looked at her searchingly, then nodded. "You've you been visiting my brother, haven't you? You don't want to believe everything you hear. I told you; he has a thing about so-called gypsies. And about me, come to that. What did he say?"

Polly shrugged, uncomfortable about revealing her conversation with Jonathan. "You know, nothing much. He was a bit concerned, that's all."

"Surprised he didn't instruct you to run them off. Ah," peering closely at her, "he did, didn't he? I hope you gave him short shrift. My advice is, take no notice. Couple of kids taking time out, that's all. No harm in that."

Finishing her drink, Polly glanced at her watch. "Is that the time? I must dash. Got a funeral visit."

He rose with her. "That'll be Jack Davidson. When is the funeral? Tuesday?"

Polly nodded. "Two o'clock. Are you going?"

"Everyone is going. The church will be packed. He was very well known in the whole area. Good luck with the grieving widow and the idolised son."

Polly shot him a puzzled glance, but had no time to question him further. "Thanks for the coffee, David. 'Bye for now. Be seeing you."

Number four Norwich Road, Anglesham, was an imposing, semi-detached, three storey Victorian villa with bay windows, gable ends, and fancy brickwork. Polly's heart sank as she drove up to the burgundy front door via a broad gravel sweep guarding an immaculate circular flower bed in a perfect lawn. Like this one, all the houses in this stretch of Norwich Road were impressive. Polly could almost smell the wealth as she climbed from her car, and was only too aware that in the majority of the population, wealth equals power. Perhaps that was what David had meant by his cryptic remark.

Unconsciously, she smoothed down her wild blond hair and tugged anxiously at her skirt as she rang the doorbell. At least it was a modern, electric bell, not one of those huge jangling affairs for summoning the servants.

As the door opened, Polly smiled warmly, holding out her hand. "Mrs Davidson? I'm Polly Hewitt."

"Come in." The tall, elderly, painfully thin woman, with greying hair dragged back austerely into a pleat, failed to respond to the smile. Dismissively, she brushed Polly's fingertips with her own before leading the way through a dark and somewhat oppressive hall into a much lighter lounge which was rather spoilt by being overstuffed with furniture and antiques. "My son, John."

A man aged around forty, but with a supercilious expression which made him look as if he had never been young, dark hair slicked back with a low parting, shorter than his mother and plump like his recently deceased father, rose from an armchair and shook hands with Polly. His palm was moist and his mouth petulant. Peering at Polly through thick spectacles as if she were a specimen, he made no attempt to smile.

Polly said, "Pleased to meet you, but not under these circumstances. It must have been a terrible shock for both of you."

"Naturally. One doesn't expect one's husband to leave for a game of golf but never return." Her face austere, Evelyn Davidson indicated Polly should sit, perching herself on the edge of the only upright chair in the room. Polly all but disappeared into a depth of chintz. Evelyn added in a courteous voice, but one which invited a negative response, "Would you like a cup of tea?"

"No thank you. I've just had coffee." Polly settled herself as best she could and flipped open her notebook. "I believe the air ambulance was called?"

There was an impatient sigh from John. "It was a sudden collapse. What else would you expect?"

Evidently there was no means of establishing friendly contact through compassion. Polly switched tacks. "If I could confirm the details with you?" From her notebook she read the little information she had, and both mother and son nodded.

The preliminaries over, Polly began to guide the meeting into the delicate area of talking about the service for the deceased and gleaning some information about his life, for the eulogy. "Had you thought of any hymns you might like?"

John Davidson snorted. As Polly eyed him, Evelyn handed her a piece of folded notepaper from the rosewood table. "It's all here."

"Oh. I see you have the whole service written out."

John Davidson snorted again. "You didn't imagine my mother would be unprepared at this late date, surely?"

"It's unusual." Polly smiled at him as warmly as she could. "Death is a confusing time. Many people feel so bewildered that they don't know where to start. This information is very useful for me, though, so thank you for that. Shall we just run through the service?"

"Is that necessary? My mother and I have worked it out perfectly well, thank you. I can't understand why you've come."

Polly continued to smile at him, but she could feel anger beginning to mount inside her. Why couldn't he let her do her job without all this unnecessary hostility? "Perhaps you could bear with me. I do understand that you have completed the service between you, but I need to familiarise myself with it. If I go over it with you now it will save me having to trouble you again later."

Evelyn Davidson inclined her head, almost, Polly thought, like the queen. After an uncertain glance at his mother, John subsided into a sulk.

Feeling she had regained some control, Polly glanced over the paper, reading it aloud and adding her own comments. "Have you decided whether you want to follow the coffin into church, whether you want to be in church first, or whether you'd like the coffin to be in church prior to the service?"

At the perplexed looks, it was clear neither of them had thought the service through to quite this extent. Evelyn said, "Surely the traditional way is for the family to follow the coffin into church?"

Polly nodded. "Many people choose to follow. It gets you into church without having to face your friends first."

"We'll do that then."

"I usually precede the coffin and read some sentences from the bible as the coffin is brought into church. Would you like that? The organist will play quietly beneath the words. Then I like to welcome everyone with an informal introduction. Funerals are hard for friends and family, so it's sensible to settle people as well as possible. All right? After that there's a short prayer, thanking God for Jack's life, then the first hymn. I see you've chosen The Lord's My Shepherd—to the tune of Crimond?"

"Of course. We want the traditional service. Obviously we must have the twenty-third psalm somewhere." Evelyn sat rigidly, staring straight ahead, as though if she allowed herself to unbend, she would collapse in a crumpled heap.

Polly nodded. "What about a reading from the bible after that?"

With an air of pomposity, John said, "We've chosen two poems, a Shakespeare sonnet—you probably won't know that—and a lesser-known piece by Tennyson. I don't suppose you'll know that either. Both appropriate, I think you'll find. The vice-chair of the parish council will read one, and the chair of the county council the other."

"I see. Well," Polly spoke directly to Evelyn, ignoring John, "you did specify a traditional funeral. Traditionally, whatever other readings there might be, there would always be a bible reading. There's a nice passage in John's gospel—in my Father's house are many dwelling places. I go to prepare a place for you—do you know that one?"

John scowled, but Evelyn said again, "Of course. Put that in, then, if you must. We'll find someone to read it."

"Or I could read it myself, if you prefer. Perhaps you could let me know about that. Then there would normally be a eulogy—"

"—that's sorted. Oswald Waters is doing that." John's air of triumph was now unmistakeable.

"I beg your pardon?" Polly was stunned.

"Reverend Waters. He was a great friend of my father and he taught me at school. We've already arranged it with him."

"I see." Polly swallowed her anger. "Then he and I will need to meet to discuss the service so that everything runs smoothly. Your next hymn is Abide With Me? Good. Then a time for prayer. It's traditional to mention family members by name in the prayers. The two of you, obviously, but do you have a wife or partner, John? Are there any grandchildren?"

Evelyn said stiffly, "Just John."

"Is there anyone else you'd like mentioned? I shall add 'all other relatives and friends' as a matter of course, but if there's a specific friend?"

"Just myself and John."

This was even harder going than she had anticipated. Polly struggled on, doing her best to maintain an outward show of relaxed calm, trying to engage with these two, and reminding herself that grief took people in many different ways. "Okay. Your final hymn is The Day Thou Gavest; we remain standing to commend Jack to God's care, and after that we go out into the churchyard for the burial. I usually say the Nunc Dimittis as I recess down the aisle, again preceding the coffin, and again, the organist will play quietly underneath the words. Do you want everyone to gather at the graveside, or just the immediate family?"

For the first time, Evelyn consulted her son. "What do you think, John?"

"Only family. The rest can start to make their way over to The Railway Arms for refreshments." He stood up. "Is that it, then?"

Refusing to be dismissed like a servant, Polly said, "I'll just say a prayer for you before I go, if I may." Without waiting for a response, she closed her eyes and asked God to bless Evelyn and John during this difficult time. Then she too rose, and walked over to Evelyn with outstretched hand, saying, "You know where to find me. If there's anything you need, or you think of anything you'd like to add or to change, give me a ring. Goodbye, now."

Avoiding looking at Polly, Evelyn again brushed her fingers. There was no word of thanks. John stood aloof by the door, waiting to usher Polly out. He held his arms so stiffly by his sides that Polly made no attempt to shake hands with him, contenting herself with nodding at him. He avoided eye contact, and his weak blue eyes, staring straight ahead through the heavy glasses, were stony. Polly continued to smile amiably as she climbed into her car, but inside she was fuming. She had been treated with barely courteous disdain and out-manoeuvred, and there was nothing she could do about it.

CHAPTER TWENTY-THREE

Polly stormed over to Parsondale, driving at breakneck speed, determined to confront Oswald Waters before her rage had cooled. How dare he? Who did he think he was, the bishop of Parsondale? This was more than a challenge to her authority. Oswald could not have spoken more clearly if he had extended his middle finger and mouthed the accompanying words.

Polly had no idea what she was going to say, nor could she see any way of scuppering Oswald's little scheme. A funeral with grieving relatives—however unpleasant and hostile they might be—was no time to force any personal issues. Grief could have any manner of strange effects, among which might well be the sort of frigid self-control displayed by Evelyn Davidson and even the antagonistic disdain shown by her son. Polly didn't blame them, but she had an uneasy feeling they had been encouraged by Oswald. In Polly's view, as she was his incumbent it was Oswald's job to support her in her decisions, and that meant politely indicating to the Davidsons that on this occasion, regretfully he was unable to take part in Jack's funeral, but that he had every confidence in his rector to deliver a moving tribute to the late Jack. Instead, Oswald had furthered his own cause at Polly's expense. Perhaps he didn't think she'd do a good enough job, which showed how little he knew her, since Polly had always been praised for her gentle and personal touch at funerals.

Nurturing her hurt and stoking her wrath to sustain her during what could only be an uncomfortable confrontation, she roared into the drive at the Old Rectory, screeching to an ostentatious halt outside the front door, and sending gravel flying in all directions. Slamming the car door, she marched up the steps and rang the bell, keeping her finger firmly on the button.

"Polly!" A somewhat startled Catriona, dressed in a smart suit with a pencil slim skirt which made her look like a fashion model and filled Polly with envy, flung the door wide. "Come in. It's nice to see you. I've been working, so Nina said she'd look after Brent and Emily, but I'm back much earlier than I expected. I was about to put the kettle on. Want a cuppa? Nina insisted on going to collect the kids from school—to give me time to relax before the onslaught of children, so she said—and Oswald's not due home for another couple of hours. Longer, if he knows I'm going to be here."

Polly deflated abruptly. "Oh. Well, it's your father-in-law I wanted to see, so I'd better come back later. It's hardly worth staying for all that time." Already she could feel her fury subsiding, and she was afraid that hanging around for two hours would drain it completely. Without the adrenaline boost of anger, would she have the nerve to face Oswald on his own territory? Perhaps it was better to avoid him immediately after he returned from a long day at school. Perhaps his absence was actually God's gift to her. Perhaps she needed to choose the time and venue to suit herself. Perhaps she needed to cool down and think this out again.

Catriona retorted, "Of course it's worth it! Stay and talk to me. The old goat won't be here for ages yet, thank goodness, and with any luck I'll be gone before he gets back. Come on, have a cup of tea and we'll put the world to rights."

Now very unsure of herself and feeling in need of comfort, Polly allowed herself to be shepherded into the kitchen. She took refuge in humour. "That's no way to speak of your eminent father-in-law, is it, Mrs. Waters junior? Do I take it you two don't exactly see eye to eye?"

Catriona rolled her eyes. "You could say that. We've never agreed. Mainly because he's a closet misogynist—you must have noticed? Your life with him can't be that easy."

Polly admitted, "It seems he can be difficult at times. Does he really dislike women or are you just saying that?"

"Not only women. I don't suppose I should be telling you this, him being your priest and all, but he and I have very different ideas on bringing up children. He thinks I'm far too soft—just because I cuddle my five-year-old son from time to time; won't "make a man of him" according to Saint Oswald—and I think Ozzy's out of the ark. You know he actually thumped Brent?"

Polly's eyes widened. "No! Was it witnessed? You could take him to court for that."

"Well, to be fair, I think it was more of a tap than an actual smack, but I won't have him tapping them in any way whatsoever. It's none of his business how Olly and I bring up our kids. Just because he's their grandfather and a teacher to boot, he thinks he has the monopoly on child rearing. Personally, I don't think he could be more wrong. He didn't do that good a job on his own. Anyway, in today's terms he's barely out of the cave. So we had this giant row which is still simmering, even though we just about manage to be polite to each other, for Olly and Nina's sake."

"Ah, so that's his problem—or one of them, anyway. He's been so edgy, lately, I wondered what had gone wrong. I thought it was me, but perhaps it wasn't. At least, not all me."

"You thought it was you, and I thought it must be me! Perhaps we were both wrong and something entirely different has been troubling him."

"Like what?"

Catriona shrugged. "Maybe some problem at school, I don't know. Or maybe..."

"What?"

"Nothing really. I just wondered..."

"Wondered what? Come on, Catriona, you can't leave me dangling. Finish what you were going to say."

"I don't have any hard evidence. It's just conjecture on my part, what Chloe might call circumstantial evidence, so no more than a feeling really, but I've noticed that Nina has been genuinely worried. She's always timid and anxious, as you know, but this is different. Her eyes dart all over the place as if she's constantly looking for something, her hands are never still, and she keeps glancing back over her shoulder as though she's afraid of something or someone."

"Wow! I hadn't noticed any of that."

"You wouldn't. You don't see as much of her as I do. I don't suppose anyone else has noticed anything."

"What about Oliver? Has he noticed? Have you discussed it with him?"

"I've tried, but he walks away. That's always his pattern over any disagreement or anything he'd rather not hear. His face kind of tightens and his lips pinch and he clears off, then when I see him again it's as though nothing has happened."

"He must be concerned about his parents, surely?"

Catriona nodded. "That's what I find puzzling. I'm certain he is concerned about them—keeps making excuses to go round and see how they are—so I think it's more than that. I think whatever it is, Olly is in on it."

"Phew!" Polly blew out her lips. "It's beginning to sound like a conspiracy. You have no idea what this is all about?"

"No, but I do know that it dates from that vagrant arriving at Anglesham. It did occur to me that Oswald might know him, an ex-pupil, perhaps. Maybe he has some sort of hold over Oswald."

"Funny you should say that. I thought Oswald was a bit odd over that young man, and come to think of it, yes, my difficulties with Oswald date from around that time, too. And I thought it was just me! Well, this is all very interesting and I shall ponder further. Still, if he really is a misogynist as you say, he won't care much for having me around as his boss, and I'm afraid he's made that perfectly clear."

"Why, what has he done now?" Catriona wanted to know.

Polly swallowed. Catriona was her friend and she dearly wanted Catriona's support, but she didn't want to be disloyal to Oswald. She chose her words carefully, adopting a nonchalant tone which belied her real feelings. "He's been a bit funny lately, that's all. Perhaps I'm being over-sensitive, especially in the light of what you've just told me. He seemed to accept me all right to begin with, but recently he's been—difficult."

"In what way, especially? I mean, more than his usual obnoxious arrogance."

Polly giggled, and lifted her shoulders in a helpless shrug. Catriona would soon know anyway, so what was the harm in Polly putting her point of view first? Besides, the very definition of a friend was that you could say anything to them, wasn't it? "The worst thing is next week's funeral. Jack Davidson was chair of the parish council so it's bound to be a big turnout and an ideal opportunity for me to show the non-churchgoing public the caring and benign face of the church, as well as beginning to get myself known in all the villages. I could do a really good job, too. Oswald's been taking all the funerals so far because he knows everyone from school, but that means I don't get a look in. This is a big occasion, and I think the rector needs to be seen to be conducting it. I did discuss all this with Oswald and explained the position to him. I thought we'd agreed, but I've just come from visiting the Davidsons and it seems they've arranged directly with Oswald—without a word to me, mind—to deliver the eulogy, which as you know, is the major part of the service. Plus there are all sorts of important people doing readings, so I'm left with almost nothing. He really has stymied me. What annoys me more than anything is that he's gone straight over my head and there's nothing I can do about it—except have a deep and meaningful conversation with him. I certainly intend to do that. I don't suppose all this matters much in the grand scheme of things, but I am a bit put out about it."

"I should think so! It's the rector's place to preside at big events, not the OLM's. I'm afraid that's Oswald all over, though. Always has to be in the limelight. Can't stand it if someone else takes centre stage. He's not a team player, never has been. He practically ran the interregnum single-handed, and loved every minute of it. He likes the prestige, does our Oswald. Typical schoolteacher, if you ask me."

Polly laughed, feeling much better, but uneasy at discussing her OLM like this, with his daughter-in-law. "I thought Oliver was a schoolteacher?"

"Oh, Olly's different. Well, not so different, actually. He's very much like Oswald, but I keep him straightened out. I soon tell him if he comes the high horse with me or the kids. Nina's a dear and I love her to bits, but she's so timid around Oswald. Won't stand up for herself, just lets him bully her. I suppose in a way that makes them the perfect pair. He orders, she obeys!"

Laughing again, Polly finished her tea and rose to go. "You do me good, Catriona. Look, I think I'll make my way now, before Nina gets back. I don't want to have to explain my visit to her. I need to get Oswald on his own at the right time. I'll come back sometime. You will keep quiet about all this, won't you?"

Catriona hugged her. "Of course I will! And just remember, any time the old goat gets too much for you, come to me and we'll stick pins in him together. I know what he can be like."

Polly waved to her friend and was still grinning as she climbed into the car, but her mind was puzzled. Was that last remark as innocent as it sounded, or was Catriona somehow sending her a subtle message? And if so, what was the message she was trying to convey?

CHAPTER TWENTY-FOUR

"And you have absolutely no idea of where these caravans might be?" After tramping Anglesham Common for nearly three hours, Tom's feet were hurting since his usual daily exercise was nothing greater than manipulating his car pedals. Mindlessly criss-crossing narrow deer tracks all morning did not feature highly in his list of fun things to do. Growing increasingly exhausted by the minute, he was more than ready for the nearest pub.

"They're definitely on the common, but away from the road. That's what Jonathan and David both said and it's all I know, I'm afraid."

"You don't know which road? The Anglesham road or the Parsondale road?"

Polly shook her head. "Sorry, Babes. But we must find them. I feel like the answers to all my problems lie in those vans, and I really do need answers if I'm going to survive. Not sure you realise how scary life has been here in Anglesham. My life, anyway. Tell you what. Let's just follow this one last track over here, and if that turns up nothing, we'll call it a day. Worst case scenario, I'll go over to Coot Farm after lunch and get David Tunbridge or one of his sons to lead us to the camp site."

Tom sighed. "Anything for you, Sweet Pea, but I do wish you'd warned me. I'd have brought my walking boots with me if I'd known we were in for an all-day hike. These city shoes are rubbing blisters on my little toes; I can feel them forming as I speak."

"Tom! I'm so sorry. Do you want to stop now?"

But Tom was already striding ahead of her down the track she had indicated, wondering whether it really was a new path or whether it was one they had already negotiated about fifty times. Everything looked the same in this wilderness of tufted grass punctuated by brushwood and undergrowth, spinneys and copses. As they pushed their way through a thicket which might or might not be new ground, Tom stopped so abruptly that Polly cannoned into him.

"What is it? Have you seen a caravan?"

Tom was looking ahead. "No vans, but there is someone over there, I caught a movement. Look, beyond the clearing, just to the right of that oak. Do you see? A man, I think, although it's difficult to tell from here. Let's go and ask him whether he's from the vans, or whether he's come across this camp."

He was off before Polly could reply. Running to catch up with him, Polly squinted over at the figure on the far side of the clearing, and caught her breath. She was convinced she knew that loping gait.

Clutching at Tom's sleeve, she whispered, "I think I know him. I reckon it's Byron Henderson, Cheryl's partner. What in the world is he doing out here? Never took him for a lover of nature. Not this sort of nature, anyway."

Tom had made up his mind before she had a chance to warn caution. "Why don't we ask him? Come on. Let's see what he knows—if anything."

Leading the way at a run he crashed out of the spinney and across the open grassland, waving at the man on the far side, whooping and hollering to attract his attention. Startled, Byron Henderson looked up. Then he glanced behind him, furtively in Polly's view, as though he was undecided whether to stay or flee. Polly was certain he decided to stay put only when he spotted her, but it gave him time to compose his features and act out a surprised welcome.

"Polly! Fancy seeing you here! What brings you out this way?

Breathless from the run, Polly gasped, "I was about to ask you the same question, Byron. Never pegged you as a walker. Let me introduce you to Tom. Tom, this is Byron."

The two men shook hands, but Polly was amused to notice Tom surreptitiously wiping his hand down the side of his trousers after contact with Byron's sticky palm. Was Byron sweating more than usual, and if so, why? What was he hiding?

Tom said, "We're looking for caravans. Have you seen them? We've been traipsing this common all morning without the hint of a caravan. Do you happen to know where they are?"

"Me? No, certainly not. I haven't seen or heard anyone or anything. There's nothing out here."

"Are you sure?" Polly was certain he was lying; he had replied too quickly. "Only, both the Tunbridge brothers know about them, and David has met at least one of the inhabitants."

"They may have been here, but perhaps they've gone now. Caravans don't stay around for long. That's the point of a caravan, Polly. Caravanners like to move around from place to place whenever they feel like it."

Ignoring his patronising tone, Polly said, "You're sure you don't know where they are?"

"Polly my darling, if I'd seen a couple of caravans you'd be the first to know."

Polly frowned. Neither she nor Tom had mentioned a number, had they? "It is rather important, Byron. You remember that vagrant? The young guy who tore up the bible and nicked some cash? If you recall, he appeared out of nowhere. I have a theory that he lives in one of these vans. It would make perfect sense. It would explain why he settled on somewhere as small and out of the way as Anglesham, rather than Norwich where the pickings must be more lucrative. I don't want to harangue him, but I really need to speak with him, so if you know anything, Byron, please tell us."

Byron's lips set in an obstinate line and his shoulders squared. "Sorry, Polly. I haven't seen anyone or anything."

"So what are you doing here, Byron? Not walking, surely?"

"Lovely day for a walk, isn't it?" Byron glanced up at the overcast sky, adding, "that is, if it doesn't rain."

"No chance of that, more's the pity. The weather gurus have been promising rain for weeks now, but it hasn't materialised. If this spell goes on much longer, I'll be praying for rain soon, in church."

"With a rain dance in the aisles, I hope." Byron sniggered, and again his gaze raked Polly from top to toe.

Her amiable smile disappeared and her tone sharpened. "So come on, Byron. What are you doing out here? Not a twitcher, are you?"

"What?"

"A twitcher. You know, bird spotter. They travel all over the country whenever rare species are seen, to get a tick in their birdwatching notebooks. You must have heard the term. Norfolk is so rich in bird life that we have loads of them descending from time to time."

"Oh! Twitcher, yes, of course. Well, as a matter of fact, I am a bird watcher. I love our little feathered friends."

Tom, who had not missed the offensive glance Byron had given Polly, joined the conversation. "Really? Without binoculars or a camera? I was under the distinct impression that serious bird watchers never travelled without them."

Byron laughed, uneasily. "I left them in the car, I'm afraid. Cheryl always says I'll forget my head, if I'm not careful."

"Where are you parked, Byron? Polly didn't think there were any roads crossing the common."

"There aren't. I'm—uh," he waved vaguely behind him, "over there, somewhere. Hope I can find the car again. I drove over rough grass, you know."

Polly said, "Perhaps you could give us a lift back, then? Poor Tom's feet are giving him hell."

Dismay flitted across Byron's face. He stammered, "Well, I would, of course, but—it's rather embarrassing." He gave a nervous glance over his shoulder.

Polly pulled a disbelieving face. "What could possibly be embarrassing about giving us a lift in your car, Byron?"

He ran his tongue over his lips. "As I said, I'd be only too pleased, normally, but—well, to tell you the truth, there's someone with me."

Glancing at his distended belly and his pudgy features, Polly allowed a smile to hover over her lips. "Not a secret assignation, Byron? Whatever would Cheryl say?"

At this, his eyes looked guilty and his face took on a pleading quality. "You won't say anything, will you? I'm really sorry about the lift, but now you know my little secret, I think I'd better go. I only nipped out to relieve myself, and um, my friend will wonder where I am. Please don't follow me, Polly. I don't want you to see my—friend. I don't want to put you in a difficult position, and it's only fair that I keep her identity secret."

Tom made to follow him, but Polly laid a restraining hand on his arm. "Let him go. If we hear him start the car we'll know he's parked somewhere near, and we'll soon find out where. My guess is that he's in the vicinity of those vans. He's obviously lying through his teeth, but let him think we believe his story."

As they watched Byron go, Polly called after him, "Fair to whom, Byron? Have you thought at all about Cheryl? Is it fair to her? You need to think about that," and was rewarded by a wave of acknowledgement as Byron disappeared through the trees in the nearby copse. A moment later the sound of a car revving up filled the air.

"Well? What do you think?"

Tom pursed his lips. "I agree with you. He's lying, all right. There's no lady friend in his car. He seized upon that explanation like a drowning man. Probably got the car stacked high with drugs. But he may have outwitted us even so. He went back through that copse, but that may only have been to put us off the scent. If he'd really left the car to relive himself, he'd hardly have walked any distance to do so. I'm sure you're right and the car was around here somewhere, but where? We might have heard it start up, but he'll have gone by now and we can't follow the sound. Assuming it wasn't through that copse, where do you think we should try?"

Making their way towards the edge of the copse, they peered for signs of tyre tracks, but the ground was so hard after weeks without rain, that there was nothing. Undeterred, and with Tom's sore feet all but forgotten in the surge of excitement produced by the chance meeting with Byron, they decided to spread out around the edge of the copse, Polly moving west and Tom moving east.

"Don't go haring off on some sidetrack," Tom warned. "We don't want to lose each other. I'm not at all sure I could find my way back now, so I need your expertise. If you find anything, yell at the top of your voice. I'll do likewise. To start with, we'll just circle the copse. If we don't find anything, we'll think again."

"After lunch in the nearest pub?"

"Definitely. I'm nearly faint from lack of nourishment. Let's give it another half-hour, then pack it in for today. We should have finished this area at least, by then."

Polly's heart quickened when she discovered a grassy track wide enough for a vehicle, to the west of the copse. She was about to shout for Tom when she thought better of it. Suppose someone was there? Someone who had stuck pins in dolls, or worse, knew about dead babies. Despite Tom's warning, she veered off along the track, keeping out of sight along the tree line and creeping as quietly as she could.

The track continued for two hundred yards with, towards the end, unmistakeable signs of vehicular activity causing noticeable ruts. Her heart pounding, Polly crept further forward. She thought she could detect the smell of wood smoke on the air, denoting habitation. As the track opened out into a cramped clearing, she saw what she had been seeking all morning. Two dilapidated caravans occupied the area.

Set end to end, they were small vans; two berths, about nine foot by six foot, seven foot high, and completely covered in camouflage markings making them difficult to spot even when stumbling upon them. They looked dark and forbidding.

There was an empty washing line strung between them, and a little to the side, a wood fire, hastily stamped out and still smoking. Beyond the fire were a few used beer cans, strewn haphazardly over the ground, and a plastic bag was ballooning in the breeze. There was no sign of life in either of the vans.

Polly hesitated. She knew she ought to go back for Tom, but if anyone was hiding in one of the vans, any evidence might be destroyed before she had a chance to return. With her heart in her mouth, she crept round to the rear of the vans, keeping low to the ground. Waiting for a few minutes to make sure there was no movement, she edged quietly forward. Pressing herself against the side of the first van, she slowly lifted her head to peer through the window.

Staring straight back at her was a pair of lifeless brown eyes in a head of straggling, unkempt brown hair.

CHAPTER TWENTY-FIVE

Polly shrieked, suddenly wishing she had minded Tom's cautionary words. She fell back from the van, her hands covering her mouth. She knew she should enter the caravan, but was reluctant to do so. It was as though her legs were comprised of lead, dragging her down, away from the van.

Polly could feel herself beginning to panic. What should she do? Who else was in the van? Where was Byron when you needed him? Clearly he'd legged it at the first sign of trouble. Typical. Sending up a quick arrow prayer—please God, help me—she took a deep breath, then forced herself to approach the caravan door. Turning the handle gingerly so as not to attract the unwelcome attention of anyone else who might be hiding inside, slowly she pushed open the door.

The stench hit her. Rotting food, unwashed humanity, an overflowing toilet system and the sickly sweet smell of dope mingled to form an odour which made her gag, but she pushed forward resolutely, covering her nose and mouth with her hand. No one else was in the van, only the vagrant she had first met in Anglesham church. On the table amidst dirty mugs and plates, was a used syringe, scraps of silver paper and the tell-tale scatterings of a white powder.

Polly quickly picked her way through the debris of squalid daily living and the litter of empty beer cans, to the young man with vacant, staring eyes. His skin was very pale, his lips blue. Clearly he was drugged up to the eyeballs, but with little experience of drugs, Polly had no idea whether he was suffering from a drug overdose or whether this was the usual result of injecting with heroin. She felt his neck. There was a thready pulse, but it seemed irregular and feeble. She needed to fetch help. Pulling out her mobile phone she rang the emergency services, but this being rural Norfolk, the signal was flickering ominously.

"Yes," she shouted to a seemingly dim recipient. "Anglesham Common. What? No, I can't give you any better directions, I don't know where I am. Ambulance, quickly please. Drug overdose. Excuse me? I'm not sure, heroin, I think. He's comatose. What? Oh yes. Perhaps you'd better send the police as well. My name? It's—" But the signal had gone. Polly prayed that enough of the message had filtered through to generate action.

Desperate to contact Tom, Polly tried her phone again, but it was no use. Every time she thought she had sufficient signal to dial, it died before she could make the call.

I'm alone and I don't know what to do. God, how can I help this man? I can't leave him. I must wait for the ambulance, but what do I do? Should I drag him into the recovery position or will that make matters worse? I've no idea. He's hardly breathing; I'm sure he's dying. Keep him alive, God, please. And please help me, God. Tell me what to do. Should I do mouth-to-mouth? Ugh! He smells vile. I don't fancy putting my mouth on his, but I suppose I could breathe through a hanky. What about Tom, God? I can't go and find him. He'll think I've deserted him. Help me God, please help me.

Even as the thoughts were flashing through her mind, Polly found herself feeling in the pocket of her jeans for a clean handkerchief. She had only a tissue, but it would have to do. She couldn't stand here doing nothing, and who knew how long the ambulance would take? Placing the tissue over the sick man's nose and mouth, she took a deep breath then breathed into the tissue. It didn't seem to make much difference, but she thought she ought to keep on, for a while at least.

Polly continued the mouth-to-mouth resuscitation for a further ten minutes. She had a vague recollection of external heart massage from a first aid course at school many years earlier, but couldn't remember enough to dare to attempt it. After ten minutes, with sudden hope in her heart she heard the distinctive drone of a helicopter flying ever closer. Praying that it was the air ambulance, she grabbed a filthy tea towel, rushed out of the van and waved frantically. She was rewarded by the sight of the air ambulance first hovering, then slowly beginning to descend, searching for a space large enough and flat enough to land.

After that, it was all action. Paramedics were soon in the van with oxygen equipment, and before long the unconscious man was lifted onto a stretcher and into the ambulance. With a sigh of relief, Polly herself was about to leave to search out Tom, when a police car screeched to a halt beside her.

Ordering her to stay put, police officers were soon exploring both vans, and wanting Polly to make a statement.

"Tell me again, Reverend Hewitt, how did you come to be in the vicinity?"

"I was out for a walk."

"On your own?"

"No," Polly hesitated. She didn't want to drag Tom into any of this, but she had no choice. "With my boyfriend, Tom Curtis."

"And where is Tom Curtis now?"

Polly looked round wildly, hoping Tom would materialise as she spoke. "Well, I'm not sure. We —er—we went in opposite directions about an hour ago."

"Why was that? A row?" The officer sounded sympathetic.

"Well, no. Not exactly."

The officer waited.

Realising she had no option but to acquiesce, Polly sighed. "We were looking for the guy I found in here. I'd heard these two caravans were parked somewhere on the common, and I thought it possible that the vagrant was using them. It was obvious he was living rough. Tom and I split up to cover more ground." She glanced at her watch. "I wish I could contact him. He'll be going spare. We were supposed to meet ages ago."

"I thought you said you didn't know the man in the van?"

"I don't, not really. I don't know his name or anything about him. I met him a few weeks ago, in the church. He tore some pages out of a bible for his roll-ups, and we suspect him of stealing church money. I did report it at the time, so you'll have it on record."

The officer nodded. "You don't know anything about the women's clothes we found both here and in the other van? Have you seen a woman here?"

"No. I was told there were two vans, but I didn't have time to look in the other one. I don't know anything about any female, I'm afraid."

"All right, Reverend Hewitt, I think that's all for now, thank you. It looks like a straightforward overdose, so no suspicious circumstances as far as I can see at the moment. Our officers will check, of course. We'll know more when the lad comes round—if he ever does." The policeman snapped shut his notebook and replaced it in his pocket. "Now, can we drop you anywhere?"

Polly's eyes brightened. "Can you get a signal on your car phone? Could you ring Tom for me? Perhaps we could pick him up and you could drive us back to the rectory? Would that be okay?"

Tom wasn't far away. After meandering around the copse for half an hour, he had reached the starting point again and waited there for Polly, as arranged. When she failed to arrive, he had set off again in ill humour exacerbated by weariness and anxiety, in the direction Polly had taken, and like her had followed the broad track. He had heard and seen the air ambulance, further heightening his anxiety, and was just emerging into the clearing as his mobile phone rang.

In the relief of finding Polly unhurt, Tom was short with her. "I thought I told you to wait. What were you thinking, to go off on your own like that?"

She snapped, "I did what had to be done. Thought you'd have the nous to realise that."

It was an uncomfortable journey home, despite the much needed luxury of being transported. After answering a few questions from the police in monosyllables, Tom subsided into an injured silence, refusing to look at Polly, and instead pointedly gazing out of the window.

The atmosphere wasn't much better when they reached home. Polly too was exhausted, with the added stress of worrying over whether the man would recover. She wanted nothing more than to pour out the whole story to Tom, but he had slumped into an armchair and was busy removing his shoes and socks to inspect the raw blisters on his little toes. Polly filled a bowl with warm water, added a spoonful of salt, and armed with a clean towel, carried it through to Tom.

"Put your feet in that. It'll help."

Tom took the bowl with a grunt.

Polly tried again. "I'm sorry, Babes. It was just that I saw the track, and I thought if I yelled out it might warn whoever was around. I didn't want to alert anyone to our presence, and I was afraid that if I came back for you, any evidence might have been spirited away."

"It didn't occur to you that Byron Henderson intended to do exactly that as soon as he left us, then? Warn the occupants and remove any evidence? I'd have thought his intention was obvious."

"Look, Tom, I'm sorry. Okay? It hasn't been easy for me, you know. Of course, no reason why you should care about that, you have your precious feet to worry about. So what do you want me to do to put things right between us? Kiss your feet to make them better?"

Tom exploded. "Have you any idea of what might have happened to you? Did it even enter your head that you might be in serious danger? No, stupid question. You don't have the sense you were born with. You just carry on regardless, going your own sweet way and not giving a damn about anyone else, don't you? Do you think I suggested we meet up and go together, for my own health? I did it for you, Polly, because it was the only safe way of going about things. But you were never hot on common sense, were you? And look where it landed you—in a horrible situation which could have been avoided completely if you'd done as we agreed."

"How in the world could you and I have prevented that guy taking an overdose? You do talk rubbish, sometimes."

"That's not what I mean, and you know it! I thought we did things together whenever possible, consulted each other and worked out the best course of action between us. The two of us could have handled it much more efficiently—"

But he was speaking to an empty room. Polly had slammed out and could be heard in the kitchen, crashing pots and pans together as she prepared a meal. Normally eager to help her, today Tom stayed in the armchair, out of the way. Unused to walking, he was beginning to ache in joints he was unaware he possessed. He groaned as he pictured the drive home to Oxford next day, and even worse, limping into the office on Monday morning. He was already regretting his hostile remarks and his pompous tone, but was not yet ready to apologise. It was time Polly learned to be less impulsive. Do her good to know how her thoughtless actions impinged on other people.

Polly reappeared an hour later, with a steaming plateful of rice and curry on a lap table, which she banged down on Tom's lap. She seated herself in the other armchair, but switched on the television, to avoid having to converse.

"That was good," Tom declared, as he finished the last mouthful, adding, "thank you for that."

Polly rose without replying, to collect his empty plate.

He said, "Leave that, Sweet Pea. I'll clear up. You sit down and rest. It's been a long day."

"Rest? I wish I could. It may have escaped your notice, but it's Sunday tomorrow. Therefore I have a sermon to write and a service to prepare. So if you'll excuse me, I'll take myself off to the study and work."

She managed to flounce out of the room, which was the last Tom saw of her until next day.

CHAPTER TWENTY-SIX

The older one caught the girl as she returned from the rectory. He'd broken his usual routine and had been to see the baby. His disappointment over the birth of a girl rather than a boy had been short-lived, and he had found he couldn't see enough of this new addition to his family, however much he deplored her conception.

When he discovered their absence, he had thought she'd taken the baby out for a walk, although he'd warned them never to let her out alone. He'd never imagined her terrible deed, and even when he caught her by stepping out from behind the tree and grabbing her around the neck, he merely thought she'd left the baby somewhere.

"Where is she? Where is the baby?"

She'd laughed then, secure in the knowledge that her child was safe from harm, that he would never be able to touch her. "Where you can't get her."

"You little fool! Tell me where she is." His grip tightened.

She'd spat out the words. "She's dead. You'll never have her."

"What? Dead? How can she be? She's only just been born. What have you done, you evil bitch?"

Shock loosened his grip and she twisted away from him, but it was a half-hearted attempt at freedom. Without her baby, she had nothing to live for. She faced him defiantly, flinging her blond hair back behind her shoulders, hatred dark in her blue eyes.

His hands were around her throat now, and despite herself, she fought for breath. Kicked out against him, wriggled and struggled in his grip, but he was too strong for her. As he squeezed the life out of her, her dying thought was for her child.

'Now! Now we shall be reunited forever, you and me, Mary Elizabeth Madison...'

Shocked, sickened and frightened both by her actions and his own, he dragged her back to his home and bundled her into the freezer. Then he sat and thought about how he could possibly dispose of her.

***

On the day of the funeral Polly was awoken early, not by sunshine streaming into her bedroom as was usually the case, but by the incessant thrum of rain beating against the window panes. It was so unusual after weeks of dry weather, that she lay in bed listening for a while. It sounded heavy. When she crossed to the window to see for herself, she found that not only was the rain torrential, but it had evidently been raining for some hours, for already little rivulets and puddles were forming on the parched earth of the rectory garden. If it continued to rain all morning, Polly hoped Francis Bancroft, the funeral director, would think to bring an umbrella. Churchyards were notorious for being exposed to howling weather, and the thought of standing at an open grave, trying to read the words of committal with rain dripping down her neck, failed to appeal to Polly.

Polly dressed in her smartest funereal outfit of black clergy shirt and black skirt suit, finished off with black shoes which had rather clumpy, three inch heels. The rector was usually invited to join the funeral bash, in this case at the local pub, and she needed to look the part, but stilettos in a graveyard would be the height of madness, especially during rain.

On this occasion it would be no good to wear her old jeans underneath her robes, for the wake was a great opportunity to meet local people who never attended church except for funerals. Most folk tended to be amenable towards church following a good funeral, and were more inclined to some interest in spiritual matters since they were all likely to become aware of their own mortality, especially when the deceased had died suddenly and at a relatively young age, like Jack Davidson. Polly wanted to become better known in the villages and to make some good links, and this, she felt, was the ideal time. Not that she had any intention of proselytising or bible-bashing, which she felt was usually inappropriate and certainly so on such an occasion; she merely wished to make personal contact with a few more of her flock.

During the morning she took her mind off the forthcoming event by spending the hours in preparation for the next service of all-age worship at Lower Parsondale. Along with Catriona, she had decided to experiment with 'Messy Church', which promised to be exactly as described in the title. On one Sunday a month, instead of the children disappearing into the tower room for most of the hour, the whole service would be in church and based around fun activities for children and adults, involving glue and paints, scissors, cardboard, and modelling clay, dressing up clothes, guitars and dancing, with a simple meal laid on at the end of the service. Polly had announced her intention to the Parochial Church Council, and had been met with resistance and grumbles from many of the PCC members who had thrown up all sorts of objections, from the pews being unsuitable for any venture which involved running around, to fears that the church building itself would become messy with paint and glue, to this sort of experiment not constituting proper worship. They had suggested forcefully that an afternoon service away from their beloved Sunday morning would be more suitable for this kind of event, but Polly was determined to acknowledge it as mainstream church and insisted on it being the principle service for one Sunday a month. She suspected that most regular church members would vote with their feet and take it as a Sunday off, but by advertising widely in the whole benefice and through Catriona's word of mouth to all her friends with school age children, Polly was hoping for a good turnout. If it was to be successful the service had to be carefully planned, and Polly needed to ensure that all the activities were based around worship and solid Christian teaching. Otherwise she knew she would be accused quickly of dumbing down worship by providing mere entertainment.

She was rather afraid that the first to denounce the new service would be Oswald. He had made clear his disgust at the PCC meeting; to Polly's relief vowing his intention of having nothing to do with the innovation, but it was one thing to stand aloof and quite another to stir up discord by actively denigrating what Polly was trying to do. She didn't want to give Oswald any excuse for that to happen, so every service needed to be properly organised, following a pattern of progressive teaching. If the service attracted large numbers of new people who were receiving sound Christian input, she didn't see how even Oswald could object.

Oswald was on her mind. She had not managed to find the opportunity to catch him alone so had been unable to take him to task over today's funeral, but she knew she must talk to him sooner or later. If she let this ride, she would lose any authority she had. However unpleasant the interview would be, it had to happen. Now it looked as though the only opportunity would be during the half hour immediately prior to the service, which was far from satisfactory. With so much going on—people arriving, extra seating to be organised, VIPs to be greeted—any consultation was sure to be hurried, and this wasn't something Polly wanted to rush. Besides, both she and Oswald needed time before the funeral to settle themselves and to spend a few moments in prayer together.

In the event, the decision was taken out of Polly's hands, for although she arrived an hour before the service was due to start, she was kept busy during the whole of that time, making sure that mourners gave their names to the funeral directors, that everyone had an order of service, that the organist had the correct tunes for the hymns, and that everyone who needed a seat had one. Even so, there were three rows of mourners standing at the back of church, for whom no seat could be found. Polly had never seen the church so full, and to cap it all, Oswald arrived shaking a dripping umbrella all over the vestry floor, with just five minutes to spare in order to robe ready for the service to begin. Polly contented herself with glaring at him, but he seemed oblivious to her annoyance. She made a mental note to collar him after the service and arrange a specific time when they could talk—at the rectory, on Polly's own territory.

It was time; the hearse was arriving. Polly swallowed her irritation, concentrating all her efforts on making the funeral as easy as possible for the mourners without losing the dignity of a solemn farewell for a greatly respected public servant. She went ahead of Oswald, greeting Evelyn and John warmly as they stepped from the limousine following the hearse, warning them that the church was packed so that they wouldn't be thrown by the huge numbers turning out to pay their respects to Jack, and reassuring them that

God would give them the strength they needed to get through the service. Then she and Oswald preceded the coffin up the aisle, while Polly said sentences of scripture, and when all were in church she invited the congregation to sit down, and informally introduced the service, telling the congregation the purpose of the service, what to expect, and inviting them all to the the Railway Arms after the service while the immediate family laid Jack to rest in the churchyard.

The service went better than Polly had dreamed possible. The congregation was responsive, and even Evelyn permitted herself a few tears, which pleased Polly since she considered part of the purpose of a funeral was to enable immediate relatives to begin to get in touch with their own grief. Polly had to admit that Oswald's eulogy was first class. He painted a graphic picture of Jack Davidson, praising his work in the community and thanking God for his life, and even used light humour at appropriate moments, which broke tension in the congregation and allowed them to relax in mild laughter. He ended the talk by retelling the Christian message of a new sort of life with God, after death.

As Polly led the way into the churchyard, reading the Nunc Dimittis, she knew it had been a moving service and a worthwhile tribute to Jack, one which couldn't have failed to bring comfort to Evelyn and John. She murmured a word of thanks to Oswald as he accompanied her to the graveside, congratulating him on an excellent talk.

"You hit exactly the right note, Oswald. Tears and laughter combined—a perfect partnership. It was good."

Oswald had no chance to reply, as Francis Bancroft hurried forward with a large, black umbrella which he held over both of them. They wended their way slowly through wet grass which slapped uncomfortably at Polly's ankles. She regretted her heels, which although chunky, were beginning to squelch into the surface mud. Having seen the mechanical digger preparing the tomb in the sunshine the previous afternoon, she hoped there was no residual water in the bottom of the grave. There was nothing more embarrassing and certain to cause distress to grieving relatives than a coffin which floated.

As they neared the plot, Oswald moved discreetly to one side while Polly carried on to stand at the head of the open grave. Two sturdy, square wooden poles ready to receive the coffin, lay across the top of the gaping hole, which was a double depth of twelve feet to incorporate Evelyn as well when her time came. Polly busied herself finding the correct place in her service book while the bearers reverentially laid the coffin on top of the poles and threaded ropes beneath it and through the handles, ready for lowering it into the space. Despite the umbrella still held deferentially over her by Francis Bancroft, Polly could feel water dripping down inside her collar. Her feet were soaking, and the pages of the book were now so wet that it was difficult to turn them.

Polly waited as the immediate family gathered under umbrellas; Evelyn and John, together with Jack's brother and family, Evelyn's brother and sister, and assorted nephews, nieces and cousins.

The rest of the congregation huddled in groups around the church porch, uneasy about repairing to the comfort of the Railway Arms until the burial was complete.

When everyone was ready and gazing at her expectantly, Polly explained that she would read a few verses from Psalm 103, then during the next reading, the coffin would be lowered. She had found it paid to alert the mourners as to the moment when the coffin would disappear from their sight. Always a difficult point for them, at least it was a little easier if folk knew what to expect and when.

She finished the comforting words of the psalm, "As for mortals, their days are like grass; they flourish like a flower of the field; for the wind passes over it , and it is gone, and its place knows it no more. But the steadfast love of the Lord is from everlasting to everlasting upon those who love him, and his righteousness upon their children's children," and began to recite the solemn words of committal, "We have entrusted our brother, Jack Farley Davidson, to God's mercy and we now commit his body to the ground." She raised her right hand to make the sign of the cross and as a signal to the bearers to begin lowering the coffin.

Francis handed the umbrella to her as he moved to the grave to pull out the two poles. Polly continued, "Earth to earth, ashes to ashes, dust to dust—"

She stopped suddenly, staring down into the grave, her mouth open and a look of horror on her face.

With a puzzled glance, Francis Bancroft prompted, "Rector?"

Polly turned anguished eyes upon him. "Stop the coffin! Stop! Bring back the coffin!"

The bearers strained to hold the weight of the coffin, glancing bemusedly between Polly and their boss.

Francis said, "What?"

"Bring it back," Polly ordered. "We have to stop the funeral. I'm sorry, but we can't bury Jack."

CHAPTER TWENTY-SEVEN

"How dare you!" John Davidson was white with rage, his lips pinched in a thin line. "How dare you interrupt my father being laid to rest? Is it not enough for you to hijack our service, that you feel impelled to interrupt the most important part? Have you no pity? Haven't we suffered enough at your hands? God save us from women priests!" He appealed to Francis, "Get on with it, please. You can't do this to my poor mother."

But Francis had followed Polly's horrified gaze, matching it with stunned disbelief of his own. For a moment he stared into the pit transfixed, his face ashen, but then he seemed to come to himself and with a quick flick of his head ordered his men to lift the coffin. He slipped the poles into position beneath the raised coffin, then looked at Polly for instruction as to what to do next. This situation was unprecedented in all his years as a funeral director, and he had no idea how to handle it. Polly quickly crossed to his side for a murmured consultation, which caused him to pull out his mobile phone and dial.

Polly moved away from him towards Evelyn and John. "I'm truly sorry about this." She laid her hand on John's arm as he made to step forward, but dropped it when he flinched. "Please don't look down there. I'm afraid there's—there's—already someone buried in this grave. We cannot proceed with your father's burial."

"What? But this is our grave. We paid enough for it. How dare you bury someone else in my father's grave? This is outrageous, and the bishop will hear about it."

Polly sighed, taking his arm to steer him and Evelyn away from the graveside, trying to turn them in the direction of the church porch. "I do apologise most sincerely, but believe me, you don't want to look. It will only add to your distress. I'm not talking about—um—a conventional burial, and I can assure you it's nothing to do with me or with the church. This is not an authorised burial, and I know nothing about it. I'm afraid—well, I've just seen a woman's hand at the bottom of the grave."

Evelyn's eyes grew wide. Her knees buckled and she retched. Polly put an arm round her to support her but she shook it off angrily and leaned against her son.

Polly said, "We'll sort this out as soon as we can, but we don't know what has happened and obviously the police will have to be involved. Francis has just called them. I'm afraid we won't be able to complete Jack's burial today, but we'll have a quiet ceremony just as soon as the grave is cleared and we're given permission by the police."

"What?" John's distress was aimed at Polly in the form of extreme anger. "You're telling me there's a body down there, and you expect us to use that same space when the body has been removed? Are you out of your mind? There's no way we want Dad put anywhere near here. This grave is defiled. You can find us another plot, over the other side of the churchyard."

Polly hesitated. Plots were dug in rows. There was no precedent for digging a plot outside the current row, but this might not be the time to argue. "Shall we talk about that later, when you're over the shock? Look, why don't you take your guests over to the Railway Arms? There's nothing more any of us can do here, and the pub is expecting you. No reason not to hold the wake. We've had the funeral; the final committal can be done at any time and is often at a different time from the funeral. Perhaps we can bury Jack tomorrow or Friday."

John spluttered, "You don't seem to realise the enormity of this. Can't you see that my mother is in torment? And all you can suggest is that we carry on as though nothing has happened! How insensitive can you be?"

Polly tried to calm him. "As I've said, I really do apologise. You're quite right; this is an appalling situation and nobody should have to put up with having the funeral of a loved one disrupted. But I'm afraid it's beyond my control. A nice cup of tea might be just what Evelyn needs."

As John went from white to red in the face and appeared ready to explode, to Polly's relief Oswald silently materialised at his side. "Come on

John, Evelyn. Let's get you over the road out of this rain. We can't do anything more here at the moment. Let's go and get dry."

Fortunately most of the mourners, still waiting under umbrellas by the church porch, had no idea what had happened and assumed the burial to be over as the family members allowed themselves to be marshalled by Oswald and began to move in the direction of the church. Those waiting at the church porch put Evelyn's pallor and John's evident distress down to the emotion of the moment. But Polly knew that such a state of ignorance wouldn't last long. She was anxious to get the churchyard cleared of the crowd before the police arrived, possibly with sirens blaring, and surrounded the grave with blue and white crime scene tape. At least Jack Davidson's family and friends could be spared that.

As Oswald ushered the family away, Polly whispered, "Can you get them all over to the pub as quickly as possible, Oswald? I'll wait for the police, and join you later. Hold the fort over there, will you? They'll all know what's happened by the time they get over there, but if you can minimise damage by formally explaining, I'd be grateful. Don't say more than you have to, at this stage. I'm sure there'll be plenty of speculation, and no doubt it'll be all our fault for failing to check the grave immediately before the service. Still, do what you can."

Oswald nodded, and hurried his steps, looking, Polly thought, distinctly pleased with himself.

Catriona was right. He really does love the limelight. He's happy when he's in charge. He'll revel in being the one to inform everyone of the current state of affairs.

Francis was hovering, along with his bearers. Polly said, "Can you put the coffin back in the hearse, Francis? We'll try and rearrange for tomorrow or Friday, if possible. I'll let you know. May have to dig another grave; John wasn't too happy about using this one, under the circumstances."

Francis was still looking stricken, but had sufficient presence of mind to murmur, "Yes, of course, Reverend Hewitt. Um, who will bear the cost of that? We have to hire the equipment and someone to work it. It doesn't come cheap."

"No, I don't suppose it does. Oh Lordy! I can't see John Davidson agreeing to cough up, and to be fair, why should he? It's hardly a problem of his making."

"But if he wishes to bury elsewhere...?"

"Yes, I see your point. You can tell him, then. Rather you than me. Look, Francis, there's no point in us all hanging around here getting soaked. Why don't you go and reassure the family? I'll wait here for the police."

Francis' relief was evident. "Thank you, Reverend Hewitt. I'm sure we'll be in touch very soon."

When she was certain all mourners had removed from the churchyard, Polly again approached the grave for a better look. Having seen the emergent hand in the mud at the bottom of the hole while she was in the process of committing Jack Davidson's body to the earth, initially she had looked away quickly, feeling a little nauseous and anxious not to disgrace herself in front of the gathered Davidson clan. Since then, she had wondered whether her eyes had deceived her. Had her mind been playing tricks? Could she really have seen a hand? Or was it such a quick glance that she had imagined something that wasn't actually there?

Tentatively, because she was afraid she might vomit if she had been correct in her original assumptions, she leaned over the grave. Yes, there it was, unmistakeable. Ugh! Polly shuddered. A bit of arm was visible too, so at least the hand was unlikely to be severed, wasn't it? Polly turned away. She was beginning to feel sick again. There was no point in standing here any longer getting more drenched by the minute; she might as well wait inside the church. If she left the door open, she'd hear the police cars easily enough.

She stripped out of her wet robes, hanging them in the vestry to dry, then for something to do while she was waiting, idly checked the collection. The plate she had left at the back of church was overflowing with ten and twenty pound notes, given in memory of Jack Davidson. Pity it wasn't for church funds, but at least it was for the British Heart Foundation, a worthy cause. Still, with over a thousand in the plate it would have been nice for the church to have received some, run as it was, entirely on voluntary contributions. Especially if the church had to fork out for a new grave, to keep the peace with the Davidsons.

Polly transferred both cash and cheques into a canvas money bag, scribbled a note to the church treasurer indicating that it was to be sent to the British Heart Foundation, and locked the bag securely in the safe, pocketing the key. She made sure the vestry was locked too, before adjourning to the back pew to await the arrival of the police.

The police team, led, Polly was thankful to see, by Chloe, were quick and efficient, but as they erected a canvas tent around the grave and applied crime scene tape to a wider perimeter, it was clear this would not be over any time soon. Polly settled down to wait, but Chloe had other ideas.

"No point in you hanging around here, Polly. We can't allow any civilians anywhere near, and that includes you, rector or not."

"But if it's a body," Polly argued, "I must be here to say a prayer to lay her soul to rest as best I can."

Chloe hesitated. "All right. Stay until we see what we're dealing with here. But even if it is a body—and we don't know that for sure, yet, it may just be a limb—it'll be ages before she's brought up. We have to wait for the pathologist, and he's somewhere in Norwich so it'll take him a while. Why don't you go home to the rectory, and I'll call you when she's ready to be taken away? You can come over then and give the last rites, or whatever you have to do."

Polly nodded. It was a reasonable compromise, and to be honest, she was pleased. It would be good to get home, have a shower, wash her hair, and change into something less formal. And it was something of a relief to have a legitimate excuse for avoiding the funeral bash, and particularly, the Davidsons. She had a feeling they would not be best pleased to see her, and just at the moment she didn't feel up to fielding any more verbal abuse from John.

She waited quietly in the church until her worst fears were confirmed by Chloe. The body of a young woman had indeed been superficially concealed under the loose soil at the bottom of Jack Davidson's grave. But for the heavy rain washing away part of the topsoil, the body might never have been discovered.

Polly walked back through the gate into the rectory garden feeling shaky. There had been some terrifying happenings in Anglesham in the short time she had lived there, but nothing like this. As far as Polly could see, there could be only one explanation for a body hidden in a grave, and that was murder. But who was this young woman? Who had murdered her, and why?

CHAPTER TWENTY-EIGHT

Polly was on tenterhooks for several hours, waiting for Chloe's summons. Unable to settle, she couldn't dispel from her mind the image of that vulnerable, pallid wrist and hand. She had no doubt that it was a female hand; even from a height of twelve feet Polly had seen that it was too light and delicate to be male, but she had no means of knowing how old the female might be. She was worried too, about the fallout from such a disastrous afternoon, having no doubts that John Davidson would be loud and public in his condemnation of the church and of Polly in particular.

At the back of Polly's mind was the unwelcome possibility that the murder might be connected with all the other events that had happened recently. Afraid to acknowledge such a thought since she was the prime victim of all previous threats, Polly tried to push it away, but it hovered around the edge of her consciousness, threatening to surface at the earliest opportunity.

She brewed a pot of tea which she contemplated taking over to the officers, but in the end decided that such a move might be construed by Chloe as an attempt to muscle in on their scene, so drank it herself. Unenthusiastically, she thought about throwing a meal together, but anxious in case the call came while she was in the middle of preparations, toasted a couple of slices of bread instead, spreading them thickly with butter and marmalade. Even that failed to produce the usual comforting effect. Normally, Polly loved to sit curled up in an armchair with toast, marmalade, and a mug of tea, but this evening she was restless, and since the toast tasted like cardboard, she threw it away.

Chloe eventually rang at eight thirty that evening. The mourners had long since returned home from the Railway Arms, several of them immediately phoning Polly, agog for the latest gossip. Polly was able to say with perfect truth that police were still on site and that she knew nothing.

Chloe was as terse as ever. "You can come now. It's the body of a young girl, and we're about to load her into the van."

Picking up her service book from the hall table as she passed, Polly raced across the garden and into the churchyard, not wanting to miss this opportunity. Chloe held the tent flap open for her, regarding her with raised eyebrows as she arrived, breathless.

"Are you certain you're up for this, Polly? Don't want you passing out or throwing up. We've got enough to do without sorting out any of that."

"I'll be okay," Polly assured her, with more conviction than she felt.

"Not sure you can do much for her at this stage, anyway." Chloe was unzipping the black body bag. Even that sent shivers down Polly's spine. "Don't know how long it takes for a soul to depart, three days, isn't it? I'm sure I read that somewhere, but it's more in your field than mine. Preliminary findings indicate she's been dead for at least twenty-four hours, so I suppose she might be hovering around here somewhere."

Resisting the temptation to look upwards to the roof of the tent, Polly said firmly, "I can still recite the prayer of commendation over her, wherever her soul is."

Taking a deep breath, she moved over to the stretcher. Although she had been in ministry for five years now, Polly had seen only one dead person, and that was a natural death, in hospital. She had stayed with old Arthur Roamer, quietly holding his hand as he slipped away, but that was different. What would it be like to see someone who had not only been dead for a whole day and a night, but who had been murdered and had been covered in earth for most of that time?

Determined not to disgrace herself, Polly held herself rigidly as she looked down at the stretcher. Much of the body was still concealed in the bag, but Polly saw a young girl, perhaps sixteen or seventeen years old, with long, fair hair like silk around her shoulders. She had no make-up, but full lips with a bluish tinge and the whitest complexion Polly had ever seen. Mercifully her eyes were closed, but soil clung to her eyelids, clogged her nostrils and gathered around her lips. Skinny to the point of emaciation, she had a classical bone structure with high cheekbones, but her collar bones showed through her thin, white tee shirt. Thinking it might be important to see all the clothes, Polly asked if she might further unzip the bag, and Chloe nodded. The girl's legs were clad in the uniform of all teenagers, ragged blue jeans with holes at the knee, and she wore dirty trainers on her feet, with no socks. Polly estimated her height as around five feet six inches. As she gazed down, Polly caught her breath. Even in death, this girl was beautiful and Polly was seized by compassion, laced with anger that she had died so very prematurely.

Polly turned to Chloe, "How did she die?"

"We're not sure yet. But there are bruises around her neck, look, here and here," she showed Polly the ugly red marks, "so she may have been strangled. We won't know anything for certain until she's been examined properly back at the lab and we have in all the reports, including toxicology. She's very thin. She may have been on drugs."

"Do you know who she is?"

Chloe shook her head. "No. We'll put out enquiries and take DNA, of course, and examine her clothes to see if there are any clues there, but they look generic to me. Do you know her?"

"Of course not. But—"

"What?"

"Nothing." Even in the face of death, Polly felt unable to break Maggie's confidence. Besides, Maggie had attended Jack Davidson's funeral, so would know by now that a body had been concealed in his grave. Surely she would be in contact soon. "I just wondered who could do this to her. She's lovely."

"She is. It shouldn't make any difference since murder is murder whoever the victim, but somehow it's doubly hard for our officers when it's someone so young and pretty.

"Polly, I don't want to hurry you, but can you do your thing so we can get her back? Every second counts in a murder investigation."

"Sorry." Polly placed her right hand on the girl's head and was taken aback by the icy coldness of the scalp even through the softness of the blond hair, although Polly's brain told her she should have expected it.

Polly chose to recite a prayer suitable for use after a violent death, expressing the anguish felt by those who had discovered the girl, and asking that having been released from the world's cruelty, she might be received into God's safe hands and secure love. Polly finished by praying that justice should be done. Then, making the sign of the cross on the girl's forehead, she recited the ancient words of commendation, *Go forth upon thy journey from this world in the name of God the Father almighty who created thee; in the name of Jesus Christ who suffered death for thee; in the name of the Holy Spirit who strengthens thee; in communion with the blessed saints and aided by angels and archangels and all the armies of the heavenly host. May thy portion this day be in peace and thy dwelling the heavenly Jerusalem.*

She knew from her experience of funerals that the words were powerful, but it wasn't until she had finished speaking and had removed her hand from the girl's head, that Polly became aware that all members of the police team had filed silently into the tent and were standing with heads bowed, listening intently to her words and reverentially sharing the moment.

"Go on your journey in peace," Polly murmured, as she left the girl's side and moved out of the way.

When Polly got back to the rectory there were a number of messages on the answerphone including three from journalists, but nothing from Maggie Brewster. Polly ignored them all except the one from Jean Bannister. It was the only message not requesting information but solicitous over Polly's well-being and inviting her over for evening cocoa, if she so wished. Polly did wish. She was desperate to talk over the day's events with a sympathetic listener, for she knew there would be no sleep that night unless she was able to at least begin to get it out of her system. Donning her waterproofs and wheeling out her bike, she cycled the short distance to Crossing-Keeper's Cottage.

Jean asked no questions, simply relieving Polly of her wet gear, embracing her in a warm hug and seating her in an armchair in front of the television. Polly tucked her feet under her as Moses came over, pushing his cold nose into Polly's lap as though wanting to give her comfort. Polly fondled his ears as Jean disappeared into the kitchen. Returning a few minutes later with mugs of cocoa and a plate of ham and cheese sandwiches—"I knew you wouldn't have eaten"—she ordered Moses to his basket and switched off the television.

When Polly had eaten her fill and her shoulders began to relax, Jean said, "Do you want to talk about it?"

Polly nodded. "It was so awful, Jean. I was in the middle of the committal when I happened to glance down into the grave and saw this hand. You know how thoughts race across your mind in microseconds at times like that? I was thinking I couldn't possibly stop the funeral, then I thought I must, then I wondered if I'd imagined it, then I thought about John and Evelyn and how terrible it would be for them, and I found I'd told the bearers to lift the coffin almost without knowing what I was doing."

"Good thing you did. If you hadn't noticed her hand, that poor girl would have been buried for ever underneath an oak coffin. She would never have been seen again, which presumably was the murderer's intention. She's someone's daughter though, and they need to know what has happened to her."

"That's the problem, Jean. I'm not certain by any means, but there's just a faint possibility I might know whose daughter she is. I hope I'm wrong, I really do. I'm worried sick about it. Jean, I don't know what to do. This mother spoke to me in confidence, so I can't tell the police that she's searching for her daughter. She hasn't involved the police, so there's no missing persons report. If I tell her that it might be her daughter, but I'm wrong, where will that leave her? Everything about her missing daughter will be in the public domain and she'll be destroyed. Can I put her through that? I don't know what to do."

"Hm." Jean drained her cocoa and cradled the empty mug. "What other options do you have?"

"I was hoping she might ring me—she was at the funeral, so must know what's happened, but she hasn't, yet."

"So you were thinking of waiting to see what tomorrow brings?"

Polly looked sheepish. "Cowardly, I know. It's just that I don't want to be the one to tell her. I suppose I'm hoping the description of the murdered girl will prompt this woman to ring the police. After all, they are the official channel."

Jean nodded slowly. She paused thoughtfully, then said, "If you were this mother, Polly, if there was the faintest possibility it might be your daughter that had been found murdered, would you want to be told straight away, even if the information was wrong, or would you want to wait? And who would you want to tell you? A trusted friend, or an unknown official?"

Polly sighed. "Oh dear, I was afraid you might say that. You're right, of course, and I suppose I knew it, deep down. Didn't want to acknowledge it, though. Such an awful task." Setting down her empty mug, she stood. "I'd better go, Jean. Best to get it over."

"I hope it's okay, Polly. And remember, you can always come back. Any time."

CHAPTER TWENTY-NINE

Shrugging back into her waterproofs and switching on her cycle lamps, Polly rode slowly through the rain along the country lane which skirted the lower end of Anglesham Common, running directly from Jean's cottage to the Brewster's manor house. Polly felt uncomfortable to be calling at such a late hour; somehow bad news seemed worse at night and in driving rain. She would have much preferred to wait until morning when both she and Maggie would be brighter and more able to face what had to be faced, but Jean was right. Maggie had to know sometime. How would she react if she thought Polly had kept such vital information to herself, if there was even the slightest chance the dead girl could be Kimberley? Not that such a realisation comforted Polly. She dreaded the forthcoming interview, unsure whether or not she wanted

Giles to be home. His presence would be a necessary comfort and support for his wife, but was he even aware that Maggie had consulted Polly?

As she cycled through the rain, Polly tried to work out in her mind just how to break the news to Maggie. *Hello Maggie, sorry to tell you that your daughter may have been murdered.* No, that would never do. How about, *Maggie, I'm really sorry to spring this on you, but there is a slight possibility that we might have discovered Kimberley's body.* Oh dear, no! Far too harsh. Um, what about, *Maggie, you do know that we discovered a teenage girl in Jack Davidson's grave this afternoon, don't you? Now I don't want you to worry unduly, but I think you need to prepare yourself. I'm afraid she was blond and about Kimberley's height... Of course, we don't know who she is.* No. It was impossible to break news like this gently.

Standing on the doorstep with rain dripping down her neck, Polly felt at a distinct disadvantage, but in the event she had no need to agonise. The door was opened quickly, almost as if Maggie had been waiting. One look at Polly, and Maggie's face crumpled. Words were unnecessary.

Maggie turned away, hiding the tears. "You'd better come in."

"I'm very wet."

Maggie shrugged. Damp carpets were the least of her worries. "Come into the kitchen."

Taking a deep breath, Maggie stood with her back to the Aga, gripping the rail as though afraid she might fall. "Just tell me. I need to know. Have you—have you found her?"

Polly eased herself onto a kitchen chair, her knuckles white as she gripped the edge of the table. "I don't know, Maggie. Maybe. That's why I've come."

Maggie's legs buckled. She hung onto the Aga rail, then fell heavily onto a chair, facing Polly.

"Tell me." She whispered the words.

Polly moistened her lips. In the end, the words tumbled out. "I'm sorry, Maggie. I'm so very sorry. There was a young girl at the bottom of Jack Davidson's grave, a teenager, sixteen, seventeen. We don't know how she got there, or who she is, but I've seen her, Maggie. She's medium height, very thin, has long blond hair and was dressed in a white tee shirt and jeans. Now before you leap to any conclusions," she hurried on, afraid to stop talking, "that description applies to half the teenage female population. I don't know whether or not it's Kimberley. I've only seen that photo of her you have on your piano. The one with her holding her pony, with her hair whipping in the wind. This girl looks similar to the photo, but I think your photo was taken a year or two ago, in happier times. I—I can't tell whether it's her or not. Kimberley was slender in the picture, but not like this. This girl is painfully thin. I—er—thought you'd want to know what—who—we found."

Maggie's blue eyes were huge in her stricken face. She seemed to shrink visibly, and she turned deathly pale.

"Can I get you something? A glass of water? How about a nice cup of tea?" Polly blanched as she heard herself. A nice cup of tea? A stiff brandy might be more to the point.

She was about to apologise when Maggie said in a distracted tone, "Thank you, yes. A cup of tea would be nice."

Polly jumped to her feet, relieved to be doing something. It was almost more than she could bear to look at Maggie's forlorn face. She said nothing more as she busied herself making and pouring tea, giving Maggie time to adjust to the shock of the new information.

When they were both sipping tea and a little colour had returned to Maggie's cheeks, Polly said, "What do you want to do?"

Polly waited for a moment or two, but when nothing further was forthcoming, offered, "Would you like me to contact Chloe? She's in charge of the investigation. I'm sure she would be discreet."

Maggie frowned. "Discreet? What about?"

"Well, about Kimberley being missing."

"Oh, that. It doesn't matter any more."

Polly could have kicked herself. Of course it didn't matter. She should have realised how quickly priorities change. "Shall I ring her, then? Or do you want to phone Giles first?"

"Um," Maggie was having difficulty concentrating. "Um, yes, all right. Chloe, I think. Giles is probably in the House. I think he said they have a debate tonight and he has to be there to vote. I don't want to worry him until we know for sure." She looked beseechingly at Polly. "I'll have to go, won't I? Identify the—the body?"

"Which may not be Kimberley," Polly reminded her. "But yes, you'll have to go. I'll come with you, if you like."

Maggie seemed to reach a decision. "It's nearly ten o'clock. Is it too late? No? Better phone, then. We'll go now, if they'll let us. I'd rather get it over with tonight. No point in dragging it out; besides, I'll never sleep now."

The body was being held in the hospital mortuary, ready for the post mortem. As Maggie was in no fit state, Polly drove Maggie's BMW as fast as she dared along the country lanes, praying nothing untoward would happen, since she was unsure whether or not her own driver insurance covered her. Reaching the Norfolk and Norwich hospital without incident, due to the lateness of the hour she was able to park easily.

Chloe was waiting in the foyer to greet them. "She's in the chapel of rest. I'll take you there."

They followed Chloe's decisive steps along the long corridors, Polly holding fast to Maggie's arm, afraid to let go in case Maggie collapsed.

Chloe paused outside the door of the small chapel. "Take your time. No need to rush—you can spend as long as you like in here. I'll come in with you, then if you confirm that it is indeed Kimberley, I'll leave you with her. There's no need to fear. Her face hasn't been damaged in any way. She—she looks lovely."

Maggie nodded. Her jaw was clenched and her eyes terrified, despite Chloe's words.

Chloe pushed open the door, ushering them both into the tiny room. Moving over towards the plinth, Polly felt a tremor run through her friend's frame as she steeled herself for her coming ordeal. Then Chloe lifted the sheet covering the body and they were gazing down into the newly washed face of the murdered girl.

She looked so young and vulnerable, lying there on the snowy pillow, a white sheet covering her up to her neck and her blond hair spread out around her head like an angel's halo. With her eyes closed it was as though she was asleep in bed, and yet... Suddenly, Polly was aware as never before of the difference between life and death. Although the girl looked as though she was peacefully sleeping, there was something missing. Her soul? Her life force? She was beautiful but empty, an alabaster shell with no breath in her. The real person had gone, departed into some other realm, some other dimension. Polly bit back a sob.

For a long moment nothing was said as the three women, each with her own thoughts, gazed down upon the lifeless form. Polly scarcely dared to breathe. Then a sigh escaped Maggie's lips, and she turned away. "It isn't her."

"What? Are you sure?" Chloe was startled out of her reverie.

Maggie laughed, a brittle sound. "I do know my own daughter, Chloe. This isn't Kimberley. I don't know who this girl is; I've never seen her before. But it isn't Kimberley."

Polly said, "Then who is it?"

Chloe had snapped back into professional mode. She was already covering the body. "That's something we'll have to discover. We'll check all the missing persons meeting the description. That may turn up something. See whether her clothing offers any clues. There'll be a post mortem, of course, so we'll get her DNA in due course. That's the next step. If she doesn't match anyone on the database, we'll invite all men living in the area to voluntarily submit their DNA for analysis. I imagine we'll find out who she is before too long."

The three of them walked back along the dimly lit and silent hospital corridors in sombre mood. It wasn't until they reached the entrance and the two friends turned to say goodbye to her, that Chloe spoke.

She said abruptly, "Tell me about your daughter, Maggie. When did she go missing? Why haven't you reported her absence before now?"

Maggie had recovered some of her equilibrium. She tossed her head, giving Polly an unexpected glimpse of the lady of the manor. "Precisely because Kimberley is not really missing. It's true she has gone from home, but she went of her own volition and I feel sure she will contact us when she's ready. She's an adult now—well, nearly, and she's always been very independent, so this is not entirely out of character. Don't worry, Chloe. She'll turn up before too long, I'm certain of it." She hesitated before adding, "I don't want her temporary disappearance to be made official. You can be confident I'll contact you when I deem it necessary, Chloe. I do care about my daughter, you know."

Chloe raised one eyebrow, darting a look at Polly, but forbore to comment. "I'll say goodbye, then."

She nodded somewhat curtly and swung away across the deserted hospital car park towards her own car. Polly wanted to call after her, asking for assurances that she'd tell them when she discovered the identity of the murdered girl, but felt it wasn't the moment. Chloe needed to get home to bed. They all did.

Polly yawned. It had been a long day. She drove back to the manor house at Hartshead more sedately than on the outward journey, refused Maggie's offer of yet more tea, retrieved her bike, donned her waterproofs and set off through the rain, now easing. But she was puzzled as she cycled home from the Brewster's.

What had precipitated Maggie's lightning change of mood? Was it merely the relief of knowing that the dead girl was not her daughter, or was there something more? Did she know something that she had failed to mention to Polly? Recently Maggie had been so anxious about Kimberley's whereabouts, but she had brushed off Chloe's expertise this evening as though nothing was the matter. And if it wasn't Kimberley, who was the dead girl? She was someone's daughter, that was for sure. Obviously it was a terrific relief for Maggie, but Polly was less sanguine. Whoever the girl was, she deserved justice and Polly was determined to ensure that she received it.

CHAPTER THIRTY

After a restless night filled with images of dead babies and murdered teenagers, Polly slept late. She was awakened by the insistent ringing of the telephone, forcing her to clamber out of bed and race downstairs in her pyjamas. Glancing at the clock as she lifted the receiver, she was shocked to discover it was already nine thirty. Having missed morning prayers yet again, she offered a mute apology to God.

She managed a breathless, "Hello?" into the phone even as she wondered whether she'd be subjected to yet more non-verbal abuse, but realised with a sense of wonder that silent phone calls had somehow lost their dread, when compared with the enormity of the events of the past few days.

Oswald said, "Polly, I've organised Jack Davidson's committal for this afternoon. I've been on to Francis Bancroft; it's all arranged, so no need for you to worry. They're going to leave the original grave empty for the moment and dig a new one next to it, so still in line but leaving a gap. We can use the original grave in later years, when all the fuss has died down. I've talked to John and Evelyn; they're happy with the new plan and I'll sort it, so no need for you to turn out."

Polly blinked. Having just woken from a deep sleep, she felt bemused, unable to get her brain into gear. As her thoughts slowly started to untangle, the principal thought was that this arrangement meant she wouldn't have to face the Davidsons. Underneath that relief was the uneasy feeling that she had been manipulated yet again, but this was such a generous offer of help that she couldn't think sufficiently quickly of a courteous way to counter it.

She tried, "I'm not sure—"

But Oswald continued smoothly, "I do hope this will help you, Polly. I know how difficult the Davidsons can be, and with yesterday's awful discovery, I thought you might need some support. It is okay with you, isn't it?"

Polly heard herself saying lamely, "Thank you, Oswald, very thoughtful of you. I hope it goes well," before replacing the phone with an irritated clatter.

As she stood under the shower letting hot water cascade over her, cleansing and refreshing her for the day ahead, Polly reflected that she was more angry with herself than with Oswald. She had been caught on the hop, allowing Oswald to take control once again. At this rate, she would end up with no say at all over what happened in the benefice. During the interregnum everyone had looked to Oswald for leadership; unless Polly stamped her authority soon, there would be a complete power shift and Oswald would be rector effectively in everything but name.

The problem, Polly realised, was that Oswald always offered something to help her, just like those people who did something terrible then said, "I did it for you." Oswald hadn't done anything terrible, and it was difficult to know whether or not her anger was justified. She was uncomfortably aware of feeling sidelined, but did that matter? Was it just her ego that was bruised? If so, it would be a sin to refuse Oswald's offer, wouldn't it? Polly felt bewildered. Or was this what temptation was all about? Was the sin more to do with being offered something you wanted even if you didn't admit it to yourself, so that you meekly acquiesced allowing yourself to be manipulated into putting aside any uneasy feelings about it?

If only she had woken earlier! If she had been alert when Oswald phoned, Polly felt she might have parried his manipulation, at least long enough to give herself time to think. As it was, Oswald had yanked not only the rug, but the entire carpet from beneath her feet, and Polly was conscious that by failing to challenge Oswald over his earlier devious manoeuvrings, probably she herself was responsible for the present situation. Anyway, it was too late now. She could hardly ring him back and say, "I've had second thoughts..."

Too annoyed with herself to settle to any paperwork and not in the mood for visiting, Polly decided on a long walk to clear her head. It would give her an opportunity for quiet prayer, and maybe she would come up with a suitable plan of action which would make her feelings clear to Oswald without alienating him.

The previous day's rain had ceased. With her mind made up and the sun beating on her back, Polly's spirits quickly began to lift. By the time she was striding across Anglesham Common, her eyes were sparkling and she was humming to herself.

Deep in thought, feeling harmoniously in tune with God, and without any clear idea of the direction she was taking, unexpectedly Polly found herself close to the spinney where she and Tom had spotted Byron. Suddenly remembering the young man with the drug overdose—temporarily forgotten in the shock of discovering a murder victim—Polly strolled along the green sward leading to the dilapidated caravans. Perhaps if she had a good look inside the van, she might discover some clue as to the man's identity. Of course, the police might already know his identity, but they were hardly likely to share such information with Polly. If she knew for herself, she could visit him in hospital. He seemed such a loner that she doubted he had any visitors at all.

The door to the caravan was hanging as drunkenly as Polly remembered. She pushed against it tentatively at first, then with more force. It soon yielded, and she stepped inside. Clearly no one had been inside the van since its owner had been carted off to hospital. It was still utterly disgusting, and the foetid stench was, if anything, even stronger. Holding a handkerchief over her nose, Polly began to root about amidst the clutter.

There was nothing relevant on the table or in the few cupboards. Polly walked through to the bedroom, where the unmade double bed was covered with a filthy under sheet and heaped with a rank duvet. Wishing she'd thought to bring a pair of gloves, Polly reluctantly lifted the mattress to search the drawer beneath the bed.

She was disturbed by a sudden noise behind her, causing her to drop the mattress with a thud. Whirling around, she found herself face to face with a scowling young woman of indeterminate age. With heavy black eye-liner, thick mascara and black lipstick, Polly decided the girl might be a Goth, except that she was wearing tattered blue jeans and unexpectedly, a skimpy pink tee shirt.

The girl flicked curtains of lank, black hair away from her face, revealing a row of earrings in each ear, with long, gold hoops dangling from the lobes.

"What do you think you're doing?" Her voice was harsh, but surprisingly modulated. Then, as she spotted Polly's dog collar, she added in an insolently bored tone, "Oh, it's you. What do you want now?"

Polly's eyebrows rose in surprise. "Do I know you? Or more to the point, do you know me?"

The girl turned her back, retreating to the main room. Polly followed.

Pushing aside a pile of old magazines and empty beer cans, the girl slumped onto the only seat. "'Course I know you. You're the vicar, the one that called the ambulance for Dezzy."

"You were here? You saw that? Why didn't you come forward? You might have been able to help. Where were you, anyway? The police said there was a woman living in the other van, but nobody saw you."

"I'm not that stupid. You think I'd come forward with cops crawling all over the place? No thanks. Besides, I could see you had everything under control."

Polly regarded her thoughtfully. "How is—what did you call him? Did you say he was dizzy? Odd. That's what he said in church when I first met him. How's he getting on?"

The girl shrugged. "How would I know? Should've thought you might know that. You're supposed to visit people in hospital, aren't you?"

With the dawning realisation that the reason the girl had come to challenge her was to find out about the young man's state of health, Polly said, "I would if I knew his name. That's why I'm here; to find out who he is. I can hardly go up to the reception desk and ask for someone who's dizzy, can I? That description must apply to half the population of the hospital."

The girl's lips twitched, but her blue eyes remained suspicious. "How come you don't know him? He told you who he was when you caught him in church that day. And you told his dad."

"What? I have no idea who he is. And I certainly have no idea who his father is! I haven't told anyone anything, because I don't know anything. So why don't you enlighten me?"

"Don't suppose it'll matter, since his dad won't have anything to do with him. And Dezzy isn't a description, by the way. It's his name. That's who he is. He's not dizzy, but Dezzy." The girl looked at her expectantly, but when Polly lifted her eyebrows and shrugged, continued, "Desmond. Desmond Waters. Are you sure you didn't tell his dad? 'Cos Dezzy saw his old man come charging over to the churchyard and he swore his dad was looking for him."

Polly's eyes widened and her mouth fell open. "His dad is Oswald?"

"Yeah, 'course. Not much of a dad though, if you ask me. I mean, Dezzy needed help, not to be booted out of his own home. He went to his brother, but precious Olly won't give him the time of day, either. Frightened Daddy might get cross. All of them are dead scared the neighbours will find out they've a drug addict in the family. They'd do anything to keep that quiet. More concerned about their status than about a member of their own family, the lot of them. Bloody hypocrites, if you ask me. All that Sunday stuff in church about loving your enemy, and they don't even love their own son."

Polly's thoughts raced, as some past oddities began to slot into place. Oswald's strange behaviour, looks she had intercepted between Oswald and Oliver, Nina's nervousness. All could be explained by this startling revelation.

She said, "I didn't even know Oswald and Nina had another son. I only know Oliver. They've never mentioned anyone else and there are no photographs displaying another son. I thought Oliver was an only child. So what's your place in all this? Are you and Dezzy an item?" She glanced at the girl's slender build, and the nervous way her eyes flitted. "Are you on drugs too?"

The girl banged the table in front of her with an angry gesticulation, causing Polly to flinch. "What? You think just because I live in a caravan I must be a smack head? You're all alike, you lot."

"Sorry." Polly raised her hands in a conciliatory gesture. "Didn't mean to offend you. Just wondered what your place was in this set up."

"I've known Dezzy for years. We're good friends, always have been. Couldn't leave him alone like this, could I? I care about him. Only one that does."

Polly risked, "You're not his supplier, then. Wonder how he gets his drugs, stuck out here?"

The girl snorted. "You think you can just cut off his supply and everything will be fine? Fat lot you know. You saw him; he was nearly dead when you picked him up. Might be dead now for all I know. No. He'll have to go into rehab—if anyone can persuade him, and if he can get a place. He'll have to wait months, though. They cut back on the rehab centres in the aftermath of the recession. Blokes like Des aren't worth any votes, see." The girl's voice was full of scorn. "They're only fit for the scrap heap. So the likelihood of rehab is remote. Until then, he needs his stash."

"I see what you mean." Clearly there was no mileage in pursuing this line of enquiry for the moment. Polly tried another tack. "I'm Polly, by the way. Who are you?"

A cunning look came into the girl's eyes, and she laughed, a harsh sound. "You mean you haven't worked it out yet?" She stood up and moved to the door. Slipping out of the door she flung over her shoulder, "Wouldn't you just like to know?"

CHAPTER THIRTY-ONE

"Hey, wait!" Polly sprang up, but the girl was already running lightly across the open grass towards the anonymity of the woodland.

Polly bounded after her, determined not to let her quarry escape, but the girl was fast.

Cupping her hands around her mouth, Polly yelled, "Kimberley! Your mum's really worried about you."

The girl skidded to a halt and turned, warily. Polly waited where she was, as the girl slowly ambled back to her.

The girl said accusingly, "So you did know, all the time. Just stringing me along, were you?"

Polly shook her head. "It was a happy guess, a shot in the dark. I didn't want you rushing off before I had time to ask you a few more questions. There's so much I don't know yet. I certainly didn't recognise you. You do know your mother is looking for a blond? I suppose that's why you dyed your hair."

"Do you like it?"

"I think I might have preferred the blond, to be honest. But I have no problems with it—it has a certain Gothic attractiveness. Each to their own, in my opinion."

Kimberley reverted from a semi-sophisticated, bored teenager, to an eager child. "That's what I think. But you should hear my parents. You'd think anyone with an opinion different from theirs should be cast into outer darkness with wailing and gnashing of teeth. I knew what they'd say if I told them I'd met up with Dezzy again, so it seemed simpler not to tell them. Besides," she squared her shoulders, "I have my own life to lead."

Good job it's summer, Polly thought. *Wait until the winter comes. You might be less enamoured of an ancient caravan with no heating when the temperature plunges below zero.*

"And it looks like you're turning your back on privilege. Fancy talking about it? Could we sit out here perhaps, for a while? It may be sadly middle-class of me to admit it, but I don't think I can bear another moment of the stench inside that van."

Kimberley laughed. "I know what you mean. No way I was going to clear up that mess, whatever I think of Des." She scowled, suddenly. "Look, I don't want you telling my parents where I am."

Polly said slowly, avoiding eye contact, "You may not know this, but a girl has been murdered, Kimberley. A teenager, with long, blond hair. She was about your height and slim like you. I took your mother to the morgue yesterday to identify the body."

There was a sharp intake of breath. Kimberley turned startled eyes upon her. "I didn't know. Who was it? Is she—I mean, is my mother all right?"

"Very relieved it wasn't you, naturally. Pretty shaken up, though. It wasn't a particularly pleasant experience. We don't know yet who the girl is, but it's likely to be someone local. Your mother has been trawling the internet to try and find you and as far as I know, posting messages asking your whereabouts. She might like to know you're safe."

"But if you tell her that, she'll know I'm somewhere around here and she'll come looking for me. Or worse, tell my father. He'd call the troops out to find me, but I never want to go home again. I notice you didn't say he'd gone to the morgue. I suppose he let Mum go by herself. That's typical. Never thinks of anyone but himself and potential votes to keep him in the job. It's all that matters to him. He'd want me under lock and key so that I can't embarrass him any further."

"To be fair, he didn't know anything about it. He's in London, and your mother didn't want him worried unnecessarily. As it turns out, she was right. No point in him haring back here at the rate of knots only to discover it was someone entirely different. Anyway, was it that bad at home?"

Kimberley frowned. "They were always pushing me to be someone I wasn't. Forever on at me to succeed, as though success and making money is the only thing in life that's important. At least, my father was—and Mum never stood up to him. Never took my side. You know they sent me away from all my friends? I was only eleven. I hated it. And when I came back for the holidays, none of my old friends wanted to know me. They'd all moved on, and they treated me like the stuck up bitch they thought I must be just because I went to a posh school. I was so lonely. I felt like a leper when I came back here."

"Is that where Des came into the picture?"

"He used to babysit me when I was little. He was so nice, really gentle and kind, and I always knew he was genuinely interested in me. He read me stories and played with me. He was the best babysitter I ever had." Kimberley was gazing into the distance with a wistful look making her appear much younger and more vulnerable. "He'd been away for years, but when I came back from school in the holidays last year, he'd turned up to see if he could get any money out of his precious family. We met by chance and got talking. After that I used to sneak out and we'd meet up here. He went away again after the summer, but we kept in touch and this year, he'd got these vans from somewhere—one for each of us—and it's been brilliant, except for his drugs. He's a bit weird when he's high. He gets kind of spaced out, and afterwards he never remembers what he was doing. Then when he needs a fix, he gets really ill, and that's a bit scary. Especially the last time. I thought he was dying. I didn't know what to do, then you turned up."

"I thought he was dying, too. Let's hope the medics got to him in time. What did your parents think of your friendship with him?"

"My parents didn't like him, naturally, since he'd already dropped out of high school when he babysat me, but beggars can't be choosers, so they made the best of it. He's ten or twelve years older than me though, and as soon as I turned eleven they had this weird idea that any guy over thirteen was after my body and I was certain to get pregnant, but it wasn't like that. Des was the only good thing about coming home. He and I, both black sheep. Saint Oswald thinks the sun shines out of Olly's bum, but poor old Des was never quite good enough, whatever he did. No wonder he started on drugs."

Polly argued, "But you say you had a similar background as far as parental pressure went, and you didn't take drugs."

"I've tried pot, 'course I have. Everyone has. But I didn't like it. And I saw the change in Des, so I never wanted to get hooked on anything stronger." She sighed. "Poor Des. I wish I could help him."

"I could take you to the hospital, if you'd like to visit him. I'm going anyway, but I could make myself scarce if you want to see him alone."

"Would you? Would you really?" Then her face darkened and she said fiercely, "What's the pay off? You gonna tell my parents, or what?"

"Of course not! I'd like to tell your mother that you're alive, but I won't even do that without your permission. If you want your parents to report you to the police as a missing person, that's up to you." Polly stood up and stretched. "The offer stands, no strings attached. I'm going this afternoon and I'll swing by here. If you want to come, fine. If you're not here, I'll assume you're not interested." She shrugged and looked at her watch. "It's up to you. I'd better get back now since I walked and it'll take me ages, so I'll say goodbye. Nice meeting you, Kimberley."

She nodded at Kimberley, but the girl sprang up. "Doesn't take that long. I'll show you a short cut. Come on. It's only twenty minutes to the main road and another ten to the rectory. You'll be home in half an hour."

She set off at a fast pace, Polly panting a little to keep up. As they walked, Polly said conversationally, "I've only been here a few months, but some really weird things have happened to me. The weirdest—apart from discovering a body in one of the graves in the churchyard—was a baby was left on my doorstep in a wicker basket."

Kimberley barely broke stride. "A baby? Bloody hell! Er, I mean, wow! What happened to it? Did you find the mother or did social services take it? Poor kid. Fancy growing up knowing you'd been left on a doorstep."

That was one mystery partially cleared, then. Kimberley wasn't the child's mother. "As a matter of fact, she was dead. There was a note pinned to her blanket, telling me her name was Mary Elizabeth and the mother wanted me to give her a Christian burial."

"Oh my G—er, wow!" Kimberley was impressed. "Didn't know things like that happened in your job. Thought it was just preaching at people on Sundays."

Polly laughed. "You and most of the population! People seem to think we only work on Sundays, but it's a bit more complex than that. Not that I'd expect to find dead babies on my doorstep every day of the week. That was something out of the ordinary."

"Did you do what the mother asked? Give Mary Elizabeth a Christian burial?"

"Haven't yet. The police took her away for forensic examination. They have to find out how she died, whether it was a cot death or she was ill or something like that, or whether somebody killed her."

Kimberley's eyes grew wide. "Murder, you mean? Another murder? Chri—er, I mean, wow! Nothing like that has ever happened around here before. It's quite exciting, isn't it?"

Polly grimaced. "Less exciting when you're in the middle of it, believe me. Bit scary, to be honest. Not much fun when you think there might be a murderer in our midst."

"What, from here? Anglesham? You're joking! Must be someone from outside, Norwich or somewhere. Some low life who's just used us to dump the bodies—or body, since you said you don't know how the baby died."

"Perhaps. Anyway, the police are on to it, so I don't suppose I need to worry over much.

"Oh! We're here already." She turned to the girl. "Thanks, Kimberley. That was much quicker than the route I took. I'll have to remember that. I'll be passing here at about two this afternoon if you want to come. If not, don't worry."

Kimberley shrugged. "Might. I'll think about it. 'Bye, then."

As she turned to go, Polly called after her, "Oh, forgot to ask. How well do you know Cheryl Patterson?"

Did a shadow flit over Kimberley's face, or was that Polly's imagination?

Shrugging, Kimberley said in an off-hand way, "I know who she is, ' course I do. I was forced to go to church with my parents when I was younger. Don't know her well, though. Isn't she a nurse or something?"

Polly nodded. "And Byron Henderson?"

Kimberley answered a shade too quickly. "No, don't know him. Know the name, but he's a fairly recent addition to her household, I think. 'Bye now. Gotta dash."

She darted back the way they had come, leaving Polly staring thoughtfully after her.

CHAPTER THIRTY-TWO

Polly walked the short distance along the main road back to the rectory, her mind in a quandary. She had given her word to Kimberley, but how could she deny Maggie the knowledge that her daughter was alive and close by? What if Kimberley failed to show this afternoon? Would that release Polly from her promise? Was the confidentiality contingent upon taking Kimberley to the hospital? Polly had an uneasy feeling that it wasn't, that she was bound to keep the girl's confidence whether or not she ever saw Kimberley again.

She fell to wondering how Kimberley was financing her adventure. She couldn't have signed on, could she? Didn't you need a permanent address to claim social security benefits? Polly wasn't sure, and determined to find out via the

Internet when she reached home. Or maybe Kimberley was drawing money from a bank account. That was more likely. She was the child of wealthy parents; she was sure to have an allowance. But if she was withdrawing money, wouldn't Maggie have found out about it?

Polly suddenly recalled Maggie's surprisingly nonchalant attitude when she had realised that the murdered girl wasn't her daughter. Had she found out that Kimberley had been taking money from an account? Would any bank manager dare to release that sort of sensitive information, even to parents? Surely it was confidential. But the Brewsters were influential people and had many friends in high enough places. Perhaps confidentiality was relative in some circles. Perhaps a word had been dropped quietly in the interests either of friendship or of sycophancy.

After she reached the rectory Polly barely had time to open the post, reply to telephone calls (there was a wavering message from Maisie Faulkner who had been recalled to the hospital and told to take an overnight bag with her, and a much more strident one from a journalist wanting details of the body in the grave—Polly ignored that one), sort out the emails, and cobble together a bite of lunch, before getting into the car and setting off again.

She drove towards Anglesham Common without much expectation of seeing Kimberley, but the girl was waiting, leaning carelessly against the trunk of the old oak tree. Polly slowed to a halt and opened the passenger door. Kimberley gave her a shy smile as she clambered into the car.

Nothing was said as Polly negotiated the bends past the common, then Kimberley remarked, "I've been thinking."

"Mm?"

"If you like, you can tell my mother I'm okay."

"Should I say I've met you?"

"I suppose you'll have to. Otherwise how would you know whether or not I was okay? Come to that, how would you know I was still alive?"

Polly grinned. "Good point. What do you want me to say, then?"

"To be honest, I don't mind meeting up with Mum again, but I don't want to see Dad. He'll just bully me into submission. He'll keep on and on until I tell him everything. It's like water boarding with words."

Polly raised her eyebrows, but said nothing.

"I don't want either of them knowing about Des. They'd go ballistic if they thought I was living anywhere near him, so you mustn't tell them anything about him, or about where I'm living. Tell them I swore you to secrecy."

"All right. Would you like me to arrange a meeting with your mother? You could come to the rectory if you like, then no one else would know."

The girl brightened. "That would be cool. I'd been thinking we'd have to meet in a café or something, but there's always the danger someone will see us. My parents are very well known. Wherever they go, someone recognises them."

"Does that matter?"

"I suppose not, but I want to keep out of the way for a while. If people see me, I'll feel pressurised to go back home, and that'll mean something awful like going back to school. I don't know what I want to do yet. Dad wants me to try for Oxbridge, but I'm not doing that just because he says so. I need to make up my own mind. That's why I'm taking time out."

"I see. What about the Waters? Should I say anything to them? Do you think they have the right to know that their son is seriously ill?"

"Oh. Hadn't thought of that. I suppose, although they won't want to know. I told you—they don't love Des."

Polly said mildly, "Perhaps people have different ways of expressing love. Maybe wanting the best possible future for your child is one way of showing your love for them."

Kimberley said, "Huh!" in a withering voice, and her face tightened.

Polly added, "I didn't say it was a particularly good way of displaying love," and left it at that. They passed the remainder of the journey in silence.

As she marched up to the reception desk in the hospital leaving Kimberley lurking by the door, Polly reflected that there were times when a clerical collar came in very useful indeed. Most receptionists responded immediately.

Polly asked, "Could you tell me which ward Desmond Waters is on, please?"

"Just a minute." On the computer, the receptionist trawled through surnames beginning with W. "No, sorry, we don't seem to have a Desmond Waters here. Or do you spell it with an L, Walters? We have John William Walters, aged eighty eight years. Would that be him?"

Polly laughed. "I don't think so! This one is around thirty. Came in last week with a suspected drug overdose."

"Ah! Just a minute." The receptionist pressed more keys on the computer. "Do you know where he came from?"

"Anglesham Common. He was brought in by the emergency services."

"I think I might have him. They have an unknown young man in intensive care. He was brought in from Anglesham. That could be him. Keep going along this corridor to the very end."

"Thank you so much." Polly smiled warmly at the receptionist and hurried back to find Kimberley.

They were both in sombre mood as they traversed the long corridor. Polly warned, "He's still in intensive care so he must be very sick and he may still be unconscious. They may not let you in. They may restrict visiting to relatives only."

"Oh. Will you get in?"

"It's different for me. Clergy always seem to be accepted, unless the patient has particularly refused them. If you do get in, Kimberley, it might do him good to hear your voice. Remember, if he is unconscious, he may be able to hear you. Hearing is the last sense to go, so keep talking to him."

"What shall I say?"

"Doesn't matter. It's the sound of your voice that counts. Just prattle on about what you've been doing. I don't suppose you'll be able to stay long, anyway."

Clearly, the girl was nervous. As they walked into the intensive care unit with its gleaming but intimidating machinery, her eyes were huge in her pale face, contrasting markedly with her black lipstick and her long, black hair.

Polly had visited the unit on several previous occasions, so knew her way around. She approached the nurses' station. "May we visit Desmond Waters, please?"

"Who?" The ward sister frowned.

"I think he might be the young man who was brought in last week with a suspected drug overdose."

"Oh! Well, it will be good to put a name to him at last. Don't like to call him John Doe. Sounds a bit macabre, if you see what I mean. Yes, Reverend, you can go, of course. He's over there." She nodded towards a bed at the far end of the ward, then eyed Kimberley. "Who's this?"

As Polly opened her mouth to speak, Kimberley smoothly interjected, "I'm his sister. We've only just found out where he is."

Polly raised her eyebrows, but shut her mouth abruptly as the ward sister said, "Oh, good. You can fill us in with his personal details, then. Date of birth, next of kin and so on. We can't get much sense out of him yet. He's better than he was, but keeps lapsing into unconsciousness, I'm afraid. Still, a visit from his sister," she lingered over the word, "might stimulate him into awareness. In you go, then. Stay as long as you want but don't exhaust him."

They walked over to Desmond's bed. He had tubes emerging from every orifice and was hooked up to several machines. A plastic packet of clear liquid suspended from a chrome stand, was slowly dripping into a cannula attached to the back of his hand.

One glance at him was enough to terrify Kimberley, but Polly located a chair and sat her down next to the bed. "Talk to him," she instructed in a low whisper. "Just tell him what you've been doing and how glad you are to see him."

Kimberley leaned towards the bed and began to speak, slowly at first but with increasing confidence.

When she was satisfied that the girl was comfortable, Polly said, "I'm just going to visit someone else. Be back in half an hour or so. Okay?"

She slipped away, back to the reception desk to enquire the whereabouts of Maisie Faulkner, but as she turned the bend in the corridor, she glimpsed a familiar figure in the distance.

She risked a shout. "Byron!"

The figure half turned, then furtively hurried away, disappearing down an adjacent corridor. By the time Polly reached the spot, there was no sign of the scurrying figure. Was it Byron? Polly couldn't be sure.

She found Maisie's six-bedded room containing five elderly ladies and an empty bed, and was rewarded by watery old eyes filling with unshed tears, plus a tremulous smile from Maisie.

Maisie reached for her hand. "I'm so glad you've come, dear. You didn't mind me ringing? I don't know what they're going to do, but they say I may be in for a few days. Of course, they're all very kind here. Pull up a chair. That's better. Will you say a prayer for me?"

"Of course." Polly bent her head, closed her eyes and obliged.

Maisie beamed. "That's much better."

Polly said, "Did you come in this morning? How did you get here?"

"That nice Mr. Henderson brought me. He says he'll collect me too, when I'm ready. I just have to ring up and he'll come. Such a kind man, don't you think?"

"Did Cheryl come too?"

"Oh no, dear. She never comes. She works at the surgery, you know, so I don't suppose she has time. No, he always brings me alone. He's so kind to me. They're going to take some more blood and do an X-ray later today, but I might be able to come home tomorrow or the next day. I think it depends on the results."

Polly patted her hand. "Well, now. You concentrate on getting better so that you're home really soon. I'll keep you in my prayers, of course, and I'll pop in to visit you at home in a day or two, see how you're getting on."

"Thank you so much, dear. It means a lot to me, you know."

"I know."

Polly beamed at the other occupants of the ward and as she left, heard Maisie saying proudly, "That's my rector, you know. She's going to pray for me all the time I'm in here."

Feeling obliged to reassure all the other patients, Polly stuck her head back round the door and promised, "I'll be sure to pray for you all, ladies," before she made her escape.

When she arrived back in the intensive care unit, Polly was pleased to see that Desmond's eyes had fluttered open. That was surely a good sign.

Kimberley chatted excitedly on the way home, certain that Desmond had shown signs of improvement while she was there, but Polly's mind was elsewhere. Why did the Norfolk and

Norwich University Hospital apparently hold such fascination for Byron Henderson? And why did he disappear with such alacrity every time she came near? Exactly what was Byron Henderson's secret, and how much of it was to do with Cheryl?

CHAPTER THIRTY-THREE

Polly contacted Maggie immediately to let her know Kimberley was safe and well. Maggie's response was grateful but muted, a clear indication, Polly thought, that even if she didn't know her exact location, she already knew her daughter was okay. It was several days before Polly was able to organise a meeting at the rectory between mother and daughter, but she made the conscious decision to leave both Maggie and Kimberley to their own devices in the interim, thinking that some space might be beneficial for both of them.

Meanwhile, Polly was kept busy avoiding journalists who had gathered like vultures at the rectory gate, although how they had found out about the body in the grave in only the few hours since its discovery, she couldn't imagine. She fell into the habit of not answering the phone but letting it go to the recorder to ascertain who was ringing, before picking up the receiver. With so many calls from media people begging her to give an interview, Polly began to long for the silent treatment all over again.

Funny how much I dreaded lifting the receiver in case there was nobody at the other end. Now all that seems to have stopped, I'm full of fear in case I get trapped by a journalist. Sorry, God. I'm never satisfied, am I? I need to learn to trust you in all circumstances, but it's a difficult lesson to internalise. Perhaps that's why you keep returning me to it.

With that, Polly repaired to the kitchen to make a large pot of coffee. Might as well face the madding crowd, as they appeared to have no intention of departing. She poured coffee into a dozen mugs, added to the tray a bowl of sugar, a small jug of milk and a plate of biscuits, and carried it out to the waiting journalists. Their eyes widened in appreciation, but before she had a chance to hand round the coffee, microphones were thrust in her face and a television camera zoom lens was angled in her direction.

"Hey, hang on a minute. Let me just give you this coffee, then you can interview me if you like —as long as you promise to leave me alone afterwards. Is it a deal? Okay, then, here you are."

As she handed round mugs of coffee, Polly's brain raced. How much should she say? Would she be in danger of revealing sensitive information? She didn't think so, for she knew so little. There couldn't be any harm in talking to the press, could there?

Most of the questions were predictable.

"Reverend Hewitt, how did you feel when you realised there was a body already buried in the grave?"

"Reverend Hewitt, what did you say to the mourners? How did they feel?"

"How old was the dead girl?"

"When did you realise she had been murdered?"

"Was she a member of your flock?"

"Do you have any clues as to her identity?"

"Do you have any message for her family?"

"What would you like to say to her murderer?"

"Can there be any forgiveness for anyone who has committed such a heinous crime?"

The questions fired so rapidly and from so many different directions that Polly found herself answering on automatic pilot. She hoped she gave the right answers, especially to the question about forgiveness, but had no time to think before the next question was flung at her.

"What was the baby's name?"

Thrown by the unexpected change of topic, Polly blurted out, "Mary Elizabeth Madison."

In the sudden hush as all eyes fastened upon her, Polly realised she had let slip something which had not been public knowledge. She tried to escape, but now the journalists were clamouring for more. It was the first some of them knew about the dead baby; instantly they were avid for details.

"What baby? Where was she found?"

"How old was the baby?"

"Why are you involved, Reverend Hewitt?"

"Are you the common denominator? Are these two murders about you?"

"Has the mother been arrested?"
"Has the mother been found?"
"How do you know the baby's name?"
"Was the murdered girl the baby's mother?"
"Was the baby murdered too?"
"What relation are you to these two murders?"

Polly raised her hands in front of her face as she endeavoured to regain some control. "Stop! Please stop! I've told you all I know. I'm afraid I can't help you any further, because I know nothing more. I suggest you contact the police for any further information. I'm sure they'll give you a statement in due course. Meanwhile, I have four parishes to run, so you must excuse me."

Ignoring all additional cries for information, Polly fled back to the safety of the rectory. Shutting herself into the security of her study, she lifted the telephone with her heart hammering.

"Could I speak to the archdeacon, please? Yes, it is rather urgent. What? No, I can't tell you. I'm afraid it's personal. Yes, all right, thank you. I can hang on."

"Keith? It's Polly, Polly Hewitt. I think I need some help. Um, we have something of a situation here at Anglesham. I was taking this funeral yesterday..."

As she poured out her story to the archdeacon, Polly could almost see his face darkening. Keith had been her archdeacon when she was curate in Thorpemunden, but she felt he had never approved of her. In Polly's opinion, Keith was one of those straight-laced Christians sadly devoid of any sense of humour.

She heard a snort followed by a deep sigh as she finished her story, followed by, "Do I have to spell it out in words of one syllable yet again,

Polly? You are to contact me immediately when anything untoward happens. You know we have a diocesan communications officer, and Roger is very good at his job. He will prepare press statements for you and if necessary, he'll come to Anglesham. It's for your own protection, to avoid just such serious errors of judgement as the one you've made. Who knows what damage you may have done to the police proceedings by releasing sensitive information? To say nothing of the damage to the Church. How dare you pontificate on forgiveness? You may be a priest, but you're a relatively recent one and you must leave questions of theology to an authorised spokesman. Really, Polly! You should know better. You are not to say another word to the press without consulting either myself or Roger. Is that clear? Good. Remember, your job is to care for your flock, not to go seeking personal glorification through media appearances. I'll say no more about this now, but I don't expect this to happen again. Ever. Do you understand?"

Polly answered meekly, "Yes, Keith. I'm sorry," then quickly replaced the phone before she said anything she might later regret. She wasn't sure whether she wanted to weep, or to erupt in anger. No "How are you, Polly? How can I help?" No mention of God. No recognition of the bombastic attacks of journalists fighting for a story, and how difficult it was to contain them. No feeling for the dead girl's family or for the dead baby. And how was she supposed to answer when a journalist asked her point blank whether or not a murderer would be forgiven? Polly was quite proud of her answer of "Jesus said, 'Let he who is without sin cast the first stone,'" which was thoroughly biblical and which she thought neatly sidestepped the question in true political style. What more could Keith or anyone else say? It was one of those questions where you were damned if you did and damned if you didn't. If she said that murderers were forgiven, she'd probably be lynched by angry, frightened villagers who were already screaming for a return of the death penalty, yet her own Christian understanding was that anyone who truly repented really was forgiven by God. In college discussions the cries had always been, "What about Hitler? What about the Rwandan genocide? What about Milosevic?" and argument had raged furiously from side to side, but Polly couldn't recall any satisfactory conclusions. She did remember the female priest from Bristol though, who resigned because she felt unable to forgive the bombers, when her daughter was killed in the July 7th bombings in London. That event had made a great impact on Polly, who had realised for the first time that forgiveness is probably a gift from God, and that those who are unable to forgive are slowly killing themselves. Lack of forgiveness, she reflected, is like a kind of internal cancer that quietly eats away at your spirit. I have so much work to do here in Anglesham after these terrible murders, to suggest that our community might forgive the murderer. Somehow, we have to find a balance between the need for justice and punishment, and this essential ingredient of forgiveness—essential not for the murderer, but for us, for our health as a community. But there's no way I could have said all that in a two-second sound byte for the television. It'll be more like months of slow slogging, cautiously picking away at deep-seated prejudices, all the while supporting those who are unable to forgive. Oh God! I'm really going to need your help here. We all are.

She contemplated ringing Bishop Percy, with whom she had a much better relationship and who might offer soothing words of comfort as well as good advice, but decided that since Keith was probably on the phone to him right now, she would only look worse by trying to justify herself. Besides, there was one other person she had to ring immediately.

With a heavy heart she dialled Chloe's number. "Chloe? It's me, Polly. I'm really sorry, but I'm afraid I've dropped you in it. There are all these journalists parked outside my gate and they keep ringing me up, so in the end I decided to pre-empt them. I took coffee out to them and answered their questions. I suppose in a way I gave them an interview, so you're bound to hear about it. Like I said, I'm really sorry."

"What exactly did you say to them, Polly?"

"Well, I kind of got the impression they're linking the dead baby with the murdered girl, and I—um—I let slip the baby's name. It was all so fast, like they were raining down bullets on me. It just slipped out. And they seem to think I'm involved somehow, just because I was present when both bodies were found. Rubbish, I know, but there you are. I'm truly sorry, Chloe, but I thought you ought to know."

Chloe said calmly, "Not a problem. We were planning to release the baby's name anyway, so you've probably made that easier for us. As to linking the two deaths, who wouldn't? Anyone with a brain cell must assume a link. I'm sure you have! The first suspicious deaths ever to happen in the history of Anglesham, occurring within a week of each other—they must be linked, surely? And don't worry about the press. They're only seizing on you because you're the rector. Makes a better story if the church is involved. So no harm done, Polly. Relax."

Polly felt her shoulders drop in relief. "Thank you so much, Chloe. I got a right bollocking from the archdeacon, and to tell you the truth, I was expecting the same from you."

Chloe laughed. "No need! Now you can enjoy the rest of your day. Unwind and hang loose, that's my advice."

"Chloe, while you're on—have you traced the baby's mother yet? Is it the murdered girl? If it is, as soon as you find the Madison family you'll know who she is, won't you?"

"If only life were that simple! Please don't reveal this to anyone, Polly, but there are no families in the local vicinity with the surname Madison. We have a Madderson, several Maitlands, and a Madingley, but no Madison. We're widening the search, of course, but the name may be something of a red herring. So it's back to the slow slog, which is generally the way we solve crimes. Carefully sifting each piece of evidence, collecting hundreds of statements, following up a myriad useless leads until we find the one that will give us the answers. It's seldom as dramatic as displayed on the box, you know."

Polly laughed. "No, I guess not. Funny you should say that. That's just how I see my work—a slow slog. Anyway, thanks, Chloe. I'll catch up with you some time. 'Bye for now."

Replacing the phone in a happier frame of mind, Polly squared her shoulders. What was done, was done. Time now to get on with life, and the first thing she had to do, was to have that interview with Oswald.

CHAPTER THIRTY-FOUR

The man's head was sunk in his hands. With the disposal of the girl's body he had expected to experience relief, not this searing grief, this hollow pain deep inside himself. It was making him irritable and snappy. He had loved her in his way, although not in the same way as his son who was so morose now she had gone. At first, his son assumed she had run away, for she had talked about living abroad, but when her body was discovered, his son presumed it was suicide in her grief at the baby's death. His son had no idea of her part in the baby's death. He thought the baby had died of natural causes, them being so closely related.

Why had she done it? Why had she performed such an evil act? How could a mother murder her own child? His grandchild! His grief metamorphosed into rage as the questions swirled ceaselessly in his mind. Anger was easier to deal with than grief. It masked the pain and the guilt, at least for a while.

She had made him do it, by her actions. Anybody could see that. She had forced him to kill her. Not that he had intended to kill her, but he had to show her that her actions were unacceptable, he had to bring her to her senses somehow. It wasn't his fault that she had accepted death so readily. It was more like assisted suicide, really. Yes, that was it. She had forced him to help her commit suicide. It was like going to that clinic in Switzerland, except that she hadn't asked his permission, she had just manipulated him into it. No doubt the balance of her mind had been disturbed by the death of the baby, even though that death was at her own hands. Perhaps it was post-natal depression. Hormones made women do funny things. There was no accounting for them. Everyone knew that.

That name, for a start. What had made her choose that? How dare she choose a name for the baby—his granddaughter—without any reference whatsoever to him? Where did she find the temerity to choose that name of all names? The man shuddered as he pondered the significance of the name. Would anyone else put two and two together to make four? The man was worried.

She'd left him with a big problem when all should have been neatly closed, no doubt about that. With fear and dread the man had watched the television news, had heard the rector's words, had seen that look she gave the camera when she uttered the baby's name. How did the rector know that name? He hadn't known it, although he recognised it instantly as authentic and immediately realised its significance. Clearly the girl must have spoken to the rector when she dumped the baby, so obviously Polly Hewitt must know all about it. Therefore Polly Hewitt was a problem, a big problem. Somehow or other, he had to get to her before she revealed to the police all she knew.

***

"Oswald? It's Polly. How did the burial go this afternoon? Any problems?"

"None at all, Polly. Everything went very smoothly, thank you. John and Evelyn were very pleased."

Stung by the smugness in his tone, Polly was sharper than she had intended. "I need to see you soon, Oswald. We must talk. Are you free tomorrow?"

"On a Sunday? You know I have two services tomorrow, Polly. Then we're off to Oliver and Catriona's for lunch, so the answer is no, I'm very much afraid I'm not free."

"What time do you get home from Oliver's?"

There was a pause. "Polly, I do need some time to myself. I can't be expected to work for the church—for nothing, I might add—every minute of every day. I give my time on Sunday mornings. I think I owe Nina a little of my time, don't you?"

"This is important, Oswald, I wouldn't ask you otherwise. And I wouldn't need to keep you long. Some information I think you'd want to know."

"Tell me now, then."

"It isn't something I feel comfortable discussing over the phone. I really do need to see you in person."

He sounded testy. "I'm not sure how important it can be if you can't tell me now, Polly. I'm sure you think it is important, but for some of us out here in the real world there are more things in life than church. I'm exceptionally busy at the moment. I could make space for you next Friday afternoon. Or is this—thing—so important that it can't wait that long?" Without giving her time to respond, he continued, "No? I didn't think so. Shall we say next Friday at two?"

"If you're absolutely sure that's what you want?"

"Oh, I do, Polly, believe me! I've found over the course of my life that there are few things so important that they can't wait. We need to respond instantly only if something is both urgent and important. If it's important but not urgent, it can wait for a while. When you analyse them properly, most things fall into the category of neither urgent nor important. It's a useful lesson to learn."

How patronising could you get? Polly said sweetly, "I see. Thank you so much, Oswald. I'll come over next Friday then. Give my regards to Nina, would you? And if you happen to tell her that I'm coming to see you, perhaps you'll make it clear to her that I regard this matter as both urgent and important. Thank you, Oswald. Goodbye."

She heard him say in a more anxious tone, "Just a moment, Polly, perhaps—" but she ignored him and replaced the phone. After a snub such as the one he had just delivered, there was no way she would bring the appointment forward. Let him spend the week wondering and worrying, if that was what he wanted. Arrogant so-and-so. What in God's name was the matter with him?

***

On the Friday morning, Polly collected Kimberley from the caravan as arranged. The girl had made an effort to smarten up for the purpose of meeting her mother, with her hair neatly tied back, a clean, pale lemon shirt, blue jeans, and no trace of the black lipstick. Polly was impressed. It was a distinct improvement over the Gothic look, much more suited to a traditional, upper class background.

"You look nice."

"Is it all right? I'm determined to be myself, but I don't want to shock Mum so much that she sends the clothes police after me! This is the best I've got in the van. Most of my stuff is really skanky. How is she? What did she say when you told her I was prepared to meet? Is she going to go off on one?"

Recognising the girl's nervousness, Polly let her chatter on, merely saying reassuringly, "She was thrilled. I don't think you'll have any problems. She just wants to mend things between you, if she can."

"Oh!" Kimberley fell silent, caught up in her own thoughts. Then she said, "Have you told the Waters about Dezzy?"

"Not yet. I'm going this afternoon, though, so if you want me to mention anything in particular, or keep quiet about anything in particular, now's your chance to tell me."

Kimberley nodded. "Thanks. Well, if you can keep me out of it, I'd be grateful, but if you can't..." She shrugged. "I don't suppose it'll be the end of the world. They're all going to know sometime. Might be something to be said for getting all over at once. What do you think?"

She gazed anxiously at Polly.

Polly negotiated the turn into the rectory drive, giving herself time to think. "I don't see any reason why the Waters need to know where you have been living. As I see it, that's private to you and anyone you choose to tell. It's nobody else's business."

"But what if Des tells them?"

"That's up to Des. It's his business who he tells and what he says. But from what you've said, there's not much danger of him communicating with his parents at all."

The girl's shoulders sagged with relief. "No, you're right. How is Des, by the way? Have you seen him this week?"

"I rang on Wednesday. Apparently, since your visit, he's been doing much better. They seem to think you had some sort of stimulatory effect on him. At any rate, he's now conscious, although not yet ready to be discharged."

"Thank goodness! I will get in to see him again. It's just—well, it's been a bit difficult lately."

Polly nodded, and parked the car. There was no sign of Maggie's car yet, so Polly installed Kimberley in the lounge, promising to stay around if necessary and leaving Kimberley restlessly leafing through a magazine as she waited for her mother. She didn't have to wait long. Maggie was anxious to see her daughter, and arrived early. Polly ushered her into the lounge, then evaded the awkward silence by quickly disappearing to make coffee.

She deliberately lingered over the preparation, giving mother and daughter time to get reacquainted, and by the time she returned with the tray was delighted to observe that the atmosphere had lightened considerably. Maggie and Kimberley were sitting close together on the sofa, and Polly was sure they had been holding hands just prior to her entrance. Things were looking good.

"Will you excuse me?" Polly asked, diplomatically. "I have a lot to do in the study. This room is yours for as long as you want it."

Two identical pairs of eyes smiled at her in exactly the same way, and Polly was struck again by likeness between mother and daughter, despite the change in Kimberley's hair colour. Polly slipped out of the lounge, taking her own coffee into the study and preparing herself for an hour or two in front of the computer.

When she heard no sound issuing from the lounge in over two hours, no screams, no cries of rage, no irritable, raised voices, Polly ventured back. To her delight, both Maggie and Kimberley were wreathed in smiles. Kimberley was full of excitement.

"I'm going home! Mum says I can keep my hair how I want and see any of my friends I want. She's going to persuade Dad to buy me a car whether I go to university or not, so I can keep some independence. Isn't that brilliant? I'm going to really think about my future. And to be honest, I'm fed up with living alone in that yucky caravan. It's no fun by myself."

Polly hid a smile. The plan had worked, then. It had paid to leave her to her own devices for a further week. "When are you going home, then? Do you want to go now so that you don't have to go back to that van ever again? 'Cos if you like, I could drop by the caravan and pick up your things. I have to go out that way this afternoon. I could drop them off at the manor on my way back. It's up to you. Whatever you think."

"That's kind of you, Polly. Are you sure?" Maggie looked at her daughter. "What do you think, Kimberley? Would you prefer to go back yourself—I can easily drive you—or would you like Polly to collect your stuff?"

Flattered by the way in which everyone seemed to be genuinely seeking her opinion, and with no wish for her mother ever to see the squalid state in which she had been living, Kimberley hurriedly accepted Polly's proposal. Mother and daughter thanked Polly profusely for her efforts, and shortly left to go home, arm in arm.

Polly sighed. If only all problems could be resolved that easily.

Leaving the rectory early for her appointment with Oswald, Polly gave herself time to stop at the caravans. Kimberley's van was hardly tidy, closely resembling a teenage girl's bedroom, but at least it was clean. Polly had no qualms about picking up the few armfuls of clothes, mostly scattered over floor and furniture, and transferring them to the boot of her car. She checked on the pots and pans, but they were so battered and decrepit that she thought it best to leave them alone. They would hardly fit with the manor. She grinned when she picked up the black Goth make up, and wondered what Maggie would make of that. No doubt it would all be ditched and the long hair would be back to blond long before Giles returned home from Westminster.

Polly had just finished, had taken a last look around the van to make sure nothing was left, and was poised on the step to lock the caravan door, when she had that uncomfortable feeling of being watched. It was as though eyes were boring strongly into her back. In some trepidation her shoulders hunched, aware that she was alone in an isolated area where drug deals had taken place, and that there was a murderer on the loose somewhere in the vicinity.

She half expected to encounter Byron Henderson, but for a while could see no one. As she finished locking the door, she shook herself, hoping the feeling would go away, but it persisted. Taking a deep breath and sending up a short arrow prayer, *Please help me, God, Polly turned round, quickly scanning the area with a wide sweep of her eyes. She immediately spotted a movement in the margins of the copse. With no weapon but the car keys in her hand and wondering whether she would ever be capable of stabbing a key into someone's eye even in extremis, Polly marched as purposefully as she could with legs resembling jelly, towards the copse.*

There was no rapid scrabbling at her approach, no hurried fleeing, in fact, no further movement at all, so that Polly began to wonder whether she had imagined the whole thing, but as she reached the edge of the clearing she could see a figure almost hidden in the undergrowth. To her consternation she realised by the lumbering and stocky outline, that it was a figure she knew only too well. But how long had he been standing there watching her, and what did he want?

CHAPTER THIRTY-FIVE

"Jonathan!" Polly tried to inject enthusiasm into her voice, but it emerged as a kind of fearful squeak. She cleared her throat a couple of times, feigning a cough as she braced her wobbling knees, hoping she had made a mistake and it was David standing there. But there was no mistaking the morose face or the complete failure to raise any hint of a smile.

Almost as though he could read her thoughts, the sardonic gleam in Jonathan Tunbridge's dark eyes intensified. "What do you think you're doing?"

The accusatory tone was just what Polly needed to stiffen her nerve. She lifted her chin. "I beg your pardon? In fact, whatever it may look like to you, I've been doing exactly what you requested, Jonathan. Haven't you noticed? I've got rid of the gypsies for you."

"Thought I told you to keep away?"

"Yes, I've wondered about that. Given that it wasn't gypsies at all but just a couple of drop out kids, why should you have supposed I might be in any kind of danger? Or was there some other reason for wanting to keep me away?"

The sound issuing from his throat could only be described as a growl. Polly took a step back as Jonathan took a step forward. His shoulders were hunched and his head lowered. Polly longed to flee, but the thought came unbidden that you should stand perfectly still to face a wild animal.

He said, "I've been watching you. Saw you taking everything out, into your boot. What are you doing?"

Polly sighed. The moment of irrational fear had passed and she returned to something resembling sanity. He was, after all, only a local farmer and a member of her church. He couldn't harm her. "I met the girl who was staying here. She's decided to move on—of her own accord, I might add—and I volunteered to collect her stuff for her. She doesn't have any transport. Satisfied?"

She hadn't meant to taunt him, but he took it as a challenge. His dark eyes glared at her, but there was a slight quirk to his mouth. He nodded towards the other van. "And him?"

Playing her advantage, Polly said, "I'm surprised you don't know. I'm afraid he's in hospital. He's very ill."

Jonathan nodded again. "That's what drugs do for you. Stupid habit. Only for fools. Deserves all he gets."

"How kind! Perhaps he had stuff in his life he couldn't handle."

"Huh!" The scorn on his face deepened, although Polly didn't know whether it was scorn for drug takers, for those unable to cope with problems in their life, or scorn for her own naivety. "There's other ways of dealing with life's botherations. That's what you should be teaching folks. That's your job. That's what the church is for."

Why did everybody seem to know exactly how she should do her job? "Thank you for sharing that with me, Jonathan. I'll be sure to remember whenever I meet another drug user or anyone down on their luck. By the way, I've told you what I'm doing here, but I don't think you've told me what you're doing?"

He growled again, a sound deep in his throat, but he made no move towards her. Polly began to realise that perhaps Jean Bannister was right. His bark really was worse than his bite. Nonetheless, as he turned to go, it was clear he wasn't about to reveal his interest in the site or continue the conversation any further.

Recognising that this could be a critical juncture in their relationship since at least they were just about communicating, Polly offered tentatively, "Do you want a lift? I'm going past the farm."

She expected him to refuse, stomping away with the usual, "Huh!" but after a moment's hesitation he nodded and walked towards her car.

He folded himself into the passenger seat, his bulk making the car seem too small to contain him, but Polly took his acquiescence as a move in the right direction. Not wanting to wreck any chance of a closer relationship by a crass remark, Polly drove the first part of the journey in a silence which she found uncomfortable but preferred to regard as companionable.

The discomfort soon prevailed. Before long, Polly felt the urge to engage in conversation. "Did you see the news?"

"Don't watch much television. Why?"

Polly felt foolish. Now he was going to think she was boasting, when all she was doing was chancing a comment about the topic which was uppermost in everyone's mind. Still, there was no going back.

"Um, I was on, as it happens. A day or two ago. They interviewed me about the murdered girl. The one that was found in Jack Davidson's grave," she added helpfully, as though there were a hundred murdered girls in Anglesham.

As she spoke, she risked a sideways glance out of the corner of her eye. Was the contempt back in his face? Or had she touched a nerve? Was that a muscle quivering in his cheek? Was it her imagination or did his great, beefy hands clench slightly? Polly shivered. She wasn't sure, and he merely grunted in response to her remark, as though he had no interest whatsoever in a dead teenager.

They continued the journey without speaking further and Polly wondered whether she had blown it, but when she drove into his farmyard, avoiding the scattered piles of rusting machinery as best she could, Jonathan turned slightly towards her.

"Thanks for the lift," he muttered, his face averted.

"You're welcome."

Perhaps, after all, it had done something to ease the tension between them, Polly reflected, as she drove on towards the Waters' home, The Old Rectory in Parsondale.

Her welcome in Parsondale could not have been more different. Oswald answered the door with alacrity, almost as though he and Nina had been waiting for her. He greeted Polly effusively as he ushered her into the lounge, chatting about the weather—since it had broken the skies had been constantly overcast and the rain had barely ceased—the parlous state of the economy—always a fascinating subject for Oswald—and trying to prise from Polly any further information about the murder.

Charmed in spite of herself, Polly laughed. This was back to the Oswald of old, and she liked it. "Sorry, Oswald. I know nothing more. It all seems to have gone into hibernation, although Chloe assures me the police are treating it as a top priority. They may be stymied until they get the DNA results. Can't do much until they find out who she was, can they?

"No, don't get up," she added, as Nina made to rise from her armchair in the corner, where she was quietly knitting.

"I need to put the kettle on." Nina offered one of her warm smiles, and escaped into the kitchen.

"Won't you sit down?" Oswald indicated the settee and plumped up a cushion for Polly.

Polly sat. Evidently keeping people dangling was a very good move indeed. Oswald hadn't been this charming since they had first met. Just at the moment he couldn't do enough for her. Long may it last.

She continued with the small talk until Nina reappeared with the tea.

"Do you want me to go? I can easily sit in the kitchen." Nina was her usual self-deprecating and anxious self.

Polly said quickly, "No, no. I don't think there is anything private about this, is there, Oswald?"

She glanced at him to see how he would take this first challenge. His eyes flitted from her to Nina and back again, then he smiled and nodded. "Of course not. We have no secrets from each other, do we Nina?"

Polly launched into her prepared spiel. "I wanted to thank you, Oswald, for preaching so well at the Davidson funeral. As I said, I thought you hit exactly the right note and it was clear from their reaction that both Evelyn and John—indeed the entire congregation—thought so as well." She allowed a moment for Oswald to preen, noticing with some amusement the way he fingered his ridiculous line of facial hair whenever he felt particularly self-satisfied. "It was also a great relief to me not to have to bury Jack next day. The day of the funeral was somewhat traumatic for all of us."

"Only too pleased to be of assistance, Polly. Believe me, it was my pleasure, although I feel I should apologise for the Davidson's attitude towards you. They're usually so pleasant and courteous. I can only put it down to the stress of Jack's sudden death. It was a great shock to the whole village."

"Strange, isn't it? Personally, I can't imagine them being either pleasant or courteous. Evelyn was unsmiling and distant with me from start to finish, and John was positively rude. But as you say, I have met them under different circumstances from you. No doubt they are urbanity itself at the golf club or in the council chamber."

Nina continued to knit silently in her corner, her head lowered. Oswald's smile faded a little. He hadn't missed the implication. "Yes, well, as I said, grief takes us all in different ways. I hope you don't imagine I was instrumental in any way, for their attitude?"

Polly faced him squarely, her blue eyes holding him steadfastly. "I confess I was perturbed to hear from Francis Bancroft that arrangements had apparently been made between the Davidsons and yourself, without any reference to me. I understand the pressure exerted on you, Oswald, by ex-pupils and friends and acquaintances. But as we discussed before, I really do need to get known in these villages, so in future I'd appreciate it if you could explain to anyone who approaches you directly, that Anglican protocol demands that the rector is the initial point of contact. I have explained all this at length to Francis. I do hope it's okay with you, too?" She smiled to soften the impact of her words, but continued to hold his gaze.

Oswald's lips pinched, but after a moment he nodded. "Of course, Polly. On this occasion it was —er—somewhat difficult." He laughed, self-consciously. "You've met Evelyn and John! And Jack had been a particular friend for many years. I think the whole community would have considered it very odd indeed if I hadn't been involved in some way.

"Very good of you to call and bring this to my attention, Polly. As you know, I like to get these things out into the open as quickly as possible."

Polly resisted the temptation to roll her eyes. "I have another reason for calling, Oswald. A reason I consider to be both urgent and important."

"Ah, yes!" He had the grace to look slightly ashamed. "Well, Polly, I think I know what you're going to say, and the answer is, yes, of course I support you."

"Excuse me?"

"About the new service. As I think I've made clear, I can't pretend that children running about in church is quite my thing. As a teacher, I expect to see some discipline in the next generation, but I can see what you're trying to do and I applaud your efforts."

"You do?" Polly said, faintly.

Oswald nodded. "Of course. We need to get children and families into church, and your attempts are admirable. But I'm sure you can see that it would be entirely hypocritical of me to actually take part in the new service. I will applaud from the sidelines, if that's all right with you, and of course, do all in my power to promote the—" he ran his tongue over his lips "—fun and games as best I can. How does that sound?"

Polly blinked. "It sounds very good. Thank you, Oswald."

He rose. "So if there's nothing else?"

Polly rose too. "Just one very small matter. You remember that young tramp? The one in Anglesham churchyard that day, who later stole the money?" She was aware of an immediate, palpable silence, so looked pointedly at Oswald. The soft click of knitting needles had ceased. It felt as though the whole room was holding its breath. "I thought you might be interested to know that he's in hospital. He was in intensive care following a drug overdose, but I understand he's a little better now." As she walked towards the front door, Polly added over her shoulder, "As you showed such interest in him, I thought you might want to pay him a pastoral visit.

"Goodbye, and thank you both so much for your time."

CHAPTER THIRTY-SIX

Polly glanced at her watch. A quarter to three. Oswald hadn't wasted much of his precious time on her. Still, it meant she could drive to the hospital to check on Maisie Faulkner, who still wasn't home. Polly had a horrible suspicion that Maisie had been in so long for her tests, that she might have been given bad news.

Although she felt utterly inadequate and therefore dreaded it, Polly felt she ought to be there supporting Maisie and offering what comfort she could, should it prove necessary. But what on earth should you say to someone who might have been told her days are numbered? Was it right to mention death at all, especially if you couldn't discover what she had been told by the medical profession? Anyway, how could you help her without bleating platitudes? Should you begin to talk about life after death and planning for the funeral service, or was it kinder to avoid the topic of death altogether, until and unless the dying person brought it up? What if Maisie immediately went into a decline if Polly mentioned the dreaded word, death? Polly had no idea what a priest ought to do in such circumstances. Already worried before she even knew whether or not Maisie had heard her test results, Polly offered up a quick prayer.

If there was time, Polly thought she could peek in on Desmond, too, and chuckled to herself as she wondered whether she might meet Oswald and Nina there, and if so, what they would say to her. It might be quite entertaining to see Oswald hot with embarrassment.

Maisie's face lit up as Polly appeared in the doorway. The other five occupants of the ward had been discharged and their beds taken by three more elderly ladies, all of whom had visitors. Two beds were empty, awaiting newcomers. Maisie was the only patient with an empty bed on either side of her, and without any visitors, until Polly's arrival.

She began gossiping in the embarrassingly loud voice of the hard-of-hearing elderly, as soon as Polly pulled up a chair. "They're quite nice, but that one over there in the bed opposite, she snores all night. It's terrible. I'm not getting a wink of sleep. You'd think they'd move her into a side ward, wouldn't you? She's had a stroke, but she hasn't lost her speech. That's her son, Tower."

"Tower?"

The old lady giggled. "I know, it's a funny name, isn't it? You know why he's called that? All her children are named after London bridges. Her husband was an engineer, and he had a thing about bridges, apparently. They used to live in London, retired up here thirty years ago. The old man's dead. Been gone some twenty years, she was telling me. Her other children are Kingston, Chelsea, and Alexandra, which aren't so bad, but Tower was the youngest and they ran out of suitable names. Bet he had a terrible time of it at school."

Polly laughed. "It's not so bad when you say it often enough, and lots of people do things like that. I've baptised some babies with weird names, in my time, so there must be quite a few in Norfolk."

"But you'd expect something peculiar from Norfolk families, wouldn't you?"

"Would you? Why? What's so different about Norfolk people?"

Maisie leaned closer, with that conspiratorial look Polly was coming to recognise so well. "You must know. Everyone knows. They make jokes about it on television—normal for Norfolk—they say, things like that. You've got a few odd families in the benefice."

"I have?"

"The Talbot brothers, for one. Not that they were like that. Well, not as far as I know, but Ralph Talbot's grown-up son, he's a bit strange, isn't he? It's always hidden though, isn't it? Under the surface, like. You know their dad shot himself? Not because of," she whispered the word, "that, at least, I don't think so, but their mum cleared off with the window cleaner. Left a note on the kitchen table. Elliot Talbot was devastated. He came in from a PCC meeting—he was churchwarden at Parsondale at the time—read the note, fetched his gun and shot himself at the self-same table. The two boys were asleep in bed. The shot woke them, and they came downstairs to find the kitchen splattered all over in their father's blood and brains."

"Ugh!" Polly shuddered. "That's so sick. How old were the boys at the time?"

"About eight and ten, I'd say. Their grandmother took them on, brought the boys up on her own. Did a good job, too, but they were damaged by it. In and out of trouble with the police. Terrible scandal at the time."

"I should think so! I've never met the son. Ralph has never mentioned him, and the brothers don't seem at all damaged to me. I like them. Nice, cheery guys.."

"That's because you didn't see them as youngsters and because you don't see beneath the surface," Maisie warned. Warming to her subject, she added, "Then there's the Tunbridges —"

"—not sure I can take any more blood and guts today!" Polly changed the subject. "Anyway, Maisie, how are you? What did the doctors say?"

"They still don't know what's wrong with me, but they haven't said it's cancer. They've found I'm anaemic, though. Found that out from the blood tests. I'm on iron tablets now, as well as everything else. They don't know why I'm anaemic, though. They think I might be losing blood through my—you know—" the old lady blushed, and leaned even closer to whisper, "—in my—um—stools."

Clearly more embarrassed about her own bodily functions than about passing on the most heinous gossip, she glanced at Polly as if to ascertain whether Polly knew the meaning of the word. Polly nodded, solemnly.

"And there's nothing else?"

"Nothing they've discovered so far. I'm going for a whole body scan tomorrow. They've only got one machine for that so I've had to wait a day or two, but I don't mind. I like it in here. They're all so kind, the nurses and that. And you meet some interesting people."

Polly smiled and nodded, reflecting how awful it must be, to be so lonely that your primary excitements in life are passing on gossip and staying in hospital. "What's the food like?"

"Oh, it's lovely, really lovely, dear. We had cottage pie for lunch with peas and carrots and mashed potatoes and extra gravy if you wanted it, and rice pudding to follow. Mine had the skin on. I do love the skin on rice pudding, don't you? Tonight I've ordered a cheese salad followed by jelly and ice cream. You have a proper menu, you know. They bring round a menu each day and you place your order for the next day. And you can have cocoa or Horlicks or Ovaltine and biscuits at night, before bedtime. It's like a hotel."

"Goodness! You'll all be putting on weight!"

Maisie giggled again. "I know. I shall have to go on a diet when I come home. They're going to send me home when I've had the scan, so I may be in church again next week."

Polly patted her hand. "Well, just you concentrate on getting better, Maisie. Now, let me say a prayer for you before I go."

"Are you going to see anyone else?"

Polly said, "I came especially to see you, Maisie," and was rewarded by tears springing to the old lady's eyes, which she quickly blinked away.

With the visit to Maisie taking a little longer than expected, and with an idea that Tom might visit again this weekend, Polly decided to leave Desmond to the mercy of his parents, so that she could call in at the supermarket on the way home. Besides, as she was certain to meet several parishioners in there, it was a good venue for a little pastoral work.

It was, therefore, with some irritation that the moment she had parked, Polly spotted Cheryl bearing down upon her as if chased by every fiend from hell.

"Polly! You're an answer to prayer!" She grabbed Polly's arm, tugging her in the direction of the supermarket café. "Come and have a coffee. I need some advice."

"You, Cheryl? I've never known you need advice before. You're usually the one dishing it out."

"Ha, ha. Very funny. This is serious. Come on."

She steered Polly to a table and collected two lattes, not bothering to ask Polly for her choice. Resigned to a long wait before she could shop for the weekend, Polly obediently sipped her drink and prepared to listen.

"What's up then, Cheryl?"

Cheryl groaned. "It's Byron. Honestly, that man. I swear I'll kill him before I've finished."

"Why? What's he done?"

"Only emptied my bank account."

Polly gasped. "Cheryl! No! Really? How much? How do you know it's him? Could it be anyone else?"

Cheryl's face was grim. "It's him, all right. He's done it before. Not as bad as this, mind, but he has taken money out before, using my bank card. I was stupid enough to trust him with the pin number, a few years back."

"Has he completely cleared you out or can you put a stop on the account?"

"Don't worry, I've already done all that, and asked for a new pin number. And I wasn't stupid enough to leave much in there, not after the first time. So no, he hasn't taken everything I own, but only because I keep most of my money elsewhere. I was married years ago, when I was nineteen," she added, unexpectedly. "It only lasted three years, but he was a millionaire, thanks to daddy setting him up in a lucrative computer business, and I got half his money, much to daddy's fury. I invested it wisely and got some good returns when interest rates were up, and I had no intention of letting Byron get his mucky little hands on any of that."

"You sound as if you don't much care for Byron. How come he lives with you?"

For a flicker of a moment, Polly glimpsed the loneliness behind the brash façade. Then it was gone. Cheryl grinned. "He's been useful. Bit of a slug I know, but at least he's around and he's tame. Does what I tell him and makes a useful workhorse. Not for much longer, though. Just wait 'til I get my hands on him, the little creep."

Polly finished her coffee and made to rise. Perhaps her shopping could be salvaged after all. "Sounds as if you've got it all sorted, Cheryl. Good luck. Hope it works out for you."

Cheryl pulled her back. "No, you don't understand. I can't find him. He's legged it. That's where you come in. I need you to help me find him so I can wring the little runt's neck."

Polly's mouth fell open. "Um, I'm not sure—"

"—oh, for God's sake come on! Don't be such a wimp. All you need to do is show me where those caravans are. Don't pretend you don't know. He told me you saw him there once, when he was involved in one of his dirty little deals."

"You knew? You knew he was dealing and you did nothing? How could you? Why didn't you stop him? Tell Chloe or something?"

"Sounds like you knew as well, Polly! Did you do anything? No, thought not. Anyway, I was never sure, couldn't prove a thing. But I grew more and more suspicious. Being Byron, he's only small time. Very small time, I should imagine, but I reckon he might be in trouble with the bigger boys and that's why he needed the money. Serve him bloody well right, if you ask me. So come on, let's go. You're taking me to those caravans, 'cos that's where he'll be hanging out and I want to get at him and break his legs before anyone else has the pleasure."

CHAPTER THIRTY-SEVEN

"You're quiet. What's up? Cat got your tongue?"

Polly gripped the steering wheel more tightly. "I'm driving, remember? Concentrating. Besides, I'm thinking. Look, Cheryl, I'll show you where the vans are, but I don't want anything else to do with this. It's your domestic squabble, and I can't take sides."

"Afraid I'll really hurt him?"

Polly laughed. "Hardly! As a matter of fact, I'm expecting Tom tonight, so I want to get back to the rectory as soon as possible."

"You got all your shopping though, before we left, so what's the rush?"

"I do have to cook it! But what about you, Cheryl? If I drop you off, how will you get home? Have you got your phone with you? You could try giving me a ring and I'll always pick you up, but the signal isn't too hot from here."

Cheryl said airily, "I'll manage. I can walk, if I can't find Byron. If he's here, he'll give me a lift. That's the least he can do for me. You'll see. After this, he'll be that eager to please me, he'll jump in a fire if I tell him to."

"Five minutes ago you were all set to dump him," Polly retorted, laughing. "The vans are just round the next corner. Tell you what. I'll wait while you investigate them. If Byron's not there, I'll run you home."

Cheryl was out of the car almost before it stopped, striding towards the vans. She wrenched open the door of first one, then the other van, but turned towards Polly's car with a classic shrug. Clearly, there was no sign of Byron.

She loped back to the car. "Polly, you get on home. I'm going to stick around here for a while, see if I can sniff out Byron's presence. I'm sure he's been here, and it might be fun to be sitting in the van when he returns. Anyway, I can always walk back."

Polly said doubtfully, "Are you sure? Ring me if you want me to pick you up. If you do walk, keep going west—towards the sun. There's a short cut to the road. It's only twenty minutes or so that way. Much quicker than the way I brought you. Cheryl, you will be careful, won't you?"

As she drove home, Polly was faintly anxious. She couldn't put her finger on it, for Cheryl was big enough and bold enough to look after herself, and definitely had the upper hand as far as Byron was concerned. Nonetheless, Polly felt uneasy and wondered whether she had been entirely wise to leave Cheryl alone. She determined to ring her later, just to make sure she had reached home safely.

The doorbell rang soon after Polly arrived at the rectory, and before she had a chance to start cooking. Quashing her irritation at being disturbed yet again on what passed for her day off, as she opened the front door she was unable to prevent a start of surprise.

"Oswald! Nina! Whatever brings you here?" She glanced at her watch. "It's not long since we met."

Oswald seemed ill at ease. "Can we come in? We won't keep you long. There's something we need to say to you."

"Yes, of course!" Polly flung the door wider. "Come into the study. I'll put the kettle on. Won't be a minute."

"No, no tea. We don't need tea."

"Well, if you're sure." With her heart dropping, Polly led the way into the study and indicated the armchairs, seating herself in the computer chair. What complaints was Oswald bringing now?

She said pleasantly, "Fire away, then."

Oswald and Nina glanced at each other and away again. Oswald cleared his throat. "Polly, we want to thank you."

"Thank me?"

"Yes. I—we—that is, Nina and I—"

Polly had never seen Oswald at a loss for words before. She enjoyed the moment.

Oswald seemed to gather himself. Then the words came in a rush. "We want to thank you for saving our son's life. We've just been to see Desmond in hospital, and he told us all about it. About you calling the emergency services and getting him admitted, and going to see how he was, and bringing the Brewster girl to see him. He's agreed to go into rehab as soon as he comes out of hospital. I've already contacted The Matthew Project in Norwich. They offer counselling and support for adults as well as youngsters, and Desmond asked us to set it up for him. He's never done that before. Polly," he leaned towards her, "we are so grateful to you."

"I didn't do anything, really. Any concerned citizen would have done the same."

Nina suddenly spoke up. "You did much more than you know, Polly. You've given us another chance. We thought we'd lost him for good. And of course, we'll repay the money he stole and replace the damaged bible and your cassock-alb."

"Oh!" Polly smiled. "Thank you very much, but you don't have to do any of that. You're not responsible for Dezzy's actions."

"We want to," Oswald said, some of the old authority returning to his voice. "It's the least we can do. We want to do this for our son. Um, have you mentioned Desmond to anyone else, Polly?"

Ah! Here it comes. The real reason for the visit. "Er, no, I don't think so. Why, is secrecy important?"

Oswald had the grace to look sheepish. With a sidelong glance at her husband, Nina said firmly, "No it isn't, Polly. We agreed as a family, no more secrets. We're going to face it together, Oliver and Catriona too. This has been a wake-up call for all of us, including Desmond. He suddenly realised he didn't want to die. Desmond thought we were ashamed of him. Apparently he grew up thinking he was never good enough for us, that's been a big part of his problem. All we wanted to do was encourage him, to spur him on. We knew he had the ability, if only he applied himself. And with Oswald teaching, well, you can see that we wanted the best for both our sons. Perhaps, in retrospect, we did push a little too hard, but it's so difficult as a parent to assess these things. We've tried to dispel Desmond's unfortunate inferiority complex, but it will take time. This is our first step—openness and honesty. Desmond is more important to us than our reputation. We've told him that and we're going to prove it to him, no matter what happens, aren't we Oswald?"

Oswald nodded. Avoiding Polly's eye, he forced the words out, "And—and even if the police prosecute and he goes to prison, we're going to support him. We've told him that, too. But it might call in question my position as priest in the church, so we thought we ought to warn you, Polly. The diocese might take a dim view of a priest with a son in prison on drug related charges."

Polly said, "Despite the New Testament words in the letter to Timothy about a deacon being responsible for the behaviour of his family, I don't think the bishop would see your son's actions as any reason to request your resignation, Oswald. I'm sure he'd be sympathetic, and would commend you for supporting Desmond. Both of you might have to face some disapprobation in the parish—you know what people are like—but you have a good family around you, you're popular in the whole community, and of course, I will publicly support you. I think you're doing the right thing."

Nina's eyes filled with tears. "We don't deserve you, Polly."

Embarrassed, Polly stood up. "Nonsense! Where would the benefice be without you and

Oswald? You two are pillars of the church. I'm hardly being altruistic. I need you!"

As Nina began to cry in earnest, Polly handed her a box of tissues.

"You don't understand," Nina whispered, sniffing. "I've done something terrible, and I'm so deeply ashamed and so very sorry."

Polly waited, but when nothing other than sobs was forthcoming, she said gently, "I know all about that, Nina, so you needn't worry."

Nina raised a tear-stained face. "You know? How could you possible know? How long have you known?"

"A little while now."

"And—and you're still supporting us? You don't hate us—me?"

"Of course I don't hate you! I think I understand. Right from the beginning you realised Desmond was in the area, and you needed to support him. I was something of a threat, in case I discovered who he was. I'd only just arrived, so you—er—tried to persuade me to move on elsewhere. Is that about the shape of it?"

Nina nodded, her eyes wide with surprise. "Oswald didn't know anything about it, honestly. He would never have countenanced what I did. It was me alone, I want you to know that, Polly. Oswald didn't want anyone to find out about Desmond, but he's my son. I desperately wanted to see him and help him, but I wanted to protect Oswald at the same time. He has a position in the community, and we do have our own future to consider. How on earth did you find out?"

"It was when I became aware of Desmond's identity. Then everything sort of fell into place like a jigsaw puzzle, and it was obvious."

Nina's tears had given way to a small frown. "Why was it obvious? I thought I'd covered my tracks completely. Everything was anonymous."

"Nina, no one sews like you! I thought at first it was Jonathan Tunbridge, with the silent phone calls. He had been so openly hostile, and I didn't know of anyone else who was overtly opposed to female priests. But have you ever noticed his hands? They're huge, like spades. He could never sew anything. Then the ink on my cassock-alb seemed to tie in with the young vagrant, and as soon as I learned of his identity I knew it must be you, Nina. All Dezzy's posturing about the monstrous regiment of women—that had to be one of Oswald's quotes. And the clerical outfit on that Barbie doll was so meticulously and beautifully sewn. I knew you made clothes for the children and dressed Emily's dolls. As soon as I had all the parts of the puzzle, it was easy."

"And you don't hate me for it?" Nina's sobs were threatening to overwhelm her. "Can you ever forgive me? I'm so sorry. I honestly didn't realise how cruel it was. I couldn't think further than Desmond and at the time it seemed like the only way to help him. I felt I had no choice. Polly, I'm so ashamed."

Polly said easily, "Well, it's all out in the open now, so I hope you'll come to me in future if anything worries you. I confess it did upset me at the time, and to be honest, at one point I did think of giving up, but that's all in the past. I'm not going to mention any of this to anyone, so how about we all start again? What do you think, Oswald?"

Oswald's face was grey. It was clear he had no idea of the extent of his wife's activities on his behalf, and he was mortified. Yet in a strange way, he was moved, too. Who would have thought quiet, upright Nina would have done anything so reprehensible just to prevent any damage to his reputation? And was he in any way responsible himself, through his hard attitude in forbidding Nina to see her younger son? Could his strict discipline during the boys' childhood years have been one of the things that affected Desmond so badly? For the first time in his adult life, Oswald was beginning to suffer serious doubts about himself.

Hardly able to bring himself to look at either Polly or his wife, Oswald felt he would never lift his head again. 'How are the mighty fallen' sprang unbidden to his mind, and he bowed his head even lower, but then felt his hand firmly clasped.

"Come on, Reverend Oswald," Polly said softly, "I need you. Let's start over."

Oswald rose. "Polly, I—I don't know how to thank you. For the record, 'the monstrous regiment of women' was a kind of family joke—in poor taste, I admit, but a joke nonetheless—and I'm sorry. I'm sorry for everything. Please forgive me, too."

Polly merely smiled and gave his hand a quick squeeze. "I'll see you on Sunday," was all she said, as she showed them both to the door.

CHAPTER THIRTY-EIGHT

"What do you mean, you have to go into Norwich this morning?"

Tom sighed. He had known this moment would be difficult. "It's a business meeting. I can't tell you any more, client confidentiality and all that. You know what it's like."

"But it's Saturday and I've kept the day clear to be with you! You didn't say anything about this last night when you arrived."

Putting his arms around Polly, Tom hugged her and dropped a kiss on her forehead. "I'll be back by lunchtime, promise. And it was a good way of wangling an extra visit to you, Sweet Pea."

"Huh! Any excuse," Polly grumbled. Then she brightened. "Still, we'll have all the rest of the day together, won't we?"

"'Course we will. We can do anything you want. Go out, stay here, whatever."

"Hm. Just make sure you're back, then."

Tom was surprised he had escaped so easily without further probing, but with an unexpected few hours available to her, a plan was forming in Polly's mind. Unable to contact Cheryl the previous evening, Polly's anxiety about her reader had grown. She was determined to use the morning to search out Cheryl.

First, it would be sensible to ring Chloe, to alert her to the situation.

Chloe's answerphone cut in after a few rings. Polly gabbled, "Chloe, it's me, Polly. Byron nicked Cheryl's money and she thinks he might be dealing so she's gone after him but I can't contact her so I'm going to look for her at the old vans. By the way, I've had an idea about the murdered girl and the baby. I think I might know who they are. I'll follow it up and let you know. 'Bye for now."

En route to the vans, Polly tried Cheryl's mobile again, but after a few rings it went to voice mail. She left yet another message asking Cheryl to contact her, without any real hope of a response. With no sign of Cheryl at the vans, Polly sped on towards her next planned destination, Coot Farm, the nearest habitation to the caravans. Perhaps Cheryl had gone there seeking Byron.

As usual during daylight hours, the farm house was deserted. Polly rang the doorbell long and loud to alert at least one of the dogs to her presence, hoping the resultant barking might produce one of the Tunbridge boys. It didn't, but hearing a rustle behind her, Polly turned.

"Byron! What are you doing here? I thought you'd be long gone. Have you seen Cheryl? She was looking for you, not surprisingly! I can't raise her. I haven't seen her since yesterday and I'm a bit concerned."

Byron glanced all round, as if fearful someone might emerge unexpectedly. "It's all right. I know where she is. She's okay."

"Can you take me to her, then? I need to talk to her about tomorrow's services."

"Come in here. It's not safe to talk in the open." Byron grabbed at Polly's arm, to drag her into the big barn. Polly resisted.

"What are you doing? Let go of me. Just tell me where she is."

Byron dropped his hand. He backed off, but edged towards the barn. "Please, we'll talk inside. I tell you, it's not safe out here. He might hear you."

"Who might?" Despite the warning signals in her brain, Polly began to follow him.

Byron refused to say more until they were both in the barn. He swung the big door shut, making Polly blink as her eyes adjusted to the darkness after the glare outside.

"Over here," Byron called, dodging all the farm machinery and moving towards the far end.

Polly hesitated, unsure whether to trust him, but something about the urgency in his tone pushed her forward.

Byron bent down and began to heave at something on the ground. As Polly reached him, he pulled open a trapdoor hidden under mounds of straw and animal excrement.

Polly wrinkled her nose. "Pooh! Not sure I want to be quite so close to these enticing farmyard smells, Byron. What are you up to now?"

"She's down here."

"What? Don't tell me she's been in some underground hole all night, I don't believe it! That's medieval. What on earth are you about, Byron?"

Byron raised a face etched with misery. He whined, "It's true, but it wasn't me, honestly it wasn't. It was Joe. He caught Cheryl snooping around looking for me and he got paranoid. I thought he was going to kill her he was so mad, but he shoved her down here. I didn't know what to do. I wanted to rescue her, but I thought it was safer for her if I played along so I pretended to applaud what he was doing. I've come back this morning, 'cos I knew Joe would be out in the fields. Come on, help me get her out."

Polly drew back. "Do you expect me to believe Joe threw her down there and you left her there by herself all night? You can't be serious! Not even you would be that inhuman."

"You can say what you like about me, but help me get her out. Please. Please, Polly. You've got to believe me."

Uncertain whether it was a trick, but despite herself half believing Cheryl might be trapped underground, Polly inched closer to the dark opening, just as the big barn door at the north end creaked loudly.

Byron caught his breath and his hands began to shake. "Quick! He's coming back! Get down here. I'll shut you in so he won't see you."

"What?"

But before she had time to respond, Byron bundled her down into the depths of the earth. The heavy trapdoor clanged shut above her, and Polly was plunged into darkness.

"Help!" Polly screamed. "Help! Byron, let me out of here! This has gone on long enough. The joke's over now. Help me."

Even as she shouted, she knew it was futile. How stupid. Fancy allowing that brainless dummy Byron to outwit her. But as she stifled a sob, light filtered through into her basement hole. Polly blinked, then noticed that a door in her dungeon had opened.

A cultured voice said, "Polly? Are you okay? It was such a thud I thought the roof was caving in."

Polly had never been so thankful to hear her friend's voice. "Cheryl! Thank God! You really are here, like Byron said. I've been trying to contact you since last night."

"Well, it looks as though you've found me. Are you hurt, Polly? It didn't sound as though you used the ladder."

Polly grinned, despite the circumstances. It was so good to know she wasn't alone. She felt her limbs and her trunk. "No, I'm okay, I think. A bit bruised and winded, that's all. Byron pushed me and I fell. He told me Joe had locked you in here, and he was coming to rescue you. Said he had to play along with Joe to keep you safe, but in my opinion he was thinking more of his own skin than of you. Where is this, apart from being somewhere under the barn?"

"Can you stand? I'll show you. You'll never believe this." Cheryl led the way through the door she had opened.

Polly gasped. They were in an underground lounge with no windows but complete with sofa, armchair, and a dining table with a couple of upright chairs. There were three doors leading off.

"Where is this place? It's a fully furnished room."

"You ain't seen nothing yet! Follow me."

Cheryl led the way into a tiny kitchenette with oven and hobs, sink, washing machine, and refrigerator. Polly looked around in amazement at the pots, pans and crockery neatly arranged on shelves. She was about to open a cupboard, but Cheryl, so relieved to see Polly that she was like a child with a new toy, was urging her back into the lounge and through to the next room, which proved to be a combined bathroom and toilet with a shower unit in one corner. The final door off the lounge revealed a bedroom with a single bed covered by a floral duvet, and walls decorated in pale pink wash. Polly opened the large wardrobe which covered one wall, but it was empty.

"What a fabulous place," Polly breathed. "Who lives here? Is it a bolt hole for the boys? Like a kind of underground tree house?"

Cheryl shrugged. "Cosy, isn't it? Although it was jolly cold last night in here. You could survive though, no trouble. It must extend under most of the barn. I've heard of barn conversions, but this is something else."

"Is there any food?"

"Some bits and pieces in the fridge. Don't know how long they've been there, but there's some elderly cheese and a scraping of butter, and I found a few crackers in a tin. There's coffee and tea too, but no milk. Help yourself. I did."

Polly wasn't particularly hungry. "Do you want to fill me in with what's going on? What's all this about Joe? Byron sounded terrified of him."

Cheryl settled into the armchair, leaving the sofa for Polly. "I was right. There is some kind of drug deal going on, although as far as I could make out, Byron's just a go-between. I think Joe picks up stuff at one of the nightclubs in Norwich and sells it on to that tramp from the caravans. Byron's the delivery boy, which you have to admit is about his level. I waited at the vans until quite late last night but he didn't come back so I walked here, it being the nearest place. I had no idea Joe was involved with Byron. To be honest, I was about to cut my losses and cadge a lift home off David, when I heard Byron's voice. He was in the barn talking to Joe, whose voice was raised higher than I've ever heard it before, which made me think he was pretty angry. I heard him say there was no way Byron could back out now. I was just creeping nearer to hear better, when one of those wretched dogs started barking fit to bust. Joe rushed out of the barn to see what all the row was about, and caught me. He's got arms like a blacksmith, have you ever noticed? I thought he was going to kill me, he was so furious. He dragged me across the barn, threw me down here and slammed the lid while Byron stood there with his mouth open like a demented goldfish. I've been expecting Joe back ever since, to finish me off."

"Oh Lordy! I think he might be back now. That's why Byron shoved me down here—or so he said. Not sure I trust him further than I can throw him, but we don't have too many options at the moment." Polly's shoulders slumped. Then she brightened. "Ah, at least I have my phone. Now all we need is a signal."

"You're joking! Underground in rural Norfolk? There's precious little signal in this area above ground, let alone down here. Not a chance.

Anyway, I spent all last night trying that. Obviously we need to get out, so any more brainwaves, Einstein?"

"Now might be a good time to try prayer."

"I've been doing that since I arrived, but somehow I don't think God will reach down a mighty hand from heaven and pull us out."

"Good if he did, though, wouldn't it? Still, you're right. Let's hope he answers in some other way. He usually does, I've found." Polly glanced at her watch. "Tom will be missing me soon, I said I'd be there for lunch. And I left a message on Chloe's answerphone, so they'll be looking for us before too long."

"Yes, but will they find us? Who could ever find this place? At least Byron knows where we are, but he's so chicken-livered I think we need a more foolproof plan than relying on him, so we'd better start thinking. Don't know about you, but I have no wish for my skeleton to be discovered here twenty years hence."

As the minutes grew into hours, it became apparent that there was little hope of release. The combined strength of the two of them was insufficient to move the trapdoor, and there appeared to be no other exit. With no windows and no external doors, neither was there any means of transmitting a message to the outside world.

Cheryl had already explored every inch of the place. "There's air coming in from somewhere, but I think it's just those tiny holes up there near the ceiling." As Polly shivered, she added, "Are you cold, or is that fear?"

"It's a draught—thank you, God!" She grinned at Cheryl's perplexed expression. "Don't you get it? Draughts don't just happen. Come on, back into the bedroom. We need to explore further. Let's move some furniture. I'll try the wardrobe, you explore these drawers. You never know, there might be a hidden catch or something."

"And I might be Superwoman and pigs might fly."

Ignoring her, Polly had no sooner put her shoulder to the large wardrobe with the idea of shifting it, when she was interrupted by a squeal from Cheryl.

"Look at this, Polly! This is amazing. See what I've found. This settles it. It's absolutely imperative we get out of here now, before Joe comes back."

CHAPTER THIRTY-NINE

"Oh, I was wanting Polly. She left a message on my answerphone saying she was looking for Cheryl."

"Wish she'd left me a message," Tom grumbled. "I take it you don't know where she is, then? I had to go into Norwich this morning, but she promised me she'd be around for lunch. I'm getting seriously worried now."

"Wait there, I'm coming round." Chloe abruptly ended the call.

"I think we'd better compare notes and combine forces," she said, arriving on the rectory doorstep five minutes later.

Tom stood aside to let her in, and followed her into the lounge. "What do you make of it, Chloe?"

Chloe had worry lines creasing her forehead. "Did she say anything to you about the body of a teenager she found in one of her graves?"

"She told me the story of the funeral in full and lurid detail—ever the drama queen, our Polly—but she hasn't said anything much since. I believe she thought there was a tie-up between the baby that was left on her doorstep and the girl in the grave, but I don't know any more than that. Why? Has she said something to you?"

"This message she left on my answerphone. She said something about working out the identity of the murder victim, but knowing Polly, she's probably put two and two together and made a minimum of five. The problem is, I think she may be half right. We've had the DNA reports through, so I too have an idea about the identity of the girl."

"Who is she? And what does that mean anyway? Is Polly in some kind of danger?"

"I don't know, but I'm anxious. Look, I need to make a few enquiries, then I shall have a better idea of what to do. Why don't you relax, take it easy? I'll let you know if I come up with anything. I take it you've tried her mobile?"

"I'm not completely stupid." Tom grabbed his jacket. "I'm coming with you."

"This is a police investigation, Mr. Curtis. There's nothing more you can do. Let the police get on with their work."

Tom raised his eyebrows.

Chloe sighed. "Please, Tom. Don't make this more difficult than it has to be."

"Save your breath, Chloe. Wherever you're going, I'm coming too. Just think of me as your shadow until we find Polly."

"I can't take responsibility for having a civilian around during what could be a dangerous investigation."

Tom lifted his chin. "That settles it. If Polly's in danger, I need to be there. I won't get in your way, I promise. You never know, I might come in handy at some point. I'm relatively young, and I'm strong and fit. You have to take me along, Chloe."

"On your own head be it, Tom Curtis, but I tell you this. If you compromise this investigation in any way, I'll—I'll—" Unable to think of any appropriate sanctions, Chloe strode to the door followed by a grinning Tom.

As they drew up outside Abbot's Farm, Chloe instructed Tom to stay in the car. "Give me half an hour, Jonathan Tunbridge is no great talker. If I'm not out by then, you have my permission to come looking for me—I don't suppose I could stop you—but ring this number first, and take care. All these farmers have shotguns."

She scribbled the number for Norwich Police on a scrap of paper and handed it to Tom.

"I don't like letting you go in there alone if there's any hint of danger."

"Oh, for heaven's sake! This is my job, remember? I wouldn't be going anywhere without backup if I thought there was the slightest possibility of danger. This is more to set your mind at rest than for me. I'm only going to ask a few questions and I'll probably be out in ten minutes, but you know what it can be like when people get talking. Sometimes difficult to shut them up, although I very much doubt that will be the case here. See you in a bit."

Tom tried to settle back in his seat, but it was the longest ten minutes he could remember. He glanced round at the farmyard with its rusting machinery and air of dereliction, with an undefined sense of foreboding. The place felt so neglected and desolate. He was glad when Chloe returned.

She sat silently for a moment, her hands resting on the steering wheel and a small frown playing between her eyebrows.

Tom said, "Well?"

Chloe shrugged. "Didn't get much out of him. Just rambled on. Typical Jonathan Tunbridge. Didn't make much sense, to be honest."

"Had he seen Polly or Cheryl?"

"Almost got offended when I mentioned them. Makes it clear he doesn't like women, although I had a feeling Polly's grown on him a bit. Claims not to know anything, though."

"But?"

Chloe smiled. "Is it that obvious? Muttered one or two things that I need to look into."

"What sort of things?"

"Just ramblings of a possibly deranged mind. Nothing important."

She made to start the car, but Tom laid a restraining hand on her arm. "The word deranged makes me decidedly uneasy. Come on Chloe, we're supposed to be sharing. What did he say?"

Chloe sighed. "Said he thought Oswald Waters had been behaving strangely, mentioned the Talbot brothers, both of whom have shotgun licenses and both of whom have juvenile records—but that's common knowledge and it doesn't make them into adult criminals. They lost both parents at a young age and were brought up by granny. In my view, they're living examples showing that people can and do reform. Then he tossed his own brother David into the mix. No love lost there. So I guess we'd better have a chat with all of these. We'll start with Oswald, since he's the nearest. Anyway, he ought to know what's going on. If we can't locate either Polly or Cheryl before tomorrow, he'll find himself responsible for six church services. Come on. Off to see the Waters."

Evidently assuming Tom's presence would indicate church informality rather than police interrogation, Chloe allowed him to accompany her when they drew up outside the Old Rectory in Parsondale. Oswald was pottering in the garden. He didn't invite them in, but stood chatting to them over the flower beds.

"Cheryl? No, haven't seen her for days. Have you asked that useless excuse, Henderson? Never have been able to understand what she sees in him." Then, seeming to recollect his priestly persona, he added, "Still, takes all sorts, I suppose. I—um—Polly?" He pursed his lips and shook his head.

Tom had the distinct impression he was hiding something and had bad-mouthed Byron to give himself time to think, but Chloe merely nodded. "Oswald, you do realise you'll be responsible for all the services tomorrow if they can't be found?"

His face lit up, but again recollecting himself, he said, "Strictly speaking, you churchwardens are responsible for arranging services in the rector's absence, but I see what you mean. I could ring old Ernest Brigstock, if you like. He's over eighty and tends to prattle on like the proverbial babbling brook, but he has a good heart and is always glad of an outing."

Chloe nodded. "Thanks, Oswald. I can leave it with you, then? We're just off to see Alan and Ralph, as it happens, so I'll tell them. Save you the trouble. And of course, I'll ring you when

Cheryl and Polly turn up. I'm sure there's an innocent explanation. They've probably gone shopping together, or something."

Oswald said, "The Talbots are away. Not due back until late tonight, so I understand. I'll sort it, Chloe. Don't you worry."

Tom raised his eyebrows as they returned to the car. "Gone shopping?"

"Didn't want to start alarm bells ringing. You know walls have ears, but out in these villages the smallest blade of grass picks up what's been said. Interesting that the Talbots are away. Wonder where they've gone?"

"Did you think Oswald was hiding something?"

"You should have been a police officer, Sherlock! Yes, of course he was hiding something. Couldn't wait to get rid of us. Not at all like the Oswald we all know and love, whose hospitality is second to none. And where was the lovely Nina, I wonder?"

As she put the car into gear and drove off, Tom said, "Shouldn't you arrest him or something? He clearly knows much more than he's letting on. Maybe he knows where they are. Can't you lean on him? You'd have thought he'd have shown more shock or anxiety or something, but he didn't seem in the least surprised. I bet he knows where they are."

"Too many detective stories, Mr. Curtis! As you well know, I can't arrest anyone without good cause. Just because he didn't look surprised doesn't mean he's guilty of anything. Lots of people hide their feelings. We'll nip along to Coot Farm, see what tale they have to spin, then we'll stop for a cup of tea and a sandwich and regroup."

Tom was beginning to panic. "But we haven't found them! In fact, we haven't found out anything. We seem to be going round in circles—and giving up much too easily. I'm scared for Polly, Chloe."

"No need," Chloe said, concentrating on driving into the farmyard. "I think we've discovered a great deal. I have a few ideas. I think we're much nearer to sorting out this whole mess, you'll see. But for goodness sake, follow my lead. Don't go haring off on some tangent, thinking you know how to do the job better than me. In my profession you need to keep a cool head, otherwise you make mistakes. And they could be fatal, so just remember that and do exactly as I say. Absolutely no running off by yourself. Stay in the car until I reappear. You're not coming in with me on this one."

She parked out of sight, behind a bush and to the side of the large barn in the farmyard. Tom slumped down in his seat. It was all right for Chloe, she was seeing the action, what little there was. Just sitting outside in the car waiting like some tame poodle, was agonising. He closed his eyes, but was too restless to keep them shut for long.

Catching a movement out of the corner of his eye, Tom instinctively stayed low in his seat, but slowly turned his head to see a man—was it Byron Henderson, Tom wondered?—emerge from the barn. Tom watched as the man indulged in what Tom considered to be highly suspicious behaviour, nervously looking all round, then going back into the barn, reappearing and going through the whole procedure again.

When finally he left the barn and walked in the direction of the farmhouse, it was enough for Tom. Without further thought he leapt from the car and ran into the barn, intuitively aware that this had something to do with Polly, and that she was in danger.

When his eyes adjusted to the reduced light, Tom could detect nothing untoward. He forced himself to take some deep breaths and slow down, then began to search methodically, poking behind machinery, pulling at old harnesses, routing through piles of hay and kicking at the mess on the floor. But as he reached the far end, a deep voice growled menacingly, "What do you think you're doing?"

Tom swung round, to find himself facing the twin barrels of a very large shotgun.

CHAPTER FORTY

Cheryl was holding a pile of cheap exercise books. "Look at this, Polly. I found these taped under the drawers. I wonder who wrote them and why they were so carefully hidden?"

"Let's have a look." Polly was already opening the top notebook. She gasped. "Oh my goodness! It's just as I thought, but worse. See this name? Jessica Tunbridge, aged eleven. I'm sure she was the girl found in the grave, the mother of the baby left on my doorstep."

"Jessica Tunbridge? Isn't she Jonathan's daughter, the one who left to go to France with her mother? How could she possibly be the girl in the grave? She isn't even in the country. Whatever made you think she was the murdered teenager?"

"It was the baby, and something old Maisie Faulkner said, something about people having funny names. The baby was Mary Elizabeth

Madison, and it occurred to me that Madison might be a Christian name rather than a surname. After that it was easy to make the connections. As a matter of fact, I had it in mind to check with David this morning. If anybody knows what Jonathan's been up to, it's him."

"I still don't see what made you think it might be Jessica."

"I remembered hearing that the mother of the Tunbridge twins was called Maud and came from America. Madison is an American name meaning son of Maud, and I knew the twins had three sisters, so it was logical to assume that Mary Elizabeth Madison was named after them. I knew the sisters had religious names, because the village nicknamed them the three Graces—Faith, Hope and Charity—although I didn't know their real names. You can't get much more religious, as far as women are concerned, than Mary Elizabeth. All religious names, see, except for Madison."

"I'm beginning to. So while we all thought Jessica was in France with her mother all these years, you reckon she was held captive here all that time? By Jonathan? Surely not. He was beside himself with grief when she went. But if not him, then who? David? Joe?"

"Don't know. Shall we see what she says? There might be a clue in these notebooks, she took great care to keep them hidden. Here, look: *I can never forgive my father. I go over and over it in my mind, but all I can see is him standing there with the shotgun in his hand. I don't know what happened after that. I can't remember anything more until they brought me here.* Oh, my goodness! What do you think this means?" Polly flipped through the rest of the book. "It's a diary, and by the look of all these books, a long standing one."

Cheryl was leafing through another book from the pile. "This one says: *My baby is due soon. It is a girl, I'm sure of it. I shall name her after my aunts, that I learned about so long ago. You were right, Polly. She will be Mary Elizabeth Madison. I'll ask him if we can go away and be a proper family, somewhere abroad, I think. My daughter needs freedom. She cannot spend her life down here. Why should she? It was me who witnessed my mother's murder, not her. I shall protect her. She will never have to go through what I have been through all these years.*"

Polly and Cheryl looked at each other with similar expressions of horror.

Cheryl said, "Jonathan Tunbridge murdered his wife! We all thought she was in France with her daughter, when all the time—" she put a hand over her mouth, her eyes wide with mounting revulsion.

"Come on, we haven't time to read these now," Polly scooped up the notebooks. "You need to help me move the wardrobe. I think Jessica may have found a secret way out of here."

They pushed the wardrobe to one side more easily than they had expected. The wall appeared to be intact, but when Polly tapped gently, part of it sounded hollow.

Cheryl said, "Stand aside," and gave the wall a mighty kick, but it was a painful procedure without producing much impact. In the end they battered at it with the dining chairs until an opening appeared.

Polly led the way, still clutching the notebooks. "Jessica must have had a better way than this—

perhaps through the bathroom round the drainage pipes—but we don't have time to find it. Let's see where this leads."

They pushed their way through a hole which was little bigger than Polly's waist, and emerged at the rear of the barn beneath a large pile of brushwood and logs. Polly eased her way through, followed with even more difficulty by Cheryl.

As Polly turned to help her friend, she put her finger to her lips. "We don't know who's about. Better be careful. Don't want anyone knowing what we've found."

A thick voice muttered into her hair, "What have you found?" and the hairs on the back of her neck stood on end as she felt herself clamped by a pair of plump, sweaty arms.

Polly froze, but the effect on Cheryl was startling. Heaving herself through the narrow exit, she hissed, "Let her go, you runt!"

As Cheryl advanced menacingly, Byron took a step back. "Ssh! I can explain, honestly I can. But keep your voice down. We don't want Joe finding us here."

Polly said, "What's going on, Byron?" Then she added accusingly, "You've been dealing in drugs, haven't you? You get them from your friend at the hospital every time you drive Maisie Faulkner, then you come here and supply Joe."

"What? No, you've got it all wrong." He appealed to Cheryl. "I haven't stolen your money, love, only borrowed it for a day or two. I haven't exactly been dealing. More acting as a runner, a gopher. Earns me a bit of pocket money, I'll admit that. But I haven't been doing anything wrong. You have to believe me."

"You've been transporting and delivering drugs but you've done nothing wrong? You're a complete moron, Byron Henderson, you know that?"

Byron retreated a little further, his eyes lowered. He wiped the sweat from his forehead with a pudgy hand. "Don't you see? He needed those drugs. He would've died without them."

Polly said, "If you're referring to Desmond Waters, he nearly did die."

"You know who he is? How did you find out?"

"Never mind that now," Cheryl intervened. "How did you get involved? Do you pass them on to anyone else? Have you got anyone hooked?"

"No, I swear! I'd never do that. Only Desmond, and he's been on them for years, long before I came on the scene. It's Joe, Joe Tunbridge. He gets them from this nightclub in Norwich and he used to run them over to Desmond's caravan, but he spotted his Uncle Jonny there one day. Everyone knows how scary Jonny Tunbridge is! I met Joe in the pub and got talking, and well, I—I kind of—I—it was like I was doing him a favour, and he gave me a few quid for it. Only happened a time or two, honest. Then I saw you, Polly, and that boyfriend of yours, near the vans—I told you about that, Cheryl—and then Des passed out and I heard the air ambulance, and well, I got scared. I came here yesterday to tell Joe I wanted out, that's why I needed the money. Then you showed up Cheryl, and Joe got mad and I got even more frightened for you. That's why I'm here now, to pay Joe off once and for all, but I heard David tell Chloe that the boys are in Norwich for the afternoon and evening, so I was just trying to figure a way of getting you both out before Joe got back."

Simultaneously, Cheryl said, "You could have tried opening the trapdoor and helping us up the ladder," and Polly said, "Chloe's here?" just as a deafening shot rang out from the barn.

Shocked, they stared at each other. A moment later they heard footsteps running across the yard. Cheryl risked a peep round the corner of the barn.

"It's Chloe," she whispered to the others, "and David behind her. Isn't there a gap or a knothole or something so we can see who's in the barn?"

Byron said, "You don't have to do that. I can tell you, I saw him. It's that boyfriend of yours, Polly."

Polly's face turned ashen. "Tom? He doesn't possess a gun! Who's in there with him? He's been shot! Tom's been shot. I've got to get in there. I must get to him."

As she wrenched out of Cheryl's restraining grip, a second shot reverberated through the air. Polly was off, running for the barn entrance as if her life depended on it. She paused at the threshold, gulping back a wave of nausea as she took in an unmoving body lying in a pool of blood just inside the entrance.

Tom? Oh God, please don't let it be Tom.

Even as she thought it, Polly realised it was one of the Tunbridge twins. David? Or Jonathan? In the same instant she became aware that the other twin was holding a shotgun levelled at Tom. With a cry of rage she rushed up to the man she assumed was Jonathan Tunbridge, beating on his chest with her fists, even as Chloe screamed, "No, Polly!"

Polly ignored her. "You monster!" she cried, pummelling at Jonathan, despite his shotgun.

He pushed her away as though she was matchwood and felt in his pocket to reload the gun, but before he had a chance to do so he buckled suddenly at the knees and fell forward heavily, knocking Polly to the ground. Chloe was on him in an instant, cuffing his hands behind his back as she rolled him off Polly.

"Well done, Cheryl," Chloe said, eyeing the large piece of wood with which Cheryl had whacked Jonathan behind the knees. "Can't say the same for you, Polly," she added. "What possessed you? You could have been killed."

But Polly had run over to Tom and was unable to reply, crushed as she was in Tom's arms.

CHAPTER FORTY-ONE

"He'll be charged with murder, of course," Chloe said several days later, when they were all gathered over drinks in Polly's lounge, "but there are mitigating circumstances, and to be honest, I don't know whether he'll be considered fit to plead. He swears he didn't kill Isabel, and I'm inclined to believe him, no matter what Jessica's diaries say. By her own account she was some distance away, and I think she mistook her Uncle David for her father. We're still questioning Amos and Joe, but it's already clear they have no doubt in their own minds. Why else would David take Jessica in, without a word to his brother? It's the only explanation which makes any kind of sense. Amos was coming up eighteen and Joe twenty-two when Isabel disappeared and Jessica came to live with them, so they were both plenty old enough to make the connections."

Polly said, "David once told me Isabel was always down here when Theresa was so ill. Perhaps he made a pass at Isabel and she rejected him. Or maybe it was an accident."

"I doubt it was accidental. These farmers have been handling guns all their lives. They don't have accidents. It may have been the heat of the moment, but I think it was deliberate. Joe and Amos have told us all they know, although to be fair, Joe didn't have much to do with it. It was all Amos."

"Amos? Gentle Amos? David's youngest son? But he's so lovely! Are you sure?"

"Quite sure, he's admitted everything. He found Jessica in a state of shock after witnessing her mother's murder, although at that stage he didn't realise his father was responsible. Being a bright lad though, he soon twigged what had happened when David was so keen to keep Jessica hidden. Amos went along with David's story that Jessica would be in danger from her own father, because it suited him. He was nearly eighteen, old enough to know what was going on, but working for his father with a steady job and good pay, so not yet prepared to challenge him. Despite what she thought her father had done, Jessica couldn't bring herself to inform against Jonathan to the police, and Amos encouraged her reluctance. They'd always been close from the moment Jessica was born. He treated her like his beloved younger sister, but he was already half in love with Jessica, even though she was still only a child at the time."

"Are you saying Amos was the baby's father?"

Chloe nodded. "Bizarre, isn't it? Jessica was only sixteen when she died, so he'd been committing statutory rape for years. He'll be charged for that alone, never mind keeping Jessica prisoner all that time."

"But that was more David, surely? Amos didn't exactly snatch Jessica, did he? He was concerned for her and took her to his father. It was David who kept her hidden."

"It suited them both until Amos got her pregnant. I think David had lulled himself into a sort of false sense of security about the situation and had probably convinced himself that he really was doing Jessica a favour. Besides, he didn't see too much of her, so he could probably forget her existence for quite long periods. Amos took on all the day-to-day care of Jessica and she became very dependent on Amos even though realistically, he was her jailer. She developed a love-hate relationship with him. According to the diaries, he regularly had sex with her while telling himself—and her—it was love. The result was inevitable. Apparently David went ballistic. He could see immediately that they would be unable to keep a small child in that underground hole, so he was terrified that the whole story would get out."

Polly shivered and crept closer to Tom on the sofa, clutching his hand. "So it was David who strangled Jessica, to prevent her showing her baby to the world? Did he kill the baby too, or was the baby stillborn?"

"According to her diaries, Jessica herself smothered the baby, to save her from the underground existence Jessica had had to endure. She knew something of the family history about her aunts, so assumed that all Tunbridge females would be incarcerated in that place for at least some of their life. She was determined to spare her baby that. We'll probably never know exactly where or how David murdered Jessica, but forensics have matched his hands to the bruises on Jessica's neck. By all accounts David was quite fond of his niece, so it may have been a sudden, irrational rage when he found out she'd left the baby on your doorstep, Polly. When he realised the whole story was bound to come out, he probably thought he had no option. He'd killed once before, remember, so a second murder to tidy up wouldn't be impossible for him."

Cheryl asked, "What about Joe and Byron? What did they have to do with it?"

"Byron knew nothing about any of this. He's just a brain dead dork who thought he saw a way of making a quick buck by acting as Joe's gopher for his little drug racket. Joe knew about Jessica, but he wasn't particularly involved. He was years older than her, and not very interested. As you know, Joe is something of a loner. Never says much to anyone. He is a dealer, though, in a small way, and he was aware of Jessica's imprisonment which makes him an accessory, so he'll be charged on both those counts. The first time he set eyes on him, he clocked Byron for a lazy jerk out to make money with the least possible effort, so soon had him running errands."

Cheryl snorted, "He won't be running any more except well away from here with his tail between his legs. Good riddance to the slime bucket. I should have given him the push years ago. I'm such an idiot where men are involved."

No one disagreed with her. Tom stood up to open another bottle of wine and refill the glasses. "What made Jonathan Tunbridge turn up so soon after you'd seen him, Chloe? When he faced me with that shotgun and fired it into the roof, I thought my final moments had come."

"If it's any comfort, he had no intention of harming you. It was a way of bringing his brother out. I think he realised some of what must have happened—although not the whole story—when I asked him whether any of his sisters had had a child. He soon grasped that the murdered girl had Tunbridge DNA. I expect he checked the local press after I'd gone, and discovered the baby's name. That would have clinched it for him. I suspect he'd had an uneasy feeling deep down ever since Isabel and Jessica disappeared, but he'd suppressed it. David was always the dominant twin. For Jonathan, David was like the other half of himself, and it simply didn't occur to him that David could have snatched Jessica, although the two of them have been somewhat estranged ever since Isabel's disappearance. Perhaps he knew David fancied Isabel, but he didn't want to face the implications."

Polly said, "But why go to the barn? Why didn't he go straight to the farmhouse and threaten David there?"

Chloe took a long drink. "I'm afraid it's a pretty horrific story, and one that affected Jonathan so deeply that he's always had a problem with women."

"We all know that to our cost, especially me! He didn't exactly welcome me, remember? Is this something to do with the aunts? You said Jessica mentioned something about them in her diaries. What is the story?"

"Jessica knew some of it from her father, but he was loath to go into details with his own small daughter. All she knew was that there was an underground cottage where the aunts had stayed from time to time, and that her father hated the place, although to Jessica it sounded very exciting. For him, it's a matter of family shame. He told Jessica something of it because he'd been very fond of his sisters and she wanted to know what had happened to them, why they never came to visit. Apparently the grandfather abused each of the sisters. He built that place underground as his own little pleasure palace. He would take the girls down there one at a time, sometimes keeping them there for days or even weeks. The whole family knew about it, but were powerless to stop it. Jonathan suspected his father was actually in on it, and may have raped the girls himself. His mother spent most of her life in agony for her daughters, but was beaten whenever she tried to intervene. Jonathan was very close to his mother but hated his father and his grandfather. David was the opposite, idolised his father but despised his mother. After his marriage began to go downhill, Jonathan thought it was something to do with the Tunbridge genes, that he was somehow tainted. He was so frightened of turning out like his father and grandfather that he kept all women at a distance, and when—as he thought—his worst fears were realised because his wife and daughter ran away, he more or less became a recluse, as you all know."

"But David followed in the Tunbridge tradition?"

"So it would seem, to some extent at any rate. Unlike Jonathan, he always had an easy charm. Women liked him, and I expect Jessica both liked and trusted him. He was her uncle, and an exact physical replica of her father. I imagine that was quite a comfort to her. But the one who was really following in the family tradition was Amos. He had his father's charisma, unlike Joe who was much more like his Uncle Jonathan. Amos beguiled his young cousin so that she became utterly reliant on him, but at the same time—as her diaries show—hated him."

"Poor Jessica," Polly said, softly. "What a terrible existence for her. No wonder it pushed Jonathan over the edge. From all accounts, he doted on his daughter. I think I might have taken a shotgun to my twin brother if he'd done to me what David and his sons did to him.

"Chloe, I will be able to give Jessica and her baby a Christian burial, won't I?"

"Possibly Isabel as well, if we find her remains. I imagine she might be in another of your graves Polly, it would have been a very effective way of disposing of a body if it hadn't rained so heavily later that night. I'm afraid we may have to open up the grave nearest to the date of Isabel's disappearance four years ago, but obviously it'll be a while before we get permission for that. These things take time, so I imagine it'll be months before you can start planning any funerals."

"I hope Jonathan will be allowed to come to their funeral service when it does take place. I can't help feeling nearly as sorry for him as I do for Jessica. No wonder he was so morose all the time."

"I expect he'd probably get permission for that." Chloe glanced at her watch and stood up. "I need to go. Thanks for the drink, Polly."

Cheryl rose with her. "Me too, Polly." She appealed to Tom. "Keep her out of trouble if you possibly can, will you? I never want to go through anything like that again."

Tom laughed. "You know what she's like! There's no holding her when her mind's made up. But I do have an idea on that score."

When the door had closed behind Chloe and Cheryl, Polly said, "What idea might that be, Tom Curtis?"

Tom took her in his arms. "You never asked me what I was doing in Norwich on the Saturday morning."

"What were you doing?"

Tom beamed. "My firm is opening a branch in Norwich. They want me to run it. I was tying up the final loose ends. Didn't want to tell you until it was all settled, in case it fell through at the last minute, but it's all fixed now. I start in September."

"Tom! That's terrific!" Polly's face shone. She pulled out of his arms and gave a little dance. "I'm so happy I could cry."

"Don't do that," Tom said, "because I have something to ask you. Polly Hewitt, darling Polly, I love you so much, and when you went missing I thought I'd die. I thought of life without you and it was more than I could bear, so Polly sweetheart, will you marry me?"

So there is a God after all.

With a broad grin on her face, Polly melted into Tom's arms.

VENGEANCE LIES IN WAIT

ABOUT THE AUTHOR

Born in Rugby, Warwickshire, UK, Janice B. Scott was raised in Croydon, South London. She won a scholarship to Croydon High School, and went on to train as a physiotherapist and later as a teacher of physiotherapy.

She started writing in the seventies, winning a radio short story competition and having a short story published in the prestigious "Writers of East Anglia" edited by Angus Wilson.

She met and married her husband - also a teacher of physoiotherapy – and they set up a private physiotherapy practice together in Fakenham, a small town in North Norfolk, and produced three children, all of whom are now grown and flown.

In the late eighties Janice changed career, and was ordained as a priest in the Church of England with the first batch of women priests, in 1994. At around the same time she started her own website, offering weekly sermons for adults and stories for children. This was taken over in around 2002 by sermonsuite.com, a US publishing company, for whom she writes as "The Village Shepherd". They published volume one of a book of short stories for children and adults, "Children's Stories from the Village Shepherd" in 2009. Volumes two and three are due out this year.

Janice is also a staff writer for Redemptorist Publications, which produces weekly worship material and sermons, and which is marketed world-wide.

She worked as rector of six village churches in south Norfolk (UK), and was made Hon. Canon of Norwich Cathedral in 2008. The village churches supplied the background for her three novels, "Heaven Spent" (available in hardback and Kindle editions), "Babes and Sucklings" (available in paperback and shortly to be available in Kindle) and "Vengeance Lies In wait" (also available in Kindle). She is now working on her fourth novel in the same series.

Janice presently lives in Norwich, Norfolk, UK with her husband Ian, continuing writing, playing golf whenever possible, and visiting the family.